THE

DYING

WORLD

THE DYING WORLD

GREGORY D. LITTLE

Cursed Dragon Ship
PUBLISHING

CHAPTER 1

THE BAR KARL YONNEL limped his way into didn't seem to fit Stefani Palmieri at all. When she'd named the Prison City as the place they were to meet, he'd thought the name must be ironic, and he'd expected a cheery, modern establishment with just a hint of kitsch. What he found instead was a watering hole in the wall, the quintessential mixing of metaphors in bar form.

She said this was a place where she used to meet up with her friends. That surely included Iazmaena Delgassi. Perhaps it was Iaz, the former cop, who had selected the place for her friend group to meet once upon a time.

That notion fit perfectly. This was exactly the sort of place an off-duty cop might frequent. Unfortunately, off-duty lancers might also frequent this place. The thought ratcheted tighter the dread Karl had been feeling since receiving Stefani's message.

His former comrades-in-arms were the last people he wanted to see. He didn't want to be reminded of the life he no longer had. Particularly not tonight, when he very much suspected his public shaming was about to claim yet another victim. Even eight months gone, it would not stop carving notches into its belt.

Karl caught sight of Stefani in a cramped, dim booth in the back just as she caught sight of him. Her tremulous smile took him back to better times. And how bizarre to think of those times as better.

You're an old fool, Karl Yonnel.

"Sorry I'm late," he said as soon as he'd grown close enough to do so without shouting. With his limp, his lifelong gift from Iazmaena during her terminal spiral, it still took him an agonizing ten more seconds to reach the table, and just as long to lower himself down, concealing every jag of pain as best he could. You never missed sitting easily until you couldn't. "Tram was running slow."

It was a lie, and they both knew it. He was late because after eight months he still couldn't mentally account for how slow the limp had made him.

Too damned old to re-learn how to think.

"It's not the most accessible place," Stefani said with chagrin. "Sorry." She too had trouble adjusting. "I still come here sometimes when I need to clear my head. It helps me remember ... who I am."

It was strange, the way she sounded as though she'd meant to say something else. But so much about her was strange these days.

Or maybe not. They'd known each other for so little time before beginning this thing that was ending now. Given that tiny slice of his life, it felt profoundly unfair that the thought of it ending should hurt so much.

"So," Stefani said with a nervous gust of breath. She laughed prettily. "Do you want a drink? I want a drink. Where has Sergio gotten himself to?"

Karl restrained himself from wincing as she rose. He did not want a drink, as she very well knew. He had never been much of a drinker, and that had been before he'd watched alcohol contribute to Iazmaena's fall. Paternalistic as it was, he didn't like seeing anyone succumb to stress-drinking, Stefani most of all.

He also didn't like seeing her so eager to leave the table five seconds after he'd arrived.

But her self-imposed exile from his presence didn't last long, as she returned with what appeared to be a mixed drink, a swirling rainbow of color. Better than a straight shot, he supposed.

"Sorry," she said again. She looked so anxious that Karl felt his empathy for her overwhelm his dread. It was a blessed relief. "I'm distracted these days, I know. It's the Bridge, Karl. That device you found in the warehouse back when Iaz ... Well, it's capable of wondrous things. I shouldn't talk too much about it in public, but it's hard to think about anything else sometimes."

"It's all right," he said, and for once, his smile was not forced. "I'll start." *And I'll spare you the need to do the hard thing,* he thought. She would call it misplaced chivalry, which was why he didn't say the thought out loud.

"This isn't working," he said. "Whatever we had ... it's pretty evident it's gone now." It felt like ripping his own heart from his chest along a vector chosen to break the maximum possible number of ribs.

But she smiled in muted thanks, and so he found the strength to go on.

"You're a magistrate now, and a relationship with a pariah like myself is complicating your professional life."

She looked both as though she wanted to protest and that protesting would cause her physical pain. Karl raised a hand.

"It's all right," he said. "It's all right to be concerned about your career and what's best for your family."

He didn't add what she kept unsaid, what only Marri had been willing to tell him, and that in confidence. That Stefani had received threats directly relating to her relationship with Karl. He still reeled with guilt whenever he thought of it.

He had wanted to protect her from the blowback of his actions in attempting to take down Iazmaena. At first, they had tried to keep it secret. That had crumbled laughably fast. He knew now that it had always been a foolish hope. To protect her, he would have had to stop seeing her.

You're a weak old man.

"Do I get to talk?" she asked, her smile tight, yet fond. Perhaps she hadn't been smiling in thanks at all. He nodded for her to go on.

"What we had was forged in a different life," she said. He could not tell what she was feeling when she spoke the words. That was, he reflected, such a large part of the problem. He so often couldn't tell what she was feeling. It hadn't been that way when they first met. If anything, it had been the opposite. "Everything is different now," she went on. "And I just feel like the foundation we built 'us' on has been swept away, and there's nothing holding 'us' up anymore."

Nothing about what she said was wrong, precisely. And yet, it felt as though every word was calculated to lead his thoughts down the wrong paths. The meaning was plain enough, even if he had to read between the lines to see it. She didn't want him anymore, and she was either unwilling or unable to explain the real reason why she'd spent months pulling away.

It didn't make her decision to lie about it here, at the end, any less painful though.

"You know, maybe I will have that drink," he said.

CHAPTER 2

I AM STEFANI PALMIERI, *and I am human.*

The thought came to her at random now, whether she needed it or not. Mostly when she needed it, though. Eight months after that awful day, after Iaz's death, she worried how often she still needed it.

I am Stefani Palmieri, and I am human.

The magistrate's office in Illuminance Hall, spacious and well-lit as it was, felt suddenly stifling. It wasn't even lunchtime yet, and she had a packed afternoon. This was definitely going to be one of the bad days. At least a sense of dissociation was better than the blackouts.

"Excuse me, Madam Magistrat—oh, I'm so sorry!"

Stefani started. Her aide stood staring at her with overly wide eyes. *Not even time yet, but I must look totally out to lunch.* The banal annoyance of the thought was actually comforting. It felt normal. It was only then, snapped out of her thoughts, that she realized tears trailed down her face.

She pawed at the unfamiliar tracks of wetness. She couldn't remember the last time she'd cried. She'd cried when Iaz had died, hadn't she? Surely she had.

"Yes, Giana, what is it?" Stefani was surprised to hear hoarseness in her voice. *What is wrong with me?*

Giana's big, bright eyes normally burst with enthusiasm all the time. Now they were even larger than usual with concern.

"Are you sure, ma'am? I can—"

"Just spit it out, Giana." Stefani tried to reign in the bite in her voice. She'd gotten bad at that in the past few months. It was so rare to feel anything substantial at all that when the feelings did arrive, the force of them often took her unawares.

"I'm afraid there's been another one."

"Damn it." The words were too low and quiet to properly be called an outburst, because the truth was, Stefani had been expecting as much. *Kyne Libretta's been missing eight months, and still, she plagues us.* "In the warehouse again?" Stefani consciously unbunched her fists, which she had at her sides, thank God.

"Yes, ma'am."

"I could kill Iaz for giving her access to that facility," Stefani muttered, reddening with shame when she realized what she'd said aloud. *I'm the reason Iaz is dead. I left her alone with Kyne Libretta, and that psychopath killed her. She's dead. My best friend is dead.* It was amazing how hard it still was to accept that fact.

And then another thought, no less startling despite how common it had become.

Iaz and I should have killed Kyne Libretta when we had the chance. It was wet and tinged with red, that thought.

"I'm sorry," she said to Giana, managing to drag herself back together enough to preserve a semblance of decorum. At least the tears had stopped.

"No, please, ma'am, don't apologize," Giana said, always poise incarnate. She proffered her handheld. "I have the details here. But I'm afraid you'll have to read them on the tram ride over to Inkwell."

Stefani sighed. "It's time already?"

"Yes, ma'am." Giana tried for an encouraging smile. "But look at it this way. After today, Archon Graysteel should have no problem with you throwing all your efforts behind the Bridge reconstruction project."

"There is that," Stefani said leadenly. Time was what she needed now. What she needed and what she didn't have. And every time one of Kyne Libretta's booby traps went off, the Bridge project fell that much further behind schedule.

She just wished she understood why she believed so fervently that their time was running out.

Unbidden, it arose again.

I am Stefani Palmieri, and I am human.

⚘

"Citizens of Coldgarden, it brings me great pleasure to welcome you to this, the beginning of a normal tomorrow." Archon Ritala Graysteel's words cut through the chill of the morning but not in a warming or comforting way. Every time Stefani heard the woman speak, she remembered that Ritala did not possess the gift of speech that Archon Teodori had used to such great effect. It ought to have been a slam dunk. Eight months on from the revenant incursion, the people were surely starved for something, anything, that would prove to them that some degree of normalcy could return.

It was why Ritala had elected to hold this rally at this place and time, in Inkwell Ward and open to anyone who wanted to attend. It made perfect sense, even if the ward was not quite as rebuilt as the claim the archon was about to make. Still, Stefani felt a muffled sense of longing and loss.

Archon Teodori had held a similar gathering of his own in Illuminance, with a newly elected Iazmaena Delgassi named the magistrate of a newer, larger Watchfire. This time, Stefani sat off to the side of her archon, just as Iaz had with hers. But Stefani had been in the crowd that day, riddled with guilt over leaving Ella alone at the apartment under the care of the autodoc unit.

The memory threatened to cast her from her body like an exorcism.

I am Stefani Palmieri. I am Stefani Palmieri.

"We gather today to celebrate the beginning of that return to normalcy. Under the guiding wisdom of Magistrate William Barker of Sparks and Magistrate Stefani Palmieri of Illuminance." Ritala cut off abruptly as a cry from the crowd interrupted her.

The exact words of the shout had been drowned out by the archon's amplified voice, but something about the tone made the hairs on the back of Stefani's neck stand at attention. A worm of fear bored its way through the thick bolts of wool smothering her emotions.

Undeterred, the archon continued.

"This ward behind me, operational and livable once more, proves that our city *can* return to normal." Graysteel paused again, this time by design, to gesture at the sprawl behind her.

Despite the technical and logistical feat the return of Inkwell represented, all Stefani could see when she gazed into that tangle of buildings was a months-long delay to the Bridge project, one that prevented her from placing her ward's full resources at the disposal of that team's project lead.

But Ritala had been adamant. A full focus on reassembling the cache of materials Gene Sequencing had sequestered from the rest of the city had to wait until Inkwell was restored.

Restored enough to give a speech, at least.

"With this great ward returned to us," Ritala continued, "we can at last put the revenant incursion of eight months ago where it belongs: firmly in the past. And with the security and infrastructure improvements that have gone into the restoration, not just in Inkwell but across the *entire* city, we can ensure that any future attempts at incursion will be dealt with swiftly and mercilessly, well *away* from the city wall."

"By who?" someone shouted. Snapped out of her reverie again, Stefani scanned the crowd, trying to identify an angry face. She was surprised that she saw so many.

"There's barely any lancers left!" shouted a different voice.

"And instead of training more, you're just handing a garbage ward back to us as spit-shined refuse?"

The rapid-fire nature of the comments, and their laser-focus on key malcontent talking points, raised Stefani's hackles further. She was not a political animal, really. She was a scientist backed into a political corner as a result of some poor decisions. But even she'd been doing this long enough to realize when she was being confronted with a coordinated effort.

There was nothing spontaneous about this. The anger was real, but the barbs were too polished, the hecklers too perfectly spaced. It gave the appearance of the crowd being entirely in on it.

Ritala Graysteel was not the schmoozer Vernon Teodori had been, but she was no novice when it came to navigating the trials of elected office. Perhaps the effort was affecting her as well, or maybe Stefani's emotional distance actually worked for her in this instance, because instead of talking over her hecklers and ignoring them, Ritala Graysteel made the mistake of engaging with them.

"I can assure you, we have spared no expense to improve the infrastructure that previous administrations had let languish—" She cut off as something whizzed through the air and one of her personal security detail threw himself in between the archon and the projectile.

"Justice for Inkwell!" someone shouted.

"Down with Teodori's lackeys!"

"Down with Graysteel!"

"Down with Palmieri!"

"Justice for Iazmaena!"

"Iazmaena lives!"

"Iazmaena lives!"

"Follow me, Magistrate. Immediately, please." The large, broad, steely-eyed man who spoke was part of the archon's security detail. Stefani had no security of her own—an oversight she was seriously considering rectifying as of thirty seconds ago—but a portion of

Graysteel's detail had peeled away to encircle Stefani and Giana and steer them out of the line of fire for any more hurled objects. Stefani kept a death grip on Giana's shirtsleeve as they took welcome shelter behind the man who looked like he was ready to chew through the city wall. The crowd's sporadic shouts grew to a sustained roar. After a few moments, Magistrate Barker joined them, encased in his own, smaller detail.

"Well," Graysteel said, almost able to contain the shaking in her voice. She scratched idly at her neck as if in nervous habit. "You two didn't even get the chance to give your portions of the speech."

Which was, on balance, the only part of the debacle Stefani was pleased about. But this was hardly the time to say so.

"Given the circumstances, I think it would behoove us not to present a single target as we leave the area," the archon said. She directed a pointed gaze at Barker. After a moment's confusion, the normally gregarious man coughed uncomfortably.

"Perhaps you're correct, ma'am. I'll have my security detail escort me back to my offices."

Stefani tried not to make eye contact as the man and his team moved off in a separate direction. She knew a dismissal when she saw one. She checked to make sure Giana had stayed close.

"That escalated entirely too quickly for comfort," she said, deciding now was not the time to address Barker's dismissal either.

"Yes," Graysteel said absently. She'd abandoned the itch in her neck and was staring down intently at something on her handheld screen. Whatever she saw there made her scowl with an intensity that never meant anything but trouble for whoever was causing it. "And we should use this unexpected extra time in our schedules to discuss that very fact." She glanced back at the crowd, peering through a tiny sliver of daylight peeking through her security people. "In a more secure location, I think."

CHAPTER 3

A HALF-HOUR LATER, Graysteel, Stefani, and Giana were ensconced in the archon's spartan office in Heart Hall, which was rapidly being transformed into a fortress of heavily armed security ready to turn the angular, faux-wood and brushed-steel furniture into makeshift barricades, just in case what had begun in Inkwell spread. Stefani couldn't tell how much of what she saw was theater to preserve her peace of mind, but she found it did help.

"I'm sorry that our big event came to this," Graysteel said. She had collected herself fully, as was her talent, and was the picture of rigid poise once more. But Stefani thought the disappointment was real. The woman really had been pleased with Inkwell's rehabilitation. Either she believed in the story she told, or she wanted something permanent she could look to and say had been hers.

Stefani's guilt over the unworthy thought was as muted as the rest of her feelings at least.

"I'm less concerned about a ruined morning and more concerned about how quickly it became violent," Stefani said.

"Yes, quite. I'm passing relevant information to your handheld." Ritala swiped her finger so that the file appeared on Stefani's screen. Stefani watched the information populate. It was far too much to digest during a meeting with the archon, whose time was precious, which meant she wasn't intended to read it until later.

"What's the upshot?" Stefani asked.

Ritala's faint smile was one of pleasure that her subordinate understood her so well. She scratched idly at the back of one hand as she formulated her response with obvious care.

"If I'm being honest, this wasn't a total surprise. It's been building for some time, as I'm sure you've noticed."

Stefani had indeed noticed. There had been quite a lot of graffiti in her own ward, and if she really thought about it, such things had been escalating in the past few months.

"I'd hoped this problem would die down with time and distance from the Delgassi fiasco," Ritala said. "Instead, it's metastasized. That's why I want you to look into it closely. Along with your other work. I know your Bridge project is important to you and to the wider city. But I'm hopeful, with the Inkwell collaboration winding down, you can redirect your efforts into helping me with this problem before it becomes a true crisis."

"Me?" Stefani asked, genuinely shocked along with her dismay at yet another deferral of prioritizing the Bridge. "Why me?"

"For the same reason I sent Barker away, and that you are the only magistrate here meeting with me right now. Because you are the only magistrate I really trust," Ritala said. "Perhaps I've been too focused on the past myself. My own resources have been consumed in a very thorough investigation to determine just how rotted this city's leadership is in the wake of Teodori and Delgassi's various malfeasances. But until I have those answers, I can't afford to widen my circle of trust far."

Stefani had only a moment to wonder if that trust was real or was based more on the fact that Stefani's position—her very freedom— was owed to this woman's patronage and forbearance. Or maybe it was the fact that Stefani herself was the target of as much of the popular ire as the archon was. *I am just full of paranoid Iaz thoughts today.* Then Graysteel was talking again.

"You haven't been in this role for long, and I know I've kept you moving at breakneck pace the entire time, so you may not have had time to formulate a network of eyes and ears around the city. It's a distasteful part of the job, maybe the *most* distasteful, but it is necessary, and I can assure you the other magistrates all do it. If you lack those resources, I can make mine available to you—"

"No, I have people," Stefani interrupted. "And they have some contact with the police, I believe." It was a half-truth at best. She didn't have *people,* she had *person.* She had Karl. And he was at least as disliked by the police as she was.

And more to the point, of course, she didn't have him anymore.

But now, having uttered the words, she had a sudden fear the archon would demand she divulge the names of these people. Karl Yonnel was definitely a name Ritala Graysteel would not want to hear, from Stefani or anyone else.

"Good," Graysteel said, sounding satisfied that an unpleasant task was done. Perhaps her distaste for the practice of secret-gathering was such that she simply didn't want any more details than were necessary. "Use them. I will deploy my own people as well, of course. We need a way to nip this, if not in the bud, then before the flower manages to be pollinated. I've no idea how to do that just yet, but we need information before we can even begin to formulate a plan."

Stefani couldn't help but feel the archon should have been using this network of hers all along if this had been a fear, even a remote one. But she knew better than to say anything. It was possible the woman's network was almost as stunted as Stefani's own.

With the archon's dismissal, Stefani rose, gesturing absently for Giana to follow as her mind whirled. Once they were out of the office and past earshot of the guards, Giana leaned in close and spoke low.

"You don't have any network of informants. None that you've told me about at least." Glancing at her sidelong, Stefani saw an expression somewhere between confused and accusatory.

"I've got a friend or two I can call," Stefani said evasively.

Giana lowered her voice even further. "You're talking about Karl? Forgive me for putting my nose in, but won't that be awkward?"

Stefani gritted her teeth. She had never tried to hide her relationship with Karl from Giana. On the contrary, she'd had to relay messages to him through her assistant on several occasions, so they were at least casually acquainted. But she hadn't precisely flaunted it, either. And she hadn't mentioned the breakup at all, yet. But the woman was too damned intuitive for Stefani's own good. "And one or two others," she lied.

"If you like," Giana said diplomatically, "I have an old contact from school that might be able to help. He's in the police now. A different ward," she said, as though to both hedge what she was able to promise and avert suspicion in turn. "Renewal. We last parted on somewhat awkward terms, he and I." This came with a significant look at Stefani, which she took to mean they had parted on similar terms as Stefani and Karl had. "But I suspect he would take my call."

"I don't want you to do anything that would make you uncomfortable," Stefani began. But the look Giana gave her in reply was the woman's private brand of determined. "Do it, then."

As much as Stefani wanted to think this let her off the hook with reaching out to Karl, she knew immediately she wouldn't be spared. The archon was right about the seriousness of the situation. And two people searching for answers had to be better than one, after all.

CHAPTER 4

AFTER SEEING Stefani safely back to her office and falling into her work, Giana Novak let the door to the magistrate's office close behind her as she returned to her desk in the antechamber. She let out a long, ragged sigh once she was sure she was alone.

She went through her breathing exercises for managing anxiety, the ones she'd looked up two months prior from her anonymized handheld *just in case*, trying to calm her nerves. They didn't really work any longer on a normal day, much less after a near-attack in the streets. But deep down, Giana was afraid that maybe they actually did work, and if she stopped, her anxiety and paranoia would grow even worse.

She should never have taken this job. She wasn't here for any of the right reasons, she was putting herself in danger, and those two facts had never been more apparent than right now.

And tomorrow, it would be even worse. Somehow it would. Every day was worse than the previous.

I can leave at any time, she told herself. *I can just say I've had a new offer, or the work just doesn't suit me, or anything, really. Anything!*

But instead of doing those things, Giana turned up each day, smiling and praying that Stefani Palmieri couldn't read her thoughts on her face. She didn't understand why, but the only thing more frightening than the thought of showing up another day was the thought of walking away.

Today's terror had been a special thing, true. But Giana lived every day in fear. She felt it every time she looked into Stefani's face and saw anything but open friendliness. The mental self-interrogation would start.

Does she know? Does she even suspect? The certainty that Giana's deception would fail with time warred with the far feebler hunch that the worst of that danger had surely passed when she'd been screened prior to her hiring.

But there was no telling what kind of data Stefani could get access to now that no one in the city was tasked with safeguarding that data. And no matter how expensive Giana's false credentials had been, with enough time and determination, any false identity could crumble.

Find something productive to do. Distraction was the only thing that really helped these days. Organizing anything, no matter how small, seemed to work best as distraction.

She checked her messages, a reflex almost as deep as breathing after eight months as a magister's aide, and felt a sudden bolt of shock. Not from her work messages, which had piled up as they always did while a crowd had nearly mobbed them.

No, it was a personal email account that caused Giana's heart to skip: one she'd stopped using eight months ago out of fear, but never had the heart to totally purge. More specifically, it was a particular message's sender.

The subject line said, *URGENT: Your life may be in danger.*

The *from* line read, *Dr. Palo Hayasun.* And it was dated the day Iazmaena Delgassi had destroyed Gene Sequencing.

Giana came unmoored from reality. She suddenly wondered if she'd just dreamed the last eight months of her life, if Giana Novak, the last surviving member of the now-destroyed Gene Sequencing, was waking now from the most vivid dream imaginable. Or maybe she was having a psychotic episode, and this was just another day in her windowless office at Gene Sequencing. Sweat stood out all over her as she grappled with sudden and intense vertigo, a sense of falling upward into endless sky.

Then she reread the subject line.

URGENT: Your life may be in danger.

With effort, reason reasserted itself. Dr. Hayasun had sent a final message. *Your life may be in danger,* implied that it was just related to the danger every Gene Sequencing employee had been under at the time of the siege. Likely, if she had the capacity to check, this message had been routed through a relay server buried under Inkwell. A server which had likely just had power restored today, as the last of the grid came back online in that ward coinciding with the archon's press conference there. Dr. Hayasun had merely been doing what good bosses did, looking out for their employees' welfare. After all, Giana had been his aide the way she was now Stefani Palmieri's.

Almost certainly, nothing about Giana's circumstances had changed just because she received a months-belated message.

But hot on the heels of reasoned self-reassurance came the fear. Stefani Palmieri, once the close confidante of the now-deceased architect of Gene Sequencing's demise, Iazmaena Delgassi, might open her door at any moment and find this message on Giana's screen.

I should just delete it. He's dead. Every report agreed on that, though the lack of body—his and anyone else's—had spurred many conspiracy theories Giana had tried hard not to listen to. She could do nothing to help him now, and a message from beyond the grave of a high-ranking person in Gene Sequencing might put Giana in actual danger.

Instead, she keyed the intercom button into Stefani's office before she was even aware of doing so.

"Ma'am, I'm suddenly not feeling myself. I think maybe the riot got to me more than I realized. I feel terrible for asking, but would it be possible to take the rest of the day off?"

As ever, Giana marveled at the way her words did not shake the way her soul currently was. How she called upon that inner well of reserve was a mystery she would never have answered, she knew, but just as every time she managed it, she felt a profound gratitude.

Though without the odd skill as a crutch, perhaps she'd have been desperate enough to have left for safer pastures a long time ago.

"Of course," Stefani said through the intercom speaker. *Her* voice, in stark contrast with Giana's, still sounded a bit shaky, even through the tinniness. Possibly, she was even relieved Giana was leaving. Giana hadn't missed how much the woman seemed to prefer solitude. "Take whatever time you need. Just let me know you are feeling better later, yes?"

The implicit "or if you aren't," hung in the air. While hypermutation's onset was rarely as subtle as something saying "I feel a little off," no symptom had ever been ruled out as a potential warning sign so far as Giana knew.

Had Gene Sequencing survived, she might already have known more than she had eight months prior, when she'd been half a step above a new hire. But short of Stefani being able to reconstruct any of the defunct organization's lost secrets, that hope was lost to her forever now.

"Thank you, ma'am. I certainly will."

Giana did not wait another moment, powering down her workstation screen. This was a message she didn't want to open anywhere but her secure system at home.

⋈

Safe in her apartment, with every electronic safeguard she possessed in place and a considerable quantity of bourbon in her system to calm her shaking hands, Giana at last keyed the message to open.

For a heart-stopping moment, she feared it would be video, that despite all her reasoning through the logic of such a message, she might be forced to witness a portion of the attack as it had been happening. But, blessedly, it opened as text.

Giana,
I'm sorry, I don't have time to explain. We're under attack.
Delgassi is here with ######################### opl3.
Fucking filters! We're all going to be killed, I think. I'm not
sure why you didn't come in all those days ago, but even
though it meant you missed out on this delightful party, I'm
concerned what it might mean. I don't think I'm going to get
out of here to explain it to you, but you're owed an explana-
tion. When you first onboarded, you recall the
m3d1#@######## Something happened there. To
###############nly a few were affected. Only you that I can
find, though there must be more. There's a $##1nt3r g#o#p.
Been operating within Gene Sequencing for who knows how
long? I guess they'll die with the rest of us. Except maybe you.
I still don't have all the information and never will, now.
######################## did to you, it made you
####################################. I'm sorry I can't
tell you more. If we make it out of this by some miracle, maybe
I can find out more. If not, goodbye. Corner of
Pro$##################. Inkw3ll.
Gods below save us, and you too,
Dr. Palo Hayasun

The shaking in Giana's hand had resumed and grown to encompass her whole body by the time she finished reading. She closed it at once, fumbling with the controls so badly she almost deleted it instead. Then her finger hovered, quivering, on the point of deleting it on purpose. If it was gone, if the information within it was gone, there was nothing to do, nothing she could act on. She could pretend it had never arrived.

She had never felt so strong an urge.

No! I was his assistant. Assistant-in-training, technically. But she had felt the bond forming between them day by day. She had burned with pride at that feeling once. Before Iazmaena Delgassi's actions had found all the cracks within Giana and shattered her without ever having laid eyes upon her.

Tears burned in her eyes. It had been a while since that had happened, but no matter how long in between, every time they came, the loss felt as fresh as a still-warm corpse. *Even though Dr. Hayasun knew he was about to die, he was trying to tell me something important about myself.*

Her thoughts slid from deleting Dr. Hayasun's cryptic warning, latching instead onto a desperate desire to send Stefani a message of her own, resigning right now, plausible excuses be thrice-damned. She could wash her hands of all of it. A promise of relief warred with a sense of alarm, a battle that seemed to play out in her mind while Giana Novak was a mere spectator, watching from outside herself.

In the end, she neither deleted the message from Dr. Hayasun nor sent a letter of resignation. Instead, she shut down her terminal, made her unsteady way to the bathroom, vomited, rinsed her mouth out, then retreated to her bedroom and sobbed, screaming into her pillow until her voice was hoarse.

At last, weak with exhaustion and grief, darkness descended, and she knew no more.

CHAPTER 5

THE FOREST around her was cool and black. Its dangling fronds cloaked her in welcoming darkness as she scented her target and its spike of filthy panic. She picked through underbrush with unconscious skill, limbs like jointed scythes making no noise beyond the faintest whisper. Soon would be the time to abandon stealth, to move fast: the last stretch, the final striving before the reward.

Destruction. Scouring. Purification.

The filth had been foolish to leave its fastness. It was not truly safe anywhere, of course. Nowhere was safe across the vast wildernesses of this world. But secure in its fortress city, at least it would have had a chance.

The forests belonged to her.

By the mix of scents, the filth had ranged far, left its group. These parasitic infestations were creatures of groups. They believed those groups brought them safety. To be one of many was to ensure another was more likely to be targeted. But this filth had no group any longer. Separated, cast out, or merely foolish, it made no matter.

For the invader, it was too late.

She broke into a scuttling run. They never expected the speed. Their glassy eyes drifted to the bulky central mass and ignored the seemingly spindly legs, capable of moving in a blur when the moment called for it.

She could not see this filth the way it saw, but she knew it was there. Her own senses told her this across spectra the filth couldn't perceive. All that power of thought wasted on such a narrow band of awareness. It was almost too easy. But "too easy" was a concept of the filth, a trap to dull reflexes.

Thinking did nothing but slow reaction time.

She did not think; she anticipated. She did not guess; she knew. And when the chase ended, as it would in mere instants, she would relish the ritual of purification, not lament how much more satisfying a stiffer challenge would make it.

Thick, rubbery stalks gave way to a small clearing and within it, the target, frozen in fear. She paused the barest instant, suddenly wary of a trap. But there was nothing—no other scents, no other sounds. Just defenseless putrefaction, easily destroyed, less than one leap away.

She bunched her legs to spring, only to be startled by a soft, cooing sound.

✳

Marri opened her eyes to find herself leaning over a bed in a room that wasn't her own. Her entire body was tensed as if for a fight. A rank, impure smell filled her nose. It spoke of foulness in need of cleaning. Her eyes picked out details in the blackness quickly as her ears sought to make sense of the sound that had wakened her from ... something.

Memory crashed home of where she was, of where *precisely* she was.

Again. It had happened again. And it grew worse every time.

As though sensing her distress, Stefani shifted in her sleep, only her head and one bare shoulder visible above the covers. Stefani liked to sleep in a cold apartment. The sight of her face awakened a strange echo of the feeling Marri had felt in the … dream? Had it been a dream? How could any dream feel so real, so present and alive? At least when they'd started, these whatever-they-were, they hadn't ended in sleepwalking.

Worse than the sleepwalking, though, was the echo. It was hate. It was a desperate need for purification.

She brandished a kitchen knife over Stefani's sleeping form in one white-knuckled fist.

Nearly dropping the blade in shock, Marri forced herself to step away. Across the room, secure in her crib, Ella cooed again, still asleep. Drenched now in cold sweat, Marri fled the room, waking neither Stefani, who returned home exhausted when she returned home at all, nor Ella, who settled back into burbling slumber, thank the gods below.

Marri did not stop at the room, though. That felt entirely too close, and she didn't even understand what that feeling meant. She paused only long enough to return the knife to its safety block, marveling that she had somehow disengaged the locks in her sleep.

She had to get out of this apartment. The city scared her less than this place did when she tried to sleep. There was a feeling to stepping out into Coldgarden at night that felt like going home.

She tried to focus on her sense of her surroundings as she closed the building's armored front door silently behind herself. She had to be aware of all potential threats. It was a less scary thing to think about than wondering what might have happened if the baby's soft sounds of sleepy contentment hadn't wakened Marri in time.

The darkness of the city swallowed her, and she welcomed it.

CHAPTER 6

A ROOM FULL OF HARD, cold eyes turned to regard Karl as he stumped into the dark and dingy bar from the rain, and he cursed the limp that made it impossible to avoid attracting notice. *For a man who professes not to drink, you sure wind up in a lot of unpleasant meetings in bars.*

He picked out the man he was there to meet right away, owner of the gaze which was slowest to turn back to its drink in the corner booth. Regret at ever agreeing to this rendezvous etched the man's face. He'd been adamant about keeping a low profile, and Karl had not troubled to inform the man about his impediment.

Sorry, friend, you're star of the bar tonight. At least they didn't know who he was. If they had, he'd most likely have gotten worse than hard looks.

Resolute, Karl waved off the questioning glare of the bartender. A drink might have eased his limp somewhat, but despite his moment of weakness during the breakup, this was one bright line he remained committed to steering clear of, particularly now, when the thought could be so tempting.

Instead, he threaded his way through high-top tables and the treacherous legs of bar stools, plunking down upon the bench opposite the man in his booth, resolving not to complain about the fellow picking a table in a sunken part of the bar, forcing Karl to negotiate still more stairs. In place of a greeting, the sallow-faced man growled at Karl in a warning whisper.

"You didn't tell me—"

"I know," Karl said. "Because I needed you to agree to meet with me." He had no other leads. "In my defense, I also neglected to tell you that I'll double your pay." It wasn't something he could afford to do, but he could afford to lose this job even less.

The promised pay bump seemed to mollify the man. He lifted his glass in mock salute. "Next round's on you then," he said, throwing the glass back and gulping its contents down in one.

"You have what we agreed on?" Karl asked. He could keep his words circumspect at least. He held out a hand, expecting to be handed a sheet of scrap paper. He'd had it fixed in his mind's eye since they arranged this meeting, torn edges, brown from its thousand recyclings in Renewal Ward yet still repurposed from some other, nobler use.

Something more honorable.

But Karl was surprised when the man pulled out a handheld instead. He'd seemed far too skittish to trust electronic communications given the circles he ran in.

Those sunken eyes read Karl's confusion like a menu. "It's just an address," he said with a nasty smile. He waited until Karl proffered up his own handheld and tapped them together, transferring the information. "Scrubbed clean of metadata. Straight into the book it goes with the others you've got. No names. No way to tell where it came from." His smile faded into a more honest expression. "Now pay me and get out. This isn't the kind of place you want to linger. Awful lot of hypermutation lately in these parts, if you take my meaning."

Karl did. It was another way of saying a lot of people died in these parts for sticking their noses where they didn't belong. Karl ignored the thinly veiled threat as the man took his own turn to extend an expectant hand. Karl had no illusions he would be satisfied with an equally electronic response. Trackable funds were not exactly popular in the sort of business Karl had found himself in.

It had started by accident. Relieved of his rank and his career, he'd still been trying to find his footing amid meager and dwindling savings when a former junior officer of his, one Lance Corporal Heidegger, had found him.

The boy had been in a half-panic, telling Karl the story of a younger brother who had, courtesy of a new "friend," begun dipping his toes in with a very nasty crowd: printed narcotics cut with nastier stuff. No matter what straits humanity found itself in, that particular demand would apparently never cease. Heidegger wanted to help his brother, of course, but he was afraid of what the information would do to his own career should it come to light.

Karl still remembered how bitterly that pill had gone down. *He saw me as someone who had done his best to act according to his principles and got washed out for it. What a wonderful message the city's leaders are sending these youngsters.*

Instead of offering the boy lame advice he couldn't back up with any confidence, Karl had decided to stop feeling sorry for himself and help. With a little digging, he'd learned the younger Heidegger's contact had a burgeoning trail of bodies in his wake and had been of considerable interest to the police. Provided with a location and a time by Heidegger, who kept his younger brother tied up and safely away, it had been a simple enough thing to tip off the ward precinct.

That the information had come with a cash reward, a reward the grateful lance corporal insisted Karl keep, had started him thinking.

Karl reached into his coat pocket, pulling out a damp wad of bills. These had no doubt come from a different, less reputable corner of Renewal, but they spent well enough at any place this man would care about. Karl slapped them into the outstretched hand, then rose to leave, not wishing to overstay his welcome and invite something worse than glares.

Coldgarden was a city with a lot of criminal activity. Karl had no idea what crime rates had looked like in this city or any other before the arrival of the revenants and the obliteration of the human world beyond, but he'd had an up-close view of how desperation, real or imagined, could twist a person's morals into something monstrous. What that meant in practice was that there were a lot of criminals at large, and therefore a lot of active rewards for their capture.

Karl tried not to think too much about what happened after the capturing part. Coldgarden didn't have room for a prison of any appreciable size. High-profile criminals, the kind whose capture and imprisonment would trumpet the power of the city's police and their prowess at keeping Coldgarden's citizens safe, very publicly occupied the city's limited cells. What happened to lower-order criminals once they went into the system was somewhat ... opaque. Thus, Karl tried to restrict his bounty-hunting-by-proxy to only the nasty, violent subset of that latter group.

And mostly, this let him sleep at night.

He emerged back into the lightening rain, pulling up his hood as much to cover his face from view as to shield it from the weather. He'd never set foot in this bar before. No one there, not even his contact, knew his name. Yet, he decided to wait until the morning to deliver this information to the local precinct, hoping fervently it would keep for that long at least. His limp made him notable even to those that didn't know him, and he couldn't afford to be seen going straight from this place to the police. He already worried the precinct would clue in on who he was, like some of the precincts in other wards had.

As he'd known it would, the Graysteel administration had thoroughly publicized his punishment. No member of the Coldgarden police would soon forget the man who had attempted to take down one of their own who had climbed all the way to the rank of archon. However justified—and slow—he'd been in the attempt.

Massaging his side—the damp always made it ache worse—Karl stumped down the bar's steps into the street and out into the cramped and hostile night.

CHAPTER 7

KARL'S HANDHELD chimed as he manhandled the door to his apartment open. It had taken him a month to work out the trick of the warped door frame such that he could manage it every time. Now he did it without thought.

He juggled his takeout dinner and the door and his cane as he reversed the process, forcing the door shut, closing out the darkness of the city beyond. Perching his takeout precariously upon the small sliver of space he'd left on the side table for just that purpose, Karl checked his handheld and sighed.

His request for a permit to carry a sidearm had been denied again. Which wasn't a surprise, precisely. In a city where lethal hypermutation could be found behind any given skinned knee if your luck was out, dedicated weapons were frowned upon. Fortunately, criminals tended to be equally wary of them, and there were plenty of non-lethal options to pick from.

It was more the *reason* for the refusal that bothered him. The likely reason, anyway. That, and the fact that it had come in so late, which meant it had been auto-rejected, never even looked at by a human. Likely, his name was linked to an automatic flag in the system.

You're a bitter old man, Karl. It was better this way. He kept reminding himself. Or it should have been. Would have been, if he'd been strong enough to resist attempting a relationship with Stefani in the first place.

Thinking of Stefani started it all up again: regret, recrimination. Wishing he could do their conversation at the bar over. Wishing he could do the past eight months over. Wishing he had stood firm when Iazmaena Delgassi had wanted to promote him to lance commander.

He might be dead if he hadn't been lance commander, considering the current state of the Lancer Corps. But there were days ...

He sighed again. Like the gun permit, he supposed it didn't matter. The past was the past, and this was where he was now.

Karl took another step, intending to grab up his dinner with his free hand and camp out with it in his office chair.

But his hip had other ideas.

Had he still been in the Lancer Corps, there might have been something surgical technology could have repaired now that the initial wound had healed over the preceding months. All with an acceptably low hypermutation risk. Now, it was just something he'd have to live with, likely forever. So while the lance of pain that shot up and down his left side wasn't exactly a surprise, it was spectacularly ill-timed.

Instead of grabbing up the bag with his dinner, his hand flailed, seeking to correct his sudden imbalance as his leg went wobbly with pain. He clipped the bag and watched helplessly as both it and he sagged to the side, as though they were dance partners, perfectly synchronized.

The difference was Karl was able to catch himself with his cane, while there was nothing to stop his bag sliding from the tabletop in horrible slow motion.

He was just reconciling himself to a night of going to bed hungry when a low shape surged at him from around the corner at the table's far end, darting with such impossible speed it was almost a blur. Adrenaline surged within Karl, spurred by a lifetime of viewing inhumanly fast shapes emerging from the darkness as a one-way trip to an early grave—provided they could scrape enough of you up to burn and bury.

But his assailant stopped short, catching the bag before it could burst upon his floor and scatter noodles everywhere.

"You should be more careful," Marri said, handing him back his dinner with a self-satisfied smirk.

"Did you come all the way here by yourself?" Karl asked Marri once he'd calmed his racing heart enough to speak cogently.

The look she gave him at this question could have peeled away memory matter.

"I know you're very well acquainted with living on the streets," he said, refusing to back down. "But the city is a different place now."

"Worse than when it was overrun with revenants?"

"In some ways, yes," he said stubbornly, wishing it were not so.

"I only saw one person the whole way over."

"Exactly. Because everyone else knows better than to wander around in the dark." And then, because of the strange way she'd emphasized the statement, "Was there something strange about this person?"

Marri shrugged. "It was at the tram station, while I waited for the tram. He eyeballed me. I eyeballed him. He never got close. We were the only two people out, so what else was there to look at?" But she was hiding discomfiture. Karl could tell. He also knew that if he pressed, she would only clam up more. She had made it here safe. That was what was important. So he changed the subject.

"Well, now that you're here, I suppose I should thank you, and not just for saving my dinner. I have a huge list of must-buys on this place, and not enough money for most of them. An e-lock just went to the top of my list." Judging by her sullen look, he knew it was the right call. The girl could pick any physical lock in existence, but biometric locks were harder to breach. In Karl's new line of work, there were more dangerous people than Marri who might have reason to want to break into his home.

Or there would be, if he could keep up a steady enough stream of bounties to generate enemies.

Marri, he noted, still looked more smug than sheepish. She'd grown quite a bit in the past eight months, even if he'd seen her often enough over the course of them that he had to think back to realize it. He could swear the gangly now-teen had grown half a meter.

And had she always been that *fast*?

"Does your mother know you're here at this hour?" It was a rhetorical question. Clearly the answer was *no*.

"She's not my mother," Marri snapped, and Karl chided himself. An obvious trap, and he'd walked right into it. While they had seen a decent amount of each other, they hadn't spent much time alone. Even still, Karl had sensed a consistent tension between the girl and Stefani.

"By every legal force this city can bring to bear, she is," Karl retorted gently, refusing to relent. "And don't dodge the question. You know what I mean."

"I have nightmares when I sleep there," Marri said, not meeting his eyes. "When she's around."

Karl paused and rethought what he had been about to say before the late addition. It required a lot of unpacking. He started with the least troubling, though it was troubling enough. "When she's around? Is she gone at night often?" His impression was she'd been busy, but his unspoken assumption was she'd been avoiding him more than anything.

But life as a magistrate wasn't easy. Karl had gotten a closer view of that truth than most ever would. Not working *any* nights would surely be too much to ask. But Karl found he didn't like the idea of Marri being home alone with the baby often.

"Not often enough," she said, seemingly determined to frustrate him. "I just told you I only get the nightmares when she's there."

Karl's frown deepened. Was this some sort of cry for help? Was she trying to say something obliquely she couldn't bring herself to say directly? Such behavior would go against everything he knew of the girl, but having spent so much time on the streets didn't change the fact she was still just a kid.

He forced himself to look at her closely. She was as skinny as the day he'd met her, but taller, so she wasn't being malnourished. A growth spurt, not starvation. He felt a flash of shame at the thought.

How could you think Stefani would be mistreating the girl? Is one day after you break up enough time for you to start thinking badly about her?

But it wasn't just that. There was still that little hidden piece of why they'd failed. He couldn't let go of that idea, no matter how much he suspected it was just a sop to his ego.

"Tell me about the nightmares," he said, trying to distract himself from the sudden torrent of unpleasant thoughts.

"First tell me why you broke up with Stefani."

So much for that plan. But he wasn't going to let her get away with playing the naïf.

"You're a perceptive kid. You can't tell me you didn't sense where things were going."

Marri just shrugged, but she didn't deny his claim.

"Can I have some of your dinner?" she asked. It was her turn to deflect, apparently, but the hope in her eyes told him she was hungry in a way he dimly remembered being as a teenager.

"I don't know," he said teasingly. "I didn't order for two."

"Isn't there some rule about finders, keepers?"

Karl couldn't suppress a laugh. "If you'd wanted salvage rights, you should have let it hit the ground. Since you *saved* my dinner, it's probably a gray area. But how about you tell me about the nightmares and I split it with you?"

She shrugged uncomfortably in that way she did whenever personal details were sought after.

"I guess."

A few minutes and additional promptings later, when he'd barely started his half of the food and she'd already finished hers, she finally seemed willing to speak. "There's always a lot of blood," she said.

That was all she said, and just that quickly, Karl wondered if he should give his worries a second glance. *No! It's Stefani we're talking about here.* No person was truly harmless, but his read on Stefani told him the only path to violence she possessed was if her loved ones were threatened.

"Are you and Ella getting along?" he asked warily.

Marri snorted. "As much as you can get along with a nine-month-old." There didn't seem to be any malice in the answer, but this was hardly Karl's forte. *You need to get better at reading people if you really hope to make this bounty hunting thing a paying gig.*

Karl didn't need to ask about Ella's condition. Stefani had filled him in on it, at least as much as she was comfortable doing. He'd always sensed she was holding back. But he didn't sense that had anything to do with whatever was bothering Marri.

Unless it was simply a jealousy thing. The adopted older child versus the biological one that needed more attention.

This was really not his area.

"How about school?" he asked, flailing. "How has school been?" The face she made was more comical than traumatized, at least in Karl's experience with her.

He felt completely at sea in diagnosing the troubled statements of a teenager who had sneaked out to visit him in the middle of the night, but even just that fact seemed bad. The conversation wound down after that, the girl's stubbornness winning out over Karl's lack of willingness to push too hard. But every word out of Marri's mouth convinced him something was wrong.

CHAPTER 8

DISPUTE HER NEED for sleep though she did, Marri crashed hard once she stopped moving long enough to sit down on Karl's couch. And judging by the deep, rhythmic breathing Karl could hear all the way from his office-slash-bedroom, there were no nightmares this time.

He debated whether to call Stefani now or wait until the morning. If she noticed Marri had gone missing, Karl was one of the people she would surely contact. That she hadn't done so already suggested she was probably oblivious. Since there was no danger to the girl, he decided to leave it until sunrise and to hope he wouldn't live to regret that decision.

The fact that a part of him dreaded the prospect of speaking with her this soon after their breakup didn't enter into it.

With that can thoroughly kicked down the road, he sat down to attempt the work he'd meant to do before turning in himself. He ought to see a decent payday in the morning, but that would leave him with nothing solid to work with unless the gray spaces of the city's net had turned up something. Karl was still trying to narrow down a set of message-board rumors into something actionable on his part when age and weariness betrayed him, and he slipped off to sleep.

He woke to his handheld's insistent buzzing. *Well, that question got answered for me.*

Thanking the gods below he'd thought to silence the ringer, Karl rose awkwardly and shut the door to his bedroom. The darkness of pre-dawn was just beginning to lighten. Small chance the buzzing vibration alone had disturbed the girl's sleep, but she also had a habit of noticing everything others didn't want her to notice.

Behind the closed door, he was half-tempted to answer the phone and ream out whoever it was for calling so late when he noticed the ID.

He answered quickly, praying he hadn't been too late.

"Stefani," he said, trying not to sound shocked. No reason he should be shocked. It was obvious why she was calling, and he kicked himself for making what was now the obvious wrong call in not reaching out to her first. He'd surely catch hell for that. "Don't worry. Marri's here. She's well. She's safe. Sleeping soundly on my couch, as it happens. Listen, I'm sorry I didn't call right—"

"Karl." The sound of her voice cut him off, and he tried to calm his suddenly racing heart. *Idiot man, you'd think you were no older than Marri!* "What's this about Marri?" Stefani continued. It was her turn to sound shocked.

"I ...," he began, trailing off in confusion. "I figured that's why you called so early. She showed up here sometime last night. Broke her way into my apartment while I was out."

"She *what?*" He heard the sounds of sudden motion on the other end of the call followed by a profusion of profanity so blisteringly loud he had to hold the unit away from his head while it wound down. In the background, Ella began to cry.

"Why didn't you call as soon as you knew?"

And there it was.

"Because I ..." Finally, Karl growled and went with the truth. He was a lancer, whatever the suits said. Lancers didn't run from *conver-*

sations. "Quite frankly, Stefani, because I assumed you'd be asleep, and this was going to be an awkward enough call even without it happening in the middle of the night."

There was a deafening pause. When Stefani finally spoke, she sounded like a balloon which had lost all its air.

"Of course. I-I understand. Thank you for taking care of her."

"It's not my place," he said, reasoning since he'd already blundered into the freshly laid minefield, stepping on more mines was a given. "But I wonder if she's not feeling a little neglected. Sounds like you've been working some long hours."

No response to that, just ominous silence.

"Anyway," he said, eager to move on, "I'll take her back home just as soon as we manage breakfast, or straight to school if that works better. Just give me the details either way."

"Bring her here," Stefani said, but far from the anger he'd feared, her words were absent, as though she was lost in self-reflection. She suddenly sounded not herself.

It can't be easy to learn your adopted daughter all but ran away from home and you had no idea. Which reminded him.

"Well, if it wasn't for Marri, to what do I owe the pleasure of this call?" he asked.

A long sigh, as much static as breath over the connection. What she said next surprised him even more than Marri lunging from the darkness to save his dinner had.

"I'm sorry for the whiplash, Karl. And the early call. I recall you tend to be up before the sun, and I can't sleep with so much on my mind. I called because I have a job offer for you," she said.

Karl listened as Stefani recounted the riot in Inkwell, then her meeting with the archon afterward. "I know you have contact with the police in your current line of work," she said after finishing her story. "I'm hoping what I'm asking won't increase your risk. But there really is no one I trust more to handle this despite, well, everything."

To be honest, Stefani, I'd almost preferred you had asked me to find Kyne Libretta for you. Despite the murderous woman having seemingly vanished from the city and having not been seen since Iazmaena died, it seemed like an easier task than what was being asked of him. Safer too.

"I see," Karl said, hoping the pause hadn't been too obvious. "Well, as it happens, I'm getting ready to turn in a bounty to one of the precincts tomorrow morning. Maybe I could make a trade for information instead. It's in Renewal Ward, though, not Inkwell."

"That might work out, actually," Stefani said, her voice brightening. "Giana is going to be checking with a contact of hers in the Renewal police as well. Someone named Arjun Khatri. Maybe you can make contact with him specifically. It might smooth the way a bit."

Karl very much doubted it, but he allowed Stefani her illusions if it helped lessen her guilt.

"I know what I'm asking is difficult," she said, perhaps reading his silence correctly. "Believe me, I know they have difficulty looking past anyone they see as responsible for the downfall of their patron saint of an archon. I'm just hoping the fact you've already been punished so thoroughly will remove some of the target from your back."

More than anything, she sounded as if she needed it to be true. And, in the end, Karl knew he was just delaying the inevitable.

"I'll do what I can," he said.

"Thank you." Stefani's gratitude was palpable. "I can't tell you how much it means to have someone I can trust taking care of this."

Karl was far less sanguine about his chances of success, but it wouldn't do to say as much. Instead, it was time to nail down logistics.

"I'd like whatever formal information you have on hand before I get started." Which was little enough, by the sound of things, but anything was better than nothing.

"Of course," she said without hesitation. "I can get something together for you in time to hand it to you directly when you drop Marri off."

"I'll see you then." Karl hung up with a sigh, leaning back in his office chair to relieve the pressure on his hip, which had been building there steadily for the entire call. He took a sip of what turned out to be stale, cold coffee and let it dribble back into the mug in disgust, the remnants of his sleep thoroughly un-banished.

It was not often a single call could illuminate so much about someone. Had Karl been a normal person, he'd have been angry with Stefani for asking him to do something that would directly involve him with the police. She didn't understand, of course. Maybe, in her own way, she couldn't. The police hated her as well, but she was insulated from their anger.

Or had been, until yesterday.

Maybe she was right. Maybe the fact he had been punished while she had been promoted gave him more armor than he'd heretofore assumed in his extremely careful dealings. But whether that was true or not, sooner or later, her patronage would end. And if Karl ruined his own meal ticket, what then?

But he hadn't said that, and he wouldn't. Instead of anger at her for not knowing better, he felt a giddy elation that he would have more opportunity to prove himself useful to her, to be present in her life.

It was such an odd way to learn how deeply his judgment had been compromised.

CHAPTER 9

GIANA WOKE to a pounding headache and the feel of sheets soaked with sweat against her bare skin. Everything about the sensation immediately screamed its wrongness. She recalled all-too-vividly what kind of night Dr. Hayasun's post-mortem message had prompted: the vomit, the screaming, the collapse onto her bed.

The *fully clothed* collapse.

As though the message had prompted her to regress in time, she vividly recalled the last time she'd felt this way: on that awful day eight months ago. She'd woken in an identical state, naked in bed and hung over. Only that night, at least, she'd had an entire bottle of wine to blame. She supposed crying and vomiting could have the same dehydrating effect. Plus, there had been some bourbon last night, now that she really thought about it. Still, it seemed odd to have removed her clothes and not remember doing so. Probably she just needed to set her apartment's temperature down.

However hazy that night eight months gone had been, she still recalled her reason for downing that entire bottle of wine. She'd been seriously contemplating quitting Gene Sequencing at the time. Her anxiety that day had been particularly bad and had spiraled into wondering if they would even *let* her quit.

However immature and childish those thoughts seemed now, that day, they had started her drinking. The resulting hangover and the fit of paranoia had caused her to call out of work the next morning.

That was how Giana Novak had become the only GS employee not reporting for duty the day Iazmaena Delgassi's siege had begun.

For months now, the survivor's guilt had plagued her. A self-induced hangover had saved her life, after all, saved her life and left her utterly alone at the same time. But now, on this eerily parallel morning, with the rising sun cutting into her eyes like blades of light, she recalled something else: a memory that Dr. Hayasun's long-delayed message had unlocked.

When she'd called in sick that day, she'd missed a meeting Dr. Hayasun had set up with her, *just* her. He'd even flagged it as critically important. Remembering it now, possibly for the first time since the siege began, Giana realized it had to be related to whatever was in that final message. It was too much of a coincidence to assume that Dr. Hayasun had *two* critical messages he had to relay to her.

Giana rose with a groan, peeling the sheet away from her, relishing the soothing cool of her apartment's air conditioning—which was actually set quite low—on her pebbling skin. On unsteady feet, her muscles watery with unusual weakness, her eyes squinted against the glare of the sun, Giana made her teetering way to the bathroom.

She pushed the door open wide enough to enter, only to have another long-buried memory slam jarringly home.

Alongside the lingering smell of vomit emerging from the toilet was a second odor, even more unpleasant. It was almost like rotting meat, though blessedly fainter. With a single whiff of that stench, Giana knew with sudden clarity exactly what she would find.

The mass that had flowed the wrong way back up into the tub from the pipes below was black and sludgy like rancid oil. She could hear the slow *gulp-slurp* sounds of it draining its way back from whence it had come, whatever blockage had prompted it having apparently slunk its own way back down the pipes.

Giana turned on the water as hot and hard as it would go to help the foul mess along in its departure. A stubborn frown tugged at her brows as she did so. Perhaps she was conflating two unpleasant memories for the feelings of stress and anxiety they induced, but she knew this too had happened once before.

And she was almost positive it had happened the same day she wakened with a hangover and the Gene Sequencing siege had begun.

That seemed strange in a way that was significant. If Gene Sequencing had still existed, she'd have probably reported it to them as an oddity worth investigating.

It doesn't exist. It doesn't matter. Weird and gross things happen all the time in this city. Just forget about it. You have duties to attend to today.

All of that was very true, and surprisingly, it actually helped quiet Giana's misgivings. Even the thought of a normal day in Stefani's service blunted the edge of her hangover. The previous night's urge to resign as the magistrate's assistant had been banished as thoroughly as the night's darkness. Another childish fancy.

Maybe someday she would grow out of those.

Deciding breakfast while the tub sorted itself out would save her time, Giana headed for the kitchen with renewed purpose in her step.

She was absolutely ravenous.

CHAPTER 10

MARRI SULKED ALL the way back to Stefani's apartment. Karl congratulated himself on being wise enough not to point this out to the newly minted teenager. They rode the tram in silence instead, Karl making a point not to stare at the girl but also never quite taking his eyes off her. He knew from experience how quickly she could vanish into even a light crowd.

He was especially vigilant during the earthquake that forced the tram to briefly stop all too near an easily reachable rooftop.

For her part, Marri seemed fixated on staring blankly into the middle distance, brow furrowed slightly as though by some faraway worry. Karl wanted to say something to comfort her, but he didn't know how to talk to teenagers. He still didn't even know what was bothering her, really. As they reached their stop, he at last risked a comment, settling on a simple truth.

"I quite enjoyed the visit, you know. Next time, just get permission first."

Marri rolled her eyes as she stood, but he thought she stifled a smile too.

As Stefani opened the door to admit them, some part of Karl tried to see if she looked more tired or haggard than when she'd seen him last: signs that their breakup had affected her.

Gods below, old man, stop flattering yourself. And it's only been a day.

"You look good," he said, because it was the simple truth, and one he knew he didn't share.

Stefani's smile was wry, but she spoke first to Marri.

"Go inside. We're going to have a talk, you and I, once I've spoken to Karl."

"Thanks for sharing your dinner last night and for breakfast this morning," Marri said, turning away from Stefani to face Karl. Her words were mild and contrite, but her face was a warning thunderhead. *Don't repeat what I told you,* that face said, on pain of death.

Karl smiled as blandly noncommittal a smile as he possessed. Marri's scowl deepened, but she disappeared into the dim early morning light of the apartment beyond Stefani.

"Thank you for looking out for her," Stefani said softly. Her own smile looked as false as Karl's felt. "After all, you have to bring her back in one piece if I'm going to kill her."

Karl suppressed a wince. It was a joke, if a poorly timed one. Though there was no way she could know that. All at once, and for reasons he couldn't explain, he decided to honor Marri's request.

"I don't claim to be an expert," Karl said. "But I have heard a thing or two about kids her age and how they tend to be."

"I think if they could truly get across the magnitude of the reality," Stefani said, "we'd go extinct, because no one would have kids."

"Sounds a bit like lancer boot camp," Karl said, this time with a genuine chuckle that only hurt a little in the end.

Stefani chuckled too, seemingly against her better judgment by the way she shook herself after. "Maybe I'd better just give this to you." She reached out with a tiny data drive. "The size of the drive is symbolically appropriate, as there really isn't much. Let me know if there's anything I left out or any way I can help." She did meet his eyes then. "And thank you. You're taking a great weight off my shoulders."

"Happy to help," he said. Nothing in his heart had changed since last night, so it was a truer sentiment than he might have wished.

CHAPTER 11

"WHAT WERE YOU THINKING?" Stefani was so tired. Even raising her voice at her adopted child required more energy than she could muster. "Running off in the middle of the night like that. I had no idea where you'd gone."

"You had no idea I *was* gone, you mean," Marri countered.

Stefani bit back a curse. What she had no idea of was how the girl had worked that out. She'd specifically asked Karl not to mention it, and what a sting to her motherly pride that had been. *Nothing's changed since Ella was born. Now, you just neglect two daughters instead of one.*

Still, a tiny part of her thrilled at the exchange. It was a topic that actually let her feel strong emotions, and thus like herself. Most of the time, like herself. Sometimes, the strong emotions provoked feelings that were worse than the lack of emotion.

But Stefani had found the risk was usually worth it.

"I know I haven't been here much for you lately," Stefani said, keeping her tone measured. "And I'm going to change that. I am. I can do more of my work from here, particularly in the evenings. I can delegate some operations."

As if on cue, Ella's monitor beeped its customary twin alerts.

MUTAGEN PRIME: ACTIVE. MUTAGEN PRIME: DORMANT. Another spike of guilt lodged itself right next to her guilt over Marri.

I shouldn't have even brought Marri into this house. I've endangered her. But after Iaz, the thought of losing Marri too, even if it was to a loving home, had been too much.

When she got right down to it, the girl reminded Stefani so much of her dead friend at that age.

And nothing in Ella's strange and alarming condition had changed in eight months for good or ill.

We're still digging through Gene Sequencing's records. What's left of them. There must be something in there. There has to be!

"Giana is on her way here now," Stefani said briskly, trying to leave no room in her voice for argument. "She'll be taking you to school while I get to the office."

Marri had not taken well to the more social aspects of school so far, and recently, Stefani had been indulgent of her taking her classes remotely, from the apartment. Well, no more. She could read the girl's face like a targeted ad. She felt she was being punished.

She's always been perceptive.

"This isn't a punishment," Stefani lied. "It's so I know some adult has their eyes on you." That part, at least, was true.

"If your assistant is taking me to school," Marri said, her eyes calculating, "I guess that means all that stuff about making more time for me starts ... tonight? Tomorrow?"

Stefani gritted her teeth. She knew it was a calculated attack, but that didn't mean it didn't hurt. Worse, the fact she believed the girl was lying, that Marri *didn't* want to spend time in Stefani's presence for some reason, just made it hurt more. Had she already lost her? Was too much damage done?

The other voice chimed in, then. The one that sometimes arose when Stefani remembered how to feel real anger. It was pure rage, that voice. It whispered awful things, things no decent person should ever think. Not even for a moment.

Stefani forced it down with her own inner monologue. *Do. Not. Retaliate.*

"I know this has been hard," Stefani said. "It's a lot of change, and a lot of pain, for all of us. We all saw things we can't unsee." The way Marri broke eye contact and shifted her stance in discomfort told Stefani this, at least, had gotten through. "I'm going to try to do better, but I need you to meet me halfway. I need you not to make this transition any harder than it has to be. So no more running off, at night or otherwise. We're going to wipe the slate clean and start fresh, and we're all going to try to do better."

"You first," Marri said with sudden venom.

Teenager, Stefani thought, like a whole other mantra. She forced her breathing to slow. *Teenager. Teenager. Teenager.* Mostly, the repeated word blotted out the other voice. *I'll gut you like a fish, you little shit-stain, if you ever talk that way to me again!*

And that was why Stefani only *mostly* enjoyed the rare instances when strong emotion could punch through her shell of numbness. The other times, that other voice, frightened her terribly. It was as though a second person lived in her mind in those moments. A person that hated almost everyone, but Marri in particular.

"We're both going to do better," she said, the words measured. She tried to make them inexorable.

This time, it worked. Marri did not respond, but the way her head hung suggested that Stefani's failure to rise to the bait had finally found a path to the girl's contrition. Steeling herself, Stefani walked over, gave Marri a hug she did not return, and kissed the top of the girl's head.

"Have a good day at school," she said, the hateful voice within at last falling into an irate silence. "We'll talk more tonight."

Then she turned back to the bedroom to finish getting ready. The storm of emotions slid from her like rain off a poncho. All but the urgency, and that was always there. It was going to be another full day, and she'd already gotten a late start.

The clock was always ticking.

CHAPTER 12

"I RAN off because I'm trying to protect you," Marri said softly to the bedroom door once it slid closed with Stefani on the other side of it. She sighed. How could she explain her reasoning? *I think I might hurt you if I stay. I don't understand what's happening to me.* The answer was that she couldn't explain. Didn't make it bad reasoning, though.

She sighed again, thinking wistful thoughts of her time in the Mouse Hole with the other mice. As hungry as they'd been, as tired and stressed, she'd mattered then in a way she didn't now. Maybe that was all it was. Maybe what Marri thought was some sort of terrifying transformation going on inside her was actually just her brain's way of saying she hated her new life.

The old me would kick this me in the shins for turning up my nose at steady meals and a warm bed. But the old her was gone. This Marri, whomever she was, was all she had now.

She shook herself. No time for that. She couldn't let Karl get too far ahead of her in his investigation. Fortunately, he moved slow now. Unfortunately, a day spent in school would only give him more time to slowly investigate things without her.

Marri contemplated simply walking out of the apartment again, right now. But Stefani would probably call Magistrate Xavier of Watchfire and ask him to deploy the lancers to find her. And the last time that had happened, Magister Xavier's annoying son had really gotten on Marri's nerves about it at the City Council mixer Stefani had forced her to attend.

No, it would be better, smarter, to go to school and make use of the software she'd sneaked onto Karl's handheld when he'd been inattentive.

He had not been nearly as careful during his late-night call as he'd thought. Listening to half a conversation was not nearly as useful as listening to all of one, but after the initial awkwardness of hearing the pair of them discuss her, Marri had figured out what Stefani was telling him easily enough.

Stefani wanted Karl to figure out what the police were up to.

Marri had never had a violent run-in with Coldgarden's police, but that was not for lack of their trying. In her experience, they were both dangerous and unpredictable. And Karl was just one man, and no longer the warrior he'd been. Marri felt a flush of anger at Stefani for using Karl's feelings for her to goad him into taking this job. Stefani had a bad habit of assuming her friends could handle themselves without help, as if that kind of assumption had not already backfired badly.

That time, Marri had listened to Stefani for too long, gone along with her plan to leave Magistrate Delgassi in the presence of that ghoul. And Magistrate Delgassi had died. Died and turned into ... something.

Marri's memories of all that were admittedly blurry because of the concussion she'd suffered at the time, an injury she still didn't remember getting. But the little she recalled from Iazmaena's body seemed very different from any hypermutation she'd ever seen.

And even if she hadn't been fuzzy on the details, Stefani had told Marri never to speak about it, told her in a way that left Marri too scared to even consider defying her. It was a mood Stefani sometimes had to fight to keep down these days. She'd had to do so again just a few minutes ago. Marri had learned to spot the signs.

Anyway, the warning was barely needed. Marri didn't like to think about the thing Iazmaena's body had done when she died. It brought up other thoughts. Thoughts she didn't like. Thoughts she liked too much.

If I'd left right away, if I'd gotten there in time, if I'd never left at all, Magistrate Delgassi would still be alive, and none of this would be happening now. I can't let anything like that happen again.

If Karl was trying to expose police secrets, then so was Marri. She didn't like the idea of him, with his injury, wandering the city doing dangerous stuff without her. Revenants or not, these were not safe times in Coldgarden.

She'd seen the Strange Man again on the tram car, just as she'd seen him the night before on her way to Karl's. She hadn't mentioned the Strange Man to Karl, just as she'd never mentioned him to Stefani. That was for the very simple fact that he didn't exist.

Nobody ever saw him but Marri.

Nobody reacted to his presence, or his weird old-fashioned clothes: a brown, broad-brimmed hat and a long, high-collared coat which obscured his too-thin frame. He'd been appearing to her ever since Magistrate Delgassi had died, which meant it was likely another gift of the concussion she'd gotten that day. So much of that day was hazy.

But even as she knew the Strange Man was in her head, Marri couldn't help but think of him as a kind of harbinger of doom. He filled her with dread whenever she saw him. So the fact she'd been seeing him more and more left her on edge.

But if she wanted to protect Karl today, she needed to forget about the Strange Man and worry more about Giana. And as if thinking of devils beyond summoned them, the door to the apartment opened to a chipper, "Knock, knock!" as Stefani's assistant let herself in.

Giana looked as immaculate as always, the perfect picture of an assistant to someone important. She spotted Marri immediately, moving closer and beaming. The expression reached her eyes even less than it usually did, and close-up, Marri could see she looked uncharacteristically tired today.

"I understand you had quite the night last night!" Giana tried to make it sound like she'd been there with Marri or had at least helped her plan it.

Marri kept her face smooth to disguise her loathing of this woman, but that had stopped working months ago. She could wish Giana was stupider, but thinking your enemies were stupid because you didn't like them just made you the stupid one.

As if to prove Marri's point, Giana was too perfect to falter at the non-answer. "Well, are you just about ready for school?" She wrinkled her nose, and Marri, abruptly self-conscious, tried to remember the last time she'd taken a shower. Then she angrily chided herself for letting Giana get one over on her. She would just go to school smelly, and everyone she came across could deal with it.

"Yes," Marri said, smiling with acid sweetness.

"You don't want to put on fresh clothes?"

"I do not."

"Well, then," Giana said, her own sweetness at dangerous levels, "don't you at least need your bag?"

Out of spite, Marri tried to think of an excuse that would believably let her not bring her bag.

No. Be smart. Marri had always been good at hiding, at moving around unseen. But you were never unseen when you were the daughter of a magistrate. It was a horrible lesson to learn, but that didn't change the facts. She had to learn a different kind of hiding. So she went and got her bag, reaching for it under her bed and around the small pile of disassembled electronics she kept hidden there.

"See now?" Giana said as Marri emerged. "Following the rules isn't so bad, is it?"

Marri almost agreed, but some mimic's instinct told her that would be taking the ruse too far. If she pretended to be perfect all of a sudden, they would be suspicious. Instead, she had to pretend to be what they *expected* her to be, which was a difficult little girl who grudgingly admitted when she was beaten. So she shrugged as sullenly as she could.

"Come on, Little Miss Grump," Giana said, sighing. "The sooner we get you there, the sooner I can get back to work!"

And the sooner I get there, Marri thought, for once in complete agreement with the hateful woman, *the sooner I can get a look at what Karl is doing.*

CHAPTER 13

GIANA LEFT Marri at the school entrance, deep in the heart of Illuminance and as far away from walls or Underguts entrances as it was possible to be in this city. The horrible woman departed with a false smile and even falser well-wishes for Marri to study hard. Giana was clearly confident that all the extra security recently put in place to keep Marri there—most of it Giana's idea—would ensure Marri couldn't escape.

She climbed the school steps leadenly, in case Giana was still watching. Head hung in fake defeat, she noted how chipped and cracked the composicrete was. And this was supposed to be one of the good schools.

"Well, look who it is?" said a snide, shrill voice as the door shut behind her.

Marri hid a grimace. She hated that voice almost as much as Giana's: the school guard. Marri was sure the woman had a name, but she refused to learn it.

Attempting to look as annoyed as possible, Marri submitted to the special scan that only she received to make sure she wasn't smuggling in anything that she could use to sneak back out later. The school had learned its lessons well. The bored guard—they'd hired her just for

Marri, because apparently letting a magistrate's daughter leave to wander the city whenever she wanted was very bad—had boiled everything she was supposed to do down to a series of hand gestures.

Marri obeyed these wordlessly as the scanners searched and found nothing. The woman's boredom barely concealed her confidence in the system. Tricky as she was, Marri was a former gutter rat. She might be handy with lock-picks and unguarded valuables, but she couldn't trick machines.

So they all thought.

When these precautions had first appeared, she had considered simply waiting them out. Surely, once they thought she'd been bullied into behaving herself, they would relax, slip-up. But waiting wasn't really Marri's favorite thing.

Looking back, she realized now she had revealed too much about her own strengths and weaknesses when she'd taken work from Magistrate Delgassi to keep her mice fed. And despite all her own secrets, Magistrate Delgassi had apparently had no problems blabbing all about Marri's. To her horror, everyone had suddenly just known that basic e-locks with biometric seals or even just passcodes would keep her out. Or, in this case, in.

This was unacceptable.

Letting people know her weaknesses just gave them the means to stop her doing what she had to do. So in the months since, and especially since the school precautions had gone into place, Marri had worked hard to remove this particular weakness, and she'd worked even harder to keep that removal a secret.

She was fairly certain Karl had bought her sullenness the previous night when he'd threatened to install an e-lock that would no longer keep her out, whatever the man might think.

Sometimes all this secrecy, keeping things from people she cared about, made her sad, and getting sad over that always made her angry. After all, it wasn't her fault every adult she knew tried to restrict her so much. They should be the sad ones.

Among the things the adults wouldn't let her bring into school was her personal handheld. She'd had to scrap her old handheld after they'd confiscated it for a day, because who knew what they'd done to it in the meantime?

The daily scans had forced her to get creative, which for her, usually started with stealing something. In this case, that had been one of the school-use handhelds that were supposed to stay in her classroom.

Stealing Jerald's had been easy enough. He sat just three rows over from her and was too mean and stupid to figure out what she'd done.

She'd known the missing handheld wouldn't get discovered until a day later, which gave Marri exactly two evenings to make the stolen handheld mirror everything it did to her personal handheld she kept at home and vice versa. That had been hard, but she was getting good at these sorts of things, and she was coming to enjoy them as well.

She supposed it would have been cleaner to make her upgrades in one evening, so the missing handheld would never have been noticed at all, but she really liked the bonus of getting Jerald in trouble.

On the second morning after her theft, faced with a mandatory search that would have turned up the stolen and now-hacked handheld in her possession, she'd reverse-pickpocketed the device into Jerald's bag, letting the idiot carry it in for her.

Her plan worked perfectly—Jerald had even gotten in trouble a second time for lying because he'd denied having the device—and afterward, all she had to do was steal it again, this time swapping it with her own school handheld so nothing was missing. Then she had her own hacked device.

Simple.

Marri waited until a school-wide lesson was broadcast to everyone at once so the students' desk screens were raised, shielding what she was doing from the front of the class. Then she pulled out her corrupted device and checked to make sure the mirroring was still working.

She felt a little thrill of exultation when the tracker software opened and displayed to her the blinking red dot that was Karl, moving swiftly through the city on a tram line.

If he thought he was investigating the police alone, he was in for a surprise.

CHAPTER 14

THE DAY HAD BEGUN with hiring her newly minted ex after he'd returned her wayward daughter. Now, as she finally saw the end of it in sight, all Stefani wanted was a few hours' peace where she could get some work done. It was why she stayed so late at Illuminance Hall most days. There was just no other time when she wasn't constantly being hounded by concerns other than the ones she cared about.

"Are you sure you don't need anything else?" Giana asked with her usual solicitousness.

"No, Giana, thank you." Stefani had to mask the spike of annoyance she felt that the woman wouldn't just *go* already. It was an annoyance based on guilt over how many hours her assistant worked, which amplified Stefani's guilt over the impending breaking of her promise to Marri on the very day she'd made it. Nonetheless, Stefani tried to relish the grounding sensation both feelings awoke in her. "And thank you again for making sure Marri got safely to school. That girl will be the death of me. Go on and enjoy your evening."

Giana smiled brightly, if tiredly, and ushered herself out. This friendly ease hadn't always been the way. Even through her bouts of dissociation, Stefani had sensed tension between them almost from the moment the other woman accepted her position. Probably it was just the normal stormy opening to any working relationship between two such different people, but more than once in the first few months, Stefani had wondered if she'd made a mistake.

After Giana departed, Stefani stared at the office door she'd left open in her wake. It was an entirely appropriate decision on Giana's part. Stefani's open-door office hours were technically not over for the day, but she was still tempted to key the door closed from her desk.

Still, it was getting late. It would be very unlikely for someone to show up now, but the blowback she'd get if someone *did* show up and found a locked door would be, well, not worth the PR hassle. With a minor prayer to spare her any further visits, Stefani left the door as it was and resumed work.

Magistrate Barker of Sparks Ward—Stefani always had to resist the urge to think of him as Magistrate Sparker—had sent Stefani another half-dozen messages just in the past hour. He was one of those that thought of something he needed to say and sent it instantly. Then he would think twice and send a follow up. Then a follow up to the follow up, and on it went.

As with most of the messages they exchanged, the latest flurry regarded the last odds and ends of restoring full power and functionality to Inkwell. It was a project that was mostly under the jurisdiction of Sparks, which made sense since they were the ward focused on powering the city. But Archon Graysteel had ordered the repairs be made with an eye toward modernizing and ruggedizing the grid, exploring ways it could be kept up even in the event of another cordon. That meant consultations with Stefani's ward, focused as it was on science and engineering challenges.

Under any other magistrate, the effort would have been on autopilot long ago. But Barker was a classic micromanager.

With a sigh, Stefani scrolled down to the bottom of the message chain, determined to start at the beginning of Barker's stream of consciousness thought process.

Hi Stef,
My people are telling me that the seismometers your people
installed after the last quake have been detecting smaller
quakes (below human detection threshold) basically nonstop.
These aren't a problem on their own, I'm told, but I don't like
what they suggest. Here's hoping they are aftershocks and not
whatever the term is for aftershocks that happen before. Befor-
eshocks?
Will

Stefani pinched the bridge of her nose, trying to stay above the irritation and appreciate it for the honest emotion it was rather than simply succumb to it. An overly familiar message with no question and nothing specifically useful for her was very typical Barker. The other five messages suggested he was working his way up to something. And Stefani really did have to play nice with him. The Bridge was going to require a phenomenal amount of the city's power when it was brought online, and Sparks was key to making sure it had that power. But before Stefani could read on and learn the culmination of Barker's message chain, she became aware that she was no longer alone in the room.

A figure stood in the doorway, draped in a long, dark coat and sporting a red, wide-brimmed hat of a style that felt both timeless and archaic, both of which completely obscured any distinguishing features. The fact, and the knowledge that she was utterly alone on this floor of the office, filled Stefani with a delicious spike of fear.

Her worry abated when the figure swept her hat from her head with a flourish, revealing brilliant red hair. Memories crashed home, along with a sense of relaxation and growing warmth. Stefani shouldn't have felt either of the latter two, considering what it indicated about her mental state.

"Ali!" As ever when the woman appeared to her like this, Stefani could suddenly recall with vivid clarity all the other Ali visits since Iaz's death. They were conversations she could only remember while one of them was happening, which gave them a dreamlike quality despite the sharpness of the recollections while she was having them.

This, plus the fact that Ali Dionya had been dead for more than a year, should have alarmed Stefani far more than it did. But standing here in her office, Ali just seemed so *real*, it was hard to feel anything but pleasant emotions while she was visiting. More practically, she also only appeared when Stefani was alone and her schedule was clear. Hence, she'd never had to explain whom she was conversing with to anyone else.

Ali was a very considerate hallucination.

"It's been a while." Stefani went on into the silence. She tried to sound as though it was not a fact she was only just now recalling. "I worried you'd stopped coming for good." It was technically true, even if she was only now worrying about it retroactively.

"I'm so sorry, Steffi dear!" Ali said. "It's been hard to find chances lately, you know?" Ali had been one to tease without mercy but had always carefully shrouded her genuine criticisms in silk.

"I know my schedule has been madness," Stefani said ruefully. "I can't exactly put you on my calendar, though, can I?"

"No," Ali said, her smile a little sad. "I suppose not."

"I don't know what I'd do if I couldn't talk to you," Stefani said, fighting back a sudden glaze of tears that had formed over her eyes. "I don't know how I'd manage."

And this, also, was true. The terror of never seeing the other woman again—Stefani's last link to a past otherwise dead and gone—was all the more horrifying in these lucid moments when she could both remember to feel it and know she would soon forget it again.

God, what is wrong with me?

"Oh, don't be dramatic, you manage fine," Ali said, laughing merrily around that knowing smile. "Look at what you're getting done. Look at the Bridge. You're so close to getting it working."

"I wish I felt your confidence." *I wish I understood why it needed to work.* These meetings allowed her to drift closer to clarity, but she never fully washed ashore. And, of course, Stefani forgot nearly everything about them once they were over.

Still, she took heart from the force of conviction behind Ali's words. Even though she knew her old friend could sound that confident about *anything*, it still somehow steadied her. "It's still all thanks to you," she said. "Even if I can't remember most of the time, all these notions have come from you."

"If I'm just a hallucination," Ali said with a wink, "isn't that all just you too?" She took Stefani's hand in hers, which were warm, almost hot.

Such vivid hallucinations. Stefani should really talk to someone about this. Ali must surely be some kind of defense mechanism for some awful memory she'd suppressed. But she knew she wouldn't seek help. Even if she'd wanted to remember whatever traumatic event her brain was blocking, seeking help meant trying to make Ali go away. And Stefani didn't want that to happen.

She nodded reluctantly in answer. "I suppose so, but it doesn't feel like it. I'm just so confused all the time."

"I know, hon," Ali said, face all sympathy. "I know it's hard. But every time I visit, we get you a little bit closer to understanding, and this time's no different. I'm going to try to help you again, try to explain. I feel like we can get you there without killing you if we take it slow. Listen to me talk and try to hold onto the present. I'll go easy at first, talk as vaguely as I can, but we won't get intense about it. I don't want you to have an aneurysm. Focus on what I'm saying."

Stefani had a vague recollection of Ali saying similar words many times before, but she didn't argue.

"You made the change early," Ali said, "with Teodori's mad dog of an enforcer. And then you made it again, with Pal—"

Stefani came back to herself. Ali had been talking, but she'd drifted off. Whatever she'd heard had evaporated like dew.

"Sorry, what? Not sure where I was just now."

"Nothing, it's not important. Really, I'm just glad you can remember seeing me at all." Ali's smile made it the truth, however much such things frustrated Stefani. Then the other woman's look grew pensive as she continued to speak. "It's so odd what the mind considers acceptable and not, what oddities it will rationalize away, no matter how strange, out of yearning. If only we had more time, we might truly come to understand all this. What we were and what we've become. But we don't have time, and I'm rambling. And now it's time to get real."

Serious was not an Ali face any of her friends had seen often, but that just made it strike home all the more when she used it.

"The reason I'm here," Ali said, "is that you need to accelerate the Bridge project. As fast as you've been going, it has to be faster. Circumstances are deteriorating faster than we'd predicted. So we need you to pick up the pace."

"If not for the fucking police trying to stir up rebellion or God-knows-what, and Kyne Libretta and her fucking booby traps, I'd have the thing done already!" The words, and the tsunami of rage they rode upon, crashed out of Stefani before she was even aware they were coming. *The other one again.*

"Goodness, Stefani Palmieri with the f-bombs. That doesn't seem right." Despite the lightness of her words, concern flashed across Ali's face. "That sounds like the other you. The one before Stefani."

Dizziness rocked Stefani at the other woman's words. Her mind felt like glass teetering at the edge of the table, poised to shatter, and the sensation felt every bit as ominous.

"What," Stefani began, then had to gulp to keep down her lunch. "What does that mean? What are you talking about?" *Please. I want to understand.*

But Ali acted as though she hadn't spoken. "I'm afraid you're going to have to be a little more mercenary. This city has people to spare. And however wicked Kyne Libretta might be, the number of traps she could have set must be finite."

"You're asking me to feed my people into whatever jaws she's left lying around. Work through any remaining traps with brute force."

"Not your best, obviously," Ali said. Her shrug had the grace to be chagrined, at least. "Not the ones you can't do without. But Stefani, if the Bridge doesn't get completed on time, *everyone* is at risk. And if it docs, you won't have to worry about disgruntled police. If ever there was a time for a little utilitarianism, now would be it. I guess that's my message to you this time. I know you don't really remember these conversations when I'm not around, but you can manage the essence of a concept or two. A drive. So, let's do the thing properly, and I can give you back your evening."

She leaned over then, taking Stefani's hands in her own for the second time and locking gazes just a few centimeters away. It was always this way, Stefani recalled. Whatever message Ali arrived to impart, she did so using this method. It always felt like being hypnotized.

"Listen to the sound of my voice," Ali said, and her voice seemed to resonate in Stefani's ears. "Listen and remember. The time for caution has passed." Her words were even more like drills than her eyes. "The Bridge must be completed as soon as possible. However reckless you feel you've been, it's not reckless enough. It *must* get finished. Whatever the cost. *Whatever the cost.* As soon as possible."

Ali moved away a meter or so, breaking her gaze, and it was like a spell had been lifted. With the lifting, Stefani felt a wash of unreality pass over her. Her friend's words had strained the pleasant feelings she brought. They were unlike anything Ali would ever say. It was almost enough to make Stefani feel like she wasn't even talking to Ali.

"Please," Stefani said impulsively. "Please, what you're asking is … Help me understand. If I could just understand, *really* understand why I'm doing this, what is really happening and why, I think it would be easier on me." Her consternation must have been plain on her face, because the other woman sighed in obvious frustration.

"Pushing harder is risky. You have no idea how risky, and you are irreplaceable. On the other hand, I wouldn't need to convince you if you could just remember everything without your mind fracturing. And because I'm your Ali in all the ways that matter, I can't stand to see you in this kind of distress and not at least try to help."

Stefani watched Ali wrestle with herself for several moments before at last lowering herself again. "This definitely isn't advisable, but if there's even a chance it could help steel your resolve, maybe we need to try a bit more forcefully. Maybe we can lodge a second concept in your brain, something a bit closer to the truth."

She smiled in that way she always did when she was trying to cover up worry, and once again, the pleasant feelings threatened to drift away. Then she resumed her intense regard. That sense of hypnosis fell over Stefani again. If anything, it was even stronger this time.

"Listen to the sound of my voice. Listen, and remember. The Bridge. You know what's it's for, right?"

"I ... Yes," Stefani said, confused. She did not recall ever being asked to respond during one of these sessions. It was a challenge to find her voice. She felt an unpleasant urge to pull back, to break the spell herself. Another first. "At least, we think we do. It's an interstellar transport device. Disassembled for some reason."

"For safety reasons," Ali said. Her eyes were awls. "So this world's indigenous life could never make it back to Earth. But you already know this."

"Back to ... *what?*" Stefani felt suddenly woozy. The urge to pull away intensified. Her thoughts blurred around the edges, as though attempting to dull the coalescing promise of pain.

"Stay with me!" Ali said sharply. "You know this isn't Earth. It isn't. You *know* that. Don't let it slip away. This has never been Earth. It's a human colony, and the threat we humans face is this world's native life. And we have to leave as soon as possible."

And held by those emerald eyes, Stefani fought, strove to retain that kernel of information even as something within her fought to cast it away, smoldering dust on a burning wind. The pain was no longer merely a promise. It blossomed bright and young, with so much potential for growth. She forced the question that formed past her lips, holding onto it as a ship did an anchor.

"How could we forget that? How could we forget that this is not Earth?"

"There is an answer to that," Ali said. Despite the feel of her hands and her intimate proximity, she seemed to fall away at the far end of a dark tunnel. Her voice was thunder. Stefani's head felt as though it was splitting, first into two, then into three. The pain pulled at her, finally realizing its potential, as though it possessed gravity greater than a world's. "Can you handle that answer, Stefani?"

Stefani opened her mouth. There was a terrible pain in her throat, but she could hear nothing over the roar of the words Ali was speaking. Stefani tasted blood. Her vision reddened.

She was falling away, and then she felt pain in her elbows, palms, and knees. The sharp shock of it brought her back to herself. Ali's voice drew down to normal.

"You were definitely not ready," Ali said. "Are you all right?" And as she helped her friend rise, she sounded as shaken as Stefani felt. Stefani's breath came in ragged gasps and sweat drenched her. One of her legs spasmed, and she nearly pitched over again. But she managed a firm nod.

"Do you remember anything I said?" Ali asked.

Of course, Stefani almost said. The words were there, clear in her mind, until the moment she went looking for them. She almost howled in frustration when she realized she'd lost all but the least of them.

"We have to leave," Stefani said leadenly. "The Bridge has to be done as fast as possible no matter the cost, because we have to leave this world." It tasted as bitter as defeat, but she tried to hold onto the little sliver of victory she'd managed. "I knew before we were running out of time. But I didn't know *why* I knew it, or what it meant. You told me the whole of it just now, didn't you? I'm sorry," she said, a fresh surge of frustration making her voice raw. Or perhaps she had been screaming. "Whatever you said, all I can recall is that we have to leave this world as fast as possible."

Hopefully she would retain the memory once Ali left.

"Hey, that's progress, babe," Ali said, her smile sickly. "We got a little ballsy pushing like that. We're lucky we didn't hurt you, so let's just be happy with the progress we did make."

"You told me we have to leave. But I still don't understand why."

"Because we don't belong here," Ali said, her phrasing careful and precise, as though the wrong word choice might collapse a cabinet full of crystal stemware. "We never did. Just keep that in your mind. We need the Bridge because we need to leave. And we need to leave right now."

Ali left through the still-open office door, which Stefani closed from her desk as the other woman vanished around the corner. Stefani knew she had just a few moments to be this version of herself, the Stefani who remembered that sometimes she hallucinated her dead friend, had conversations with her, and managed to recall slivers of insight from those conversations when she became that other, more forgetful version of herself.

But there was a third Stefani too. One who existed only in the liminal space between the other two, in the brief moments as Hallucinating Stefani became Forgetful Stefani. One who recognized that Ali was no hallucination, but a real flesh-and-blood being signifying something horrible. That third Stefani could almost remember the worst thing that had ever happened to her, but it was always just a hairsbreadth away. That third Stefani prayed every time she became aware for her forgetful self to remember, to realize, so that maybe they could all become one Stefani again and understand what was happening to them, what *had* happened to them.

But that Stefani's prayers were never answered.

CHAPTER 15

RENEWAL WARD on a sunny day felt far less dangerous than it did on a rainy night, but Karl found it no less ugly to look at. Easily the most industrial of the city's wards, the people who had built it had not given much thought to aesthetic appeal as opposed to brute functionality.

He'd planned on this visit to be the last to this precinct, and this ward, at least for a while. Far from becoming used to him, he'd found that too much time spent in the presence of the same officers went over about as well as an offline recycler filled with steadily rotting meat. But now he was going to have to try to convince these officers to let him stick around, and then come around far more frequently. He only hoped the information he could present to them was still valid enough to smooth the way for what he had to do.

Deeper into the ward he limped, dread building in every hitching step he took from the tram stop. At last, he stumped in through the precinct's double doors to find a familiar face smiling widely at him.

"Well, look here. It's our station mascot." A few barks of laughter from the other officers going about their shifts punctuated the man's words. Officer Friendly—Dawkins was his actual name—was still a fairly young man but with a clear view of middle age approaching. As such, the zeal typical of young law enforcement officers—or lancers—had dulled. At least, that was Karl's assessment of the man. Dawkins was his usual level of friendliness, which was to say he still tolerated Karl.

"What have you got for us, old man? Can I assume you are here to once again help us protect and serve our fair city?" Karl had to hand it to him. In word and tone, Friendly was an expert at striding the line between good-natured ribbing and edged comments.

"Just a few locations you might be interested in," Karl said. He'd spent all day tracking down two more leads in a desperate attempt to bolster his resume, so to speak. "Assuming I'm not too old and slow, and you haven't already found Vitirelli, Parsons, and Delacruz, of course."

"You mean you don't do this out of your sense of civic duty? Gramps, I'm shocked." Still, his eyes glittered. Three open cases taken off the board was not nothing. Karl took this as an encouraging sign and gave himself the go-ahead to proceed with his plan.

He had always been as meek as a mouse—any mouse save Marri —in his precinct visits. The police didn't always start out knowing who he was, but they figured it out eventually. Be useful. Be unassuming. Be submissive. Take whatever shit they handed you as long as it was purely verbal in nature. That was his credo.

His new tasking, however, required a new approach.

"Sorry to disappoint, but sense of civic duty's about used up, I'm afraid." He gave Friendly a calculated, knowing look. "I'm sure you understand."

"Oh, we understand," Friendly said. His voice had changed. There was still humor in his tone, but only just. The edge was winning out.

Time to pull back before Karl got too far out on this limb. He raised his hands in mock surrender. "Sorry, officer. I forgot myself. I've just had a day, and I—"

"I don't think any of us here give a fuck about your day," the suddenly not-so-friendly officer said. His tone remained mild throughout, but all trace of warmth or familiarity was gone. "I'm not sure what you think our relationship is here. But just because I smile when you come limping in through that door like a dying dog, we are not at shoot-the-shit-like-we're-work-bros level, and we never will be."

"Understood," Karl said, desperate to stem the flood before it swept him away. All around the precinct lobby, hard eyes were being leveled at him.

"Do you? We had a detective go missing just last night, and you can bet he ain't showing back up alive. They never do when it goes down like that. And he's the third this month." He spat, though Karl thought it was more performance than projectile.

"Officer Dawkins, I didn't mean to offend." Karl fought hard not to flail. "To be honest, I didn't come here to see you specifically. I was told there was an Arjun Khatri here?"

Friendly's nostrils flared, and Karl realized he'd stepped in it yet again. *Of course. He gets to take credit for what you turn up. Ask to talk to a different officer, and that sounds like I'm trying to polish someone else's badge. Stupid old man!*

Friendly snapped his fingers. The sound was shockingly loud in the sudden quiet.

"Hey, Khatri!" he shouted, grabbing the attention of a dark-skinned man with curly black hair. "You expecting a message from former Lance Commander Karl Yonnel?"

"Not in the slightest," Arjun Khatri said stiffly from behind the front desk.

Great, thanks for being on top of that, Giana. Karl didn't know her well, but he knew it was unlike Stefani's assistant to be late on anything, ever. Of course, given the mood in the room, maybe Officer Khatri was just lying to avoid having Friendly's guns turned on him.

"Sorry, Gramps, looks like you're still dealing with me," Friendly said. "Give me your information, and if it's good, you can come back for the money after we take out the trash. And then I don't want to see you here again. A few lowlifes mulched ain't worth my self-respect."

Karl didn't miss the subtle threat, and his stomach churned at the seeming confirmation of so many rumors. *Maybe he's just bluffing.* It didn't matter. *Got to reel this back before I lose control for good.* The idea that he'd ever had control almost made him laugh.

"What's the name of this detective? The one that went missing. I know I'm just a broken-down old lancer, but I'd like to help find them. I can keep an ear open and let you know if I hear anything."

"How 'bout you leave that to us, old-timer?" The tone brooked no possible argument.

Karl nodded in what he hoped was a respectful manner, but the buzz of hostility rising from the other officers in earshot was only growing worse. Unable to leave well enough alone, Karl didn't know if the next words out of his mouth were an attempt to be sure or an airing of what he viewed as an unfair grievance.

"Listen," he said, this time neither backing down nor blustering. That felt like the crucial balance, not that he had any idea what the hell he was even doing. This might land him in the hospital.

Or a gutter somewhere, hypermutated beyond all recognition.

But he pressed on. "I'm sorry for overstepping myself. And I know what you all think of me. I know you hate what I did, and to be honest, I do too. But I was a soldier. Was. Why do you think that's past tense? Do you think I track down lowlifes for table scraps because they showered me with riches for what I did?"

"You had worse coming to you, traitor," another officer piped up.

Karl's heart rate jumped another few notches, ancient reflex warning him he was being ganged up on, surrounded. *Run. Run. Run.* His racing heart stamped out the beat his panicking hindbrain produced.

"Come on, guys," he said, not bothering to hide his desperation to calm the situation. "You're cops. You must get bullshit orders all the time. You're telling me you've never followed an order and been punished for it? I *liked* Iazmaena Delgassi. I didn't want to do what I did. But the other magistrates pulled out some archaic law and showed me how it meant I had to do what they said."

Forget edging back toward the trunk of the tree. He was further out on his limb than ever. It could easily have gone down that way, but it hadn't. With any luck, the extreme secrecy with which Iaz's death was treated meant none of these ward police would know that either.

"It didn't feel right," he said, "but it was a legal order as far as I could tell. I'm no fancy lawyer. If there was a way around it, I couldn't see it."

Wonder of wonders, the angry buzz abated some, replaced in part by an air of consideration.

Karl lowered his voice, trying to grab any moment of advantage. "And legal or not, they threatened to make me vanish if I didn't do what they said. It was a mistake, but I made it under duress. Then, when their dirty work was all done, they swept me aside like revenant scat."

"That true?" As though steam could simply become water again on the instant, Officer Friendly's attitude had veered back toward Karl's name for him.

"Only reason they didn't disappear me anyway was that it would be inconvenient, I figure. But they made me swear not to tell a soul."

"Then why are you telling us now?" This was Arjun, and he sounded worried, as though Karl had suddenly gone Mutagen Prime active and was hell-bent on spreading it to everyone in the room.

This was it, the crucial moment. He had to sell it, or this still might end in disaster. Running would never be an option for him again.

"Because I'm sick of these politicians and their fucking conspiracy games," he said from under furrowed brows. He tried to make his voice sound dangerous, but it wasn't something he was practiced at. Still, based on the reactions on the faces he could see, it had gotten them to think. "I'm sick of scrabbling through the streets like a gutter rat trying to survive."

Now was the moment where he could reveal some of what he knew, enough to try and put his foot in the door. But he sensed that was too aggressive. He was in the precinct's lobby. If some of the cops in the room were among those fomenting discord, it didn't mean all of them were. Besides, none of this could seem like Karl's idea. Instead, he pulled out his handheld with an air of getting a task done and moving on.

"But my problems aren't your problems. Wanting to get back at them is one thing. Actually doing it, well ..." He shrugged, trying to look defeated. "I mean, look at me. What can I do?"

For several moments after Friendly took custody of the location data and Karl turned to stump back out the door, he thought he'd been too timid at the last. Or too honest about his utility to any budding revolution.

Then Friendly approached, leaning in for Karl's ears alone. "Hold on a second, there, Gramps," he said. Karl paused, trying to look merely warily curious instead of eager.

"Let's talk."

CHAPTER 16

EVEN IN THE GATHERING DUSK, Marri could spot Karl's limp as the old lancer departed the police station. It would have been obvious from a kilometer off. She considered approaching him, but that would mean tipping him off that she was able to follow his handheld. He was old but not stupid. Besides, she had mainly come here to make sure he walked out of the police precinct he'd walked into so willingly.

So maybe he wasn't as smart as she thought.

She considered simply making for a tram station he wouldn't be headed toward and going home before Stefani caught her missing again. But she was in luck. As she matched Karl's pace, keeping to the other side of the street so no one would associate them with one another, he raised his handheld to his ear.

Thinking quickly, Marri activated her eavesdropping packet. It was rudimentary and required line-of-sight, but as long as she kept him in full view, she'd be able to hear who he talked to.

Both ends of the call this time.

"It's me," Karl said in her ear. No name. So at least he was being somewhat careful. "I made first contact."

"Anything to report?" As Marri had suspected, the other speaker was Stefani. In a sudden rash of paranoia, Marri double-checked her own handheld was muted.

"They were willing to listen," Karl said. "I think they'll give me a chance—"

"So fast? That's wonderful!"

"No, that's not what I mean," he said. "They'll give me a chance to prove that I'm serious. I'm going to have to do something. Something that would incriminate me were I ever to turn on them, understand?"

"I see," Stefani said, voice sober. "We can work something out. Set up something that looks like a crime, but in reality, you'll have formal immunity. As long as you don't have to hurt anyone ..."

"*She* would buy off on that, you think? For me?" Karl sounded skeptical and, surprisingly, bitter. It was not a tone Marri had ever heard in him. But she thought he was talking about the archon, and she knew he had no reason to love Ritala Graysteel.

"I wasn't planning on telling her who needed the authorization," Stefani said, sounding nettled. She kept almost using his name. Marri could tell. The magistrate would never make for much of a spy.

"Don't do anything yet," Karl said. "Give me until tomorrow night and let me think on this a bit. I'll let you know how I want to approach this then."

"If you're su—"

"I am," he said. There was a soft sound like a muffled curse. "I'm sorry," he said. "It got kind of dicey in there. Raw too. I'm on edge. I'll sleep it off."

"Karl, if you don't think you can—"

"I can do it," he said. "Tomorrow night, I'll give you a call with a plan."

As they wrapped up their call, Marri was already rummaging through his handheld remotely, looking for any new information he'd stored there in the past half-hour or so. When she saw a new contact number with no name attached, she smiled to herself.

The plan was already forming in her mind.

CHAPTER 17

THE SQUARE BURIED DEEP in Heart Ward was a familiar one. It was home to the warehouse in which Karl, Stefani, and Kyne Libretta had found the disassembled Bridge components, and it was as secluded a space as was possible to find in Coldgarden. On top of avoiding prying eyes, it made sense to have to move said components as little as possible from the warehouse to their point of assembly. Each of the square's four sides of abandoned buildings ringing it stood as tall as fortress walls.

In fact, Stefani had begun to suspect that this space, so near the city center and so perfectly sized for it, represented the place where the Bridge itself had been assembled at one point. Which made the mystery of why it had been *disassembled* all the more intriguing.

Stefani arrived at the observation tower overlooking the construction site at the appointed time, albeit alone. Giana had called in sick today. Though she'd worked the day before, it was still close on the heels of her taking the afternoon of the riot off. Stefani resolved to have a talk with the woman if she did so a third time, out of concern for her well-being if nothing else.

Though, perhaps Stefani was not the ideal role model for work ethic either. Despite her promises to herself and Marri, she had worked far into the night and arrived home to find her teenager too preoccupied with tinkering on her handheld to talk to her adoptive mother. Which left Stefani feeling nettled and guilty all at once.

But even worse was Stefani had no recollection of a large chunk of time she'd been at the office. She'd received a phoned update from Karl and had been startled at how dark it had become. Everything from Giana's early departure to Stefani's handheld ringing with Karl on the other end was a blank.

And here she'd been hoping her episodes of missing time were a thing of the past.

Karl's call was another reason Stefani had to talk to Giana. Before they'd hung up, he'd mentioned that the woman had apparently failed to reach out to her police contact. It was very unlike her, and the lapse had nearly blown Karl's chances of getting in good with the police.

But regardless of how the rest of her evening had gone, Stefani had woken with a reignited determination to get the Bridge completed as soon as possible, no matter the dangers that might still lie ahead. Not to understand it, or not just that. She knew, deep in her gut, they had to use it. The feeling was like a road grader in her mind, plowing over every other desire. But Stefani managed to spare a little will to wish she understood where the notion came from.

"Good to see you this morning, Magistrate," said Dolce. The Bridge project lead, a short, energetic man, could give even Giana a run for her money in being chipper. His bright tone shattered Stefani's moody self-reflection. Totally oblivious to her distraction, he gestured, beaming, to the bay windows behind himself at the towers outer wall and canted to overlook construction. "As you can see, we remain right on schedule despite the difficulties."

Through the windows and down, Stefani beheld the large series of partially reassembled concentric circles. Constructed of exotic metals and composites and lain flat as they were, they were not much taller than Stefani. The widest of the arcs, not yet fully assembled into its completed circle, skirted the edges of the buildings to one side of the secluded square. When her scientists had first inspected the hardware and hypothesized on its use, Stefani had assumed it would stand on end. Something a person could walk through. Like a gateway.

She'd quickly been disabused of that notion. Despite functioning like a door in some respects, the experts assured her it was only ever intended to lie flat. It looked like a partially built, miniature version of the vast, kilometers-long particle accelerators which had once existed, things Stefani knew about only through laughably incomplete bits of data that had survived the Loss.

"In addition to our progress, I have the results back from that drone reconnaissance scan you got archonal approval for."

Stefani felt a thrill of excitement alongside a spike of dread. "So fast?"

"Yes, ma'am. Magistrate Barker apparently put in a priority request for drone use, so if we didn't act fast, we'd miss our chance."

"And were they where we thought?"

"See for yourself, Magistrate." He indicated a screen which scrolled through aerial photos in high definition, shots of a series of hillsides where the remains of multiple destroyed buildings lay strewn about.

It was harder to look at than she'd feared, truthfully. "This is really them?" She fought to keep her voice steady. Why was it always the negative emotions that surged most easily through her fugue?

"Yes, ma'am," Dolce said, oblivious to her discomfort. "These are the three buildings Archon Delgassi destroyed with the matter-eater charges to purge Inkwell of the revenant infestation. We now have confirmation that these devices, in addition to their destructive capability, physically relocated the remains hundreds of miles away in an instant! Considering we have proof that these charges were adapted —fairly crudely, I might add—directly from the Bridge technology, this is as close a confirmation of the Bridge's capabilities as we're going to get without an actual test." He finished practically bouncing.

Stefani took a moment to gather herself. There were a lot of associations with the destruction of those buildings for her. None of them were good.

Dolce is right. It's good news. Focus on that.

"That's excellent to hear," she said before the moment could sour. "Can I assume from your mood that we've had no further incidents?" Stefani asked. She felt a muted guilt that she was about to crush his normally buoyant mood, all the more so because Dolce's cheer seemed particularly rock-solid today.

"No, ma'am," he said. "If you ask me, I'm confident we've stumbled upon the last of those. We've already unboxed and integrated everything from the ground floor, and we have no evidence she was even aware of the sub-basements."

"That's good to hear," she said, grateful he'd given her this opening. "Because we need to accelerate."

He must have believed his own statements of confidence, because to look at him, this news worried him not at all. On the contrary, Stefani had thought his eyes blazed with excitement before, but now they were bonfires.

"Do we have your permission to reduce the number of required safeguards then, ma'am?"

"I was going to order you to do it otherwise, Dolce." She crushed the feeling of unease with all the rest.

"Then I think we can get it operational in days, ma'am."

The feeling of relief washing over Stefani was, without exaggeration, the strongest emotion she had felt since Iaz's death. She nearly fell to her knees, gasping, with the force of pleasure it evoked.

"That's good. Very good," she said, struggling to control her breathing. "But tell me more about your progress. Reconstruction aside, what have you learned?"

She'd asked the magic question, apparently.

"Well, ma'am ..." Dolce began before stopping. He looked torn.

"Out with it," she said, laughing despite herself. She couldn't help it. The relief was still crashing through her in chaotic aftershocks.

"It's going to sound crazy, but I assure you, we're dead-serious."

"Dead-serious about?"

"The Bridge," he said, practically shaking with excitement. "We think it came from another world."

Because we don't belong here. We never did.

It was not Stefani's voice, but Ali's that spoke clear as day in Stefani's head. She tried to recall some instance where she'd heard the woman say that, or something like it, when she had still been alive. But there was nothing. It must just be some odd association.

Stefani blinked, trying to return to the present. "I already know it's for sending people to other worlds. But to say it came from there too, you're going to have to walk me through that one."

Dolce practically danced a jig. Apparently walking Stefani through that one was going to be the highlight of his week.

"There's quite a bit of damage to the digital files stored in the warehouse—that would be Dr. Libretta's work, of course. But whatever she removed, she didn't wipe out nearly enough to obscure the meaning of what remains. This device was being used to open a gateway to Earth from *another world entirely*. Ma'am, do you realize what this means? This device could have been what brought the revenants to Earth! Thanks to the Loss, we still don't know how they arrived, but this could be it. In fact, Occam's Razor would all but guarantee it!"

"Slow down," Stefani said, at last understanding why the young researcher was so breathless with enthusiasm. "Occam's Razor or not, that's a big leap. We still don't even know if the Bridge ever worked. Why disassemble it if it did? And if what you're saying is true, how did it *get* here in the first place?"

"I think it was disassembled to prevent more revenants from coming through, ma'am," Dolce said. He did his best not to make it sound as though this was all incredibly obvious, and Stefani appreciated the effort. He was young. There was plenty of time for him to work on his poker face.

"But how did it get here in the first place if it's the thing that opened the way?"

"Think about it like grabbing the cuff of your sleeve as you pull your arm free. The sleeve turns inside out, right?" He nodded until Stefani nodded along, though she didn't yet see where he was going with it. "Well, we call this device the Bridge, but it's really the thing that *builds* a bridge, one between worlds. If we assume that the revenants, or whatever sent the revenants—since they don't exactly seem technologically savvy themselves—were the ones that built this thing, they obviously must have done so on their world."

"Seems the most likely possibility," Stefani said.

"But like you said, if that's true, how did it end up here? That brings us back to the sleeve metaphor. If you take off the shirt too fast, you might hook the cuff, and pull the sleeve back through itself."

Stefani nodded. It was a simple enough metaphor, and she could see where Dolce was going with it.

"I think our ancestors found a way to pull the device across the very bridge it was maintaining and then shut it down," he continued. "Once we had physical control over the generator, keeping it from being used again would have been trivial, especially if the revenants themselves were just some sort of shock troops or something and not able to operate it themselves."

Stefani had to admit it made a kind of intuitive sense, even if they had no idea if what Dolce described was physically possible.

"But you assured me before that the Bridge won't be locked to one location. You can open it anywhere, correct?"

"Yes, absolutely," Dolce said, raising reassuring hands. "I mean, there's likely *some* kind of limitation, but we haven't rigorously tested its coordinate inputs for limits."

"Speaking of coordinates, last time we talked, you said you were close to a breakthrough on identifying potential test sites to open it *to*," Stefani prompted.

"Ah, yes." Dolce sounded embarrassed for the first time. "We're not quite there yet. There's a file we're still trying to crack open. Really a whole set of them that seem to comprise a program to help determine usable coordinate sets. Don't worry, the encryption is simple enough. It's just a matter of time." At Stefani's look, he added, "I will, of course, find a way to accelerate that portion of the effort as well."

Stefani nodded. It was happening. It really was. Chasing that rush of relief, or perhaps chasing *away* her lingering doubts, she scrambled for more to ask, more potential pinch points.

"What about energy requirements? Are Barker's people still playing nice with us?" She thought of a corollary before he could answer. "And what are we doing to ensure there isn't a corresponding *release* of energy on this end? I can't imagine how destructive something like that would be."

"The Sparks crew is mostly staying out of our way, which is how I prefer it," Dolce said, his voice parochial as only a scientist could be. Then his eyes sparkled. "Regarding your second question, we had the same concern. We're working to address it, but just the thought exercise led us to a different hypothesis. You're correct that a huge energy release on this side is possible, particularly if the device was brought across its own pathway. Enough energy, maybe, to wipe out the majority of all our stored electronic information. Enough energy to cause the Loss."

Stefani stared at her lead scientist. *My God. Could it be true? Could this piece of disassembled hardware be the explanation for everything?*

And if it was, did they dare to try to use it?

We have to finish it and use it. As fast as possible. No matter the cost. The words felt like walls rising up, assembling themselves into tight corridors, hemming her in.

Her next words felt like a compulsion.

"I need it done, Dolce. Do you understand me? I need it operational as fast as possible. Spare nothing, and let me know if there is anything I can do to speed matters up further. Days, you said. Make it happen." Sweat stood out on her forehead at the reckless risk of these words. But she had no choice. This was her purpose.

A tremor rocked the tower. It was brief, but it felt like a punctuation mark.

"More and more of those lately," Dolce said. It was the first time he'd sounded discomfited. Stefani wished she could offer him comfort. But she wondered if her sense of urgency and the tremors were related.

It didn't matter. "Days," she said again, her own exclamation point.

They were going to rebuild the Bridge.

And they were going to cross it.

CHAPTER 18

GIANA WAS NOT ACCUSTOMED to having a whole day to herself yawning open before her. She supposed this must be what people who shirked work on false pretenses felt all the time. In her case, the guilt was considerable, since this was exactly what she was doing.

But there were questions that needed answering.

She had hoped to tackle the message the previous day, but in between waking with that monstrous hangover, having to babysit Marri on her way to school, and a general exhaustion dogging her all through the afternoon, she'd gone home and simply crashed. It was like her work duties and her mind were conspiring against letting her devote any mental resources to understanding Dr. Hayasun's dying message to her.

So, to head off further scheduling complications, and in an eerie parallel to that terrible day eight months gone, Giana had requested the whole next day off from Stefani. With a full night's rest and a pot of coffee in her, Giana spent her ill-gotten morning poring over the message, trying to lose herself in the mechanics of the mystery rather than dwell on the emotional impact. Dr. Hayasun had made a special effort to reach out with one final message: a warning, one meant for Giana specifically.

And though Giana no longer felt even a whisper of the old urge to quit working for Stefani, she found the need to understand this warning was every bit as strong as it had been when she first read it.

Even having been employed by Gene Sequencing for just four months prior to its dissolution, she was more than familiar with their infamous communications security algorithms. All employees had been. It was a favorite target for abuse amongst them.

So with her own emotional baggage locked tightly away, several clues presented themselves to her quickly. The algorithms were very good at automatically spotting things, even complex concepts, that they considered too great a reveal of information. But they couldn't always do it instantaneously.

Dr. Hayasun had ended the message abruptly, forcing a command-level override of the normal hold the algos placed on outgoing messages until they could fully process and redact them. It was something only a high-ranking member of GS could do, and then only a truly desperate one would attempt because of the penalties for an error in this sort of judgment call. This override meant the algos hadn't completed their review before the message had been sent to a server, awaiting further input before being delivered.

So that was clue one.

Clue two involved the idea of what gave the algos more trouble. Some words were banned outright, and those were easy for the system to spot and redact, so that happened fastest. Much slower was the recognition of higher-order concepts, stuff the computer had to process and sift through. Any incompletely blocked words or phrases likely belonged in that camp, except for redactions at the very end, right before Dr. Hayasun had hit send.

Clue three revolved around the only partially blocked words. Some programmer with a flair for the dramatic had installed little flourishes into the redaction protocols. Letters to be redacted would first, if applicable, shift to other, similar-looking characters: the numeral three in place of an *e*, zero in place of *o*, and so on. Only as the process completed would they be redacted into true obscurity. In the normal course of events, this little stylistic show-off wouldn't matter, as any message outbound would have been fully vetted and redacted.

In this case, though, there looked to be several partial words Giana could work with.

For instance, the first redaction, long enough that it was likely several words, ended in *opl3*. It was unlikely that it actually ended that way, unless it was some further-encoded designation Giana was wholly unaware of. More likely, they were meant to be the letters *ople* that had not completely been obscured by the algos at the time of the override. Which meant this portion of redacted text likely ended with the word *people*.

There was another example. *M3d1#@########* apparently referenced something Giana should remember, based on the context of the surrounding text. The start of the sequence looked very much like the start of the word *medical*. Going by what Giana remembered that might relate to that and the number of characters in the sequence, it likely read *medical exam*.

This realization gave her pause as a chill washed through her.

Giana did indeed recall the intensive medical exam required before her Gene Sequencing employment could begin. To call it unpleasant would have been quite an understatement. The invasiveness had been rivaled only by the off-putting nature of the staff involved in administering the tests. Their blandly pleasant demeanors had rubbed Giana the wrong way, and judging by the inside jokes she'd heard about after being fully on-boarded— including from Dr. Hayasun himself—she'd been far from the only one to feel that way.

Invasive and obscure as it had been, any number of things could have been done to her during that exam, and she would be none the wiser. Now according to the person she'd trusted most at Gene Sequencing, she learned that something had indeed been done to her.

Momentarily derailed from her investigation, her naturally obsessive mind wracked itself for any odd symptoms or behaviors she might have observed in herself in the past year. Her thoughts flitted briefly to being sick on the day the siege began, plus the similar experience just a day ago, before darting away again.

Focus, Novak. You're all over the place, and there is still part of the message to decipher.

Unfortunately, the next section with any clues did not leave her feeling any sort of relief from her anxiety. The characters *$##1nt3r g#o#p*, particularly when taken within the surrounding context of *operating within Gene Sequencing,* almost had to read as *splinter group.* It was, in many ways, the most chilling part of the missive, in that it made every other part that much more ominous in context.

The idea that Gene Sequencing didn't really trust anyone, not even its own employees, was something that each GS employee had to come to terms with. But the ongoing assumption was the organization was the aggrieved party when someone went bad. The notion that Gene Sequencing itself was rotten, or a portion of it at least, opened whole new, unpleasant vistas in her mind.

Worse, judging by one of the few remaining guessable sections of redacted text, Giana may have been among a small handful of people affected by whatever this was.

Doesn't matter. They could all have been affected, and it still wouldn't matter anymore. I'm the only one left now. The familiar hollow feeling returned, buttressed by the fact there wasn't much left to decipher, really. Two phrases about what had been done, totally blocked. And then, a non-sequitur at the end, only partially redacted.

Looking at it, Giana almost felt as though the rest of the message was just camouflage for the final statement, something for the algos to chew on so Dr. Hayasun could slip in the real meat of the message while they were distracted.

Corner of Pro$###################. It had the sound of a location. Specifically, *Corner of* implied an intersection, and the length of the redacted portion strengthened that suggestion. Not many streets with names that long in the city. And she had four letters to go on based on her initial assumption: *pros.*

And *Inkw3ll* was certainly obvious enough.

It was simple enough to query the city database to provide a list of streets that began with those letters. It was not even that long of a list, particularly restricted to just Inkwell, but it still would have taken her days of free time she did not have to search on foot.

Giana decided to make some more assumptions, because why not? She assumed he had successfully gotten the full intersection typed in before sending. She likewise assumed only two streets were listed.

It was beyond simple to craft an algo of her own, one instructed to scan every possible intersection between two streets with a combination of the correct number of characters in their names in Inkwell. She ran it and received a glaring zero results.

Frowning, she changed the parameters. Perhaps he'd included the full name, like *street* or *drive* in each member of the intersection in question. Adding in the most commonly used "surnames" of this sort, Giana ran her algorithm again.

Zero results found.

Her annoyance spiked, and she switched to a map of the city, zooming into Inkwell and scanning the space with her eyes as though she could see the answer the computer with perfect knowledge of the map had not. She was immediately struck by how different Inkwell looked compared to so many of the other wards. Among the city's oldest wards, second to Heart, the streets of Inkwell were less grid than warren, many forming octopus-like intersections of far more than two—

Inspiration fell upon her like a hammer. *Far more than two streets.* But she'd assumed two. Quickly, she rewrote her algo, stripping it of the need to look at intersections of exactly two streets, broadening it out to intersections of twenty streets just to make sure she caught everything.

One result.

Giana stared beaming, yet filled with sudden trepidation, at the glowing words staring back at her. There were three streets at this particular intersection, but only two of them mattered to her.

Prosperity and Richmonte.

CHAPTER 19

KARL WAS NOT sure what he expected to find when he arrived at the alley Marri's message had stipulated, a few blocks from her school. Except that when he saw Marri standing there, looking nervous but excited, he realized he had always been expecting this.

She looked unharmed, which was a relief. Aside from saying it was an urgent matter and dire warnings not to say anything to Stefani, her message to his handheld had been light on details.

"Is school even out this early?" he asked by way of greeting.

"No," Marri said, "which should tell you how important this is. I only have so many ways to sneak out, and whenever they figure one out, they close it."

"All right," Karl said, pinching the bridge of his nose as if to ward off the headache he knew would be coming soon. "What's this about?"

"Your new cop friend will be here in a few minutes," Marri said. Her eyes darted around in a way that told Karl she was dead serious despite being nonsensical. "And when he shows up, you need to wait with him for me to come out. I'll be last one out of the school, so no one else should see. Pull me into the alley and rough me up a little.

Threaten me. Threaten Stefani through me. Whatever. Make it look good, so they trust you."

As bad as he'd imagined the coming headache would be, the reality was so much worse.

"Hold on," Karl said. "Just, just hold on. What did you do?"

Marri looked mulish, but at last she sighed and answered, eyes darting ever faster as if she could see the seconds melting away.

"I sent him a message as you. From your handheld. He thinks you asked him to meet you here, in just a few minutes, so you can prove you are serious about joining them."

"You *what?* How?"

"Don't worry about it." Her words were evasive.

"Have you hacked into my handheld?" Karl asked, drawing the only possible conclusion.

"All right, yes!" she said. "And admitting it should be more proof how important this is. Now are you going to do it or not? Because I have to get back into the school building before final bell rings." She stared up at him, tapping her foot impatiently.

"Marri, I would never have let you—"

"Which is why I didn't ask!" she cut in. "I'm going. Don't you dare waste this! And don't worry. I won't really be afraid."

Before Karl could forbid any of this madness, she was around the corner and pounding off down the street. He sat there, dumbstruck.

"Gramps," came the voice of Officer Friendly from behind. It was an effort of will for Karl not to jump, but he mastered himself.

Guess I'm committed now. Damn that girl!

"I must admit," Friendly said, "when I realized where you planned to meet us, I was intrigued. Why are we a block from the richest school in Coldgarden right now?"

Us. Feeling a sense of dread, Karl turned. Thankfully, it was only two, including Friendly. He thought the other one was called Harken. Then he realized he still hadn't answered Friendly's question.

"Because the daughter of one Magistrate Palmieri goes to this school," Karl said. He did his best effort at a wicked grin. "And I'm about to send the good magistrate a little message through her."

The reactions were not what he expected. Friendly's eyes widened, both surprised and, Karl thought, impressed. Harken, on the other hand, paled.

"Whoa, man, what the fuck does that mean?" Harken demanded. "I'm not down with hurting kids. I've got two of my own I barely see since the divorce." His voice was bitter. "The older one would go to this school if my ex lived in Illuminance."

"If they lived here and were rich enough, you mean," Karl said, which he thought was a nice touch.

"Trust me," Harken snapped back, "with the alimony, the bitch is doing her best."

"Well, I'm not going to hurt anyone today, kid or otherwise. A message is a message. Words. She'll be plenty shook up, though. And because of that, so will Palmieri."

"Didn't you and Palmieri work together under Archon Delgassi?" Friendly said, his brows furrowing in consideration.

"I heard they did a little bit more than work together after the archon was killed," Harken said, and from him, it was just straight hostility.

Karl mentally swore. This was exactly the sort of thing a kid, even a kid like Marri, wouldn't have thought through before dumping Karl into the middle of it. But how to play it?

"We did," he said, finding and amplifying his own bitterness to Harken-like levels. "Until she dropped me like hot rocks, just like everyone else once I wasn't useful or convenient any longer. I'm guessing the good officer there knows what I mean." He nodded at Harken with what he hoped was solidarity and was relieved to see the man's open hostility ease a little. "I've got no reason to stick my neck out for Stefani Palmieri, believe me. But the fact that we were together means I know exactly where her brat goes to school. And here we are." As explanations went, this one was hand-wavier than he'd have liked. But he only had what Marri had given him to work with. "And believe me, the kid I'm about to scare the shit out of is no angel." That had just slipped out.

"Well, I guess we'll see," Friendly said. Harken merely looked disgruntled, not murderous.

Down the street, the school's tone sounded, announcing that the secure doors were opening.

"All right, we're here, so let's see this," Friendly said. "Impress me, Gramps."

"You two might want to back down the alley far enough that she can't make out your faces," Karl said. He shrugged. "No helping that for me, but I guess that's the point of proving my dedication."

Friendly and Harken looked at one another. Friendly shrugged and began to move off. Harken, still looking uncomfortable, followed after a moment.

Then, all Karl could do was wait and sweat. He tried not to think of how shady he looked, a grown man lingering alone in an alley as a school let out nearby. He really hoped school security wouldn't be patrolling this far out.

The gangly shapes of teens and almost-teens filtered by the alley's narrow mouth on their way to the tram. Karl tried to watch them without watching them. He had to act like he didn't know where in the crowd she'd be, but not act like he was about to abduct someone also.

He recognized her shadow despite its uncharacteristic hunch. The moment she appeared in the alley mouth, Karl struck, heart pounding. Her shoulders felt too thin in his grip, and despite fearing he might break her, he spun her around, thanking the gods below that she at least had the pack to cushion her back, hoping he wasn't breaking anything inside it.

Her gaze back at him held all her characteristic defiance.

"I've got a message for your mother, gutter rat!" Karl snarled, contorting his face far more than he thought was necessary, because it seemed a time to go over the top.

"Let me go, creep!" Marri's struggle against his grip was surprisingly strong. She kicked upward, trying to tag him between the legs, succeeding only in getting the inner thigh of his good leg. He thought she'd missed that way on purpose and was glad he'd been too slow to react. He had to legitimately fight to hold her still. He didn't miss her roving eyes, trying to swallow every detail around her, particularly of the two police lingering in the alley's shadowy depths.

"You'll go when I say you go! Tell your mother we know all her crimes that were overlooked. I was there. I know, oh yes I do. I paid for what I did, but people like her got *rewarded*! So you tell her justice is coming for her! Tell her that no one she loves is safe! We know everywhere you go. We are everywhere."

Marri's struggles ceased as he snarled these words at her, and Karl felt lower than dirt as her face grew afraid. She'd been right to warn him, but even with that, it was still hard to keep the act up. *It's not real. She isn't really afraid of me.*

After he'd shaken her some more and she'd scrambled away, scrubbing away tears Karl told himself were fake, his handlers emerged from their shadowed alcove.

"I've got to hand it to you, old man," Friendly said, as Karl tried to mentally scrub himself of the filth he felt without letting self-loathing show on his face. "I didn't think you had it in you. Assuming our local brothers here in Illuminance don't get ordered to bring you in for questioning between now and then, I'd love for you to be my guest at our next ... let's call it a gathering. You'll meet us at the station day after tomorrow, quarter to seven in the evening. Sharp. You auditioned for us. Only fair we return the favor."

CHAPTER 20

AFTER RETURNING from the Bridge site, Stefani spent the rest of her day barricaded in her office. Bridge visits were always the most intellectually stimulating part of her job, the closest she ever got to real science these days.

But Dolce's infinite enthusiasm took its toll.

So, it was with no guilt at all that Stefani canceled her open-door hours for the afternoon. Giana's absence, as inconvenient as it was in other ways, made this even easier. There could be no disapproval, imagined or otherwise, if no one was around to see Stefani do it.

At first, she made the cancelation with the intent to cram hours of productive work through too small a window of time. But the more the afternoon sun lit the surrounding buildings visible from her windows in an appealing golden cast, the worse of an idea that sounded. Perhaps it was Marri's continued avoidance tactics, or Karl's carefully modulated rebuke from the other night. Perhaps Dolce's hypotheses about the nature and past usage of the Bridge had shattered any chance of focus.

Whatever the answer, Stefani decided she would go home early. She might even beat Marri home from school, and wouldn't that leave her adoptive daughter stunned speechless? Knowing the girl, Stefani might even catch her misbehavior in-progress instead of only learning about it after the fact.

One of the few benefits of running the district was that the tram ride home was short. Short didn't mean not crowded, though, so the ride was never an easy one for Stefani. Her dissociative episodes seemed to strike more frequently in groups. On the other side of the coin, the risk of recognition was high among her constituents and never guaranteed to go well.

Consequently, she tried to mix up her disguises.

Today, she pulled from her office wardrobe a set of oversized sunglasses and a ratty jacket with a deep hood she could pull up all the way. It probably made her look more suspicious than incognito, especially if anyone looked closely enough to see the expensive suit she wore underneath. But covering so much of her head gave her a sense of protection, however false.

Sometimes, tricking yourself into calming down was the best you could hope for.

Heading home when the sun was still up made her feel better in one respect, but the much larger crowds than she was used to had the opposite effect. Wedged between people in an overheated, sour-smelling tram car, unable to find a seat at all, Stefani was trying to find the balance of fearing recognition and not even recognizing herself when she was snapped out of any trace of dissociation by her handheld's buzz.

The message from Magistrate Barker was short, which meant the next was likely half-typed.

Hi Stef. Seismometers say quakes are coming more frequently, and we had an actual sinkhole start up near one of the secondary reactors.

That certainly sounded concerning, but what was Stefani supposed to do—

He messaged again.

*Requested drone access to see if anything similar was
happening outside the city, where it would be more obvious.*

Stefani tried to hold herself from forming impressions until, sure enough ...

*Pictures just came back. Definitely cracks in the ground that
don't look like they should be there. Widely distributed too.
Around the city, but also as far out as the drones can get.*

He would surely reach the point any second now.

*Pictures look odd. Not sure how to describe. Could you get
some of your experts to look?*

At last, a question. No pictures were attached, but his people could surely provide them.

The tram had arrived at her stop, so Stefani had a moment to compose her thoughts. Knowing she should cut the man more slack but finding it difficult still, she was on the verge of responding that she'd ask her people to look into it when she was distracted from her focus in the worst way possible.

As she exited the car at her stop, Stefani caught sight of a fresh burst of graffiti along a street level wall, one the ward auto-cleaning units had not gotten to scrubbing away yet. She'd grown to dread seeing any graffiti in Illuminance, and frequently wondered if the other magistrates had to deal with the same thing.

Somehow, she doubted it.

She'd tried to go to the police the first few times it had happened, hoping they could step up patrols and prevent the offenders from even getting started. The graffiti had doubled after that, almost as if her complaints had merely confirmed that it bothered her. It hadn't taken her long to realize the police were not going to catch the offenders because they likely *were* the offenders.

The first of today's two phrases was nothing new. *IAZMAENA LIVES*, it said. And, just to the right and canted to make sure any onlookers knew it was distinct: *FUCK PALMIERI*. That hit Stefani like a punch to the kidney. All thoughts of responding to Magistrate Barker or even getting home early fled her mind. Instead, she moved compulsively, not toward the tram station exit and their apartment, but toward a connecting line.

There was only one thing that could quell this sort of anxiety.

The connecting tram's doors slid open at the Gaton–Wiems stop in Inkwell. The newly rebuilt station's status was obvious in its clean, modern design aesthetic and gleaming, brushed metal surfaces, a far cry from the crumbling composicrete tram stops Inkwell had once sported. It wasn't technically the closest stop, but until the ward's street-level repairs got further along, it was the stop that offered the fastest on-foot route to her destination, and it featured a minimum of detours off of well-traveled roads.

Stefani stepped out quickly, moving her eyes as far to either side as she could, scanning for suspicious people. But she didn't turn her head unless she had a reason to. Over these past eight months, Stefani had decided trying to make sure she wasn't being followed probably also made her more likely to be, if only because of how suspicious such behavior surely made her look. She saw nothing that raised her sense of danger any higher than the graffiti already had.

Silly paranoia, surely unconnected with any real threat. It was one of the worst-kept secrets in Coldgarden that *IAZMAENA LIVES* had become a kind of slogan among a segment of the police across the city. It was just a rallying cry; she didn't think it meant anything literal except to the most conspiracy-minded. But just because she was aware of no specific threat didn't mean there was no danger. The riot had proved that.

And it wasn't as if the police would alert her if there was a new, specific threat. Particularly if they were behind it.

And imagined dangers were the least of Stefani's worries. If anyone ever discovered what she was doing when she detoured to the depths of Inkwell, prison might be the least of her worries.

If she could have gotten by never coming here at all, she would have. But regular visits had become necessary for her to feel any peace of mind at all beyond muted dissociation. Stefani knew she would feel that way only until one of these visits got her caught, but she tried not to think about that.

Her destination was a couple of blocks from the tram stop, and her path took her across one of those invisible borders the city possessed where a comfortably middle-class neighborhood transitioned into a mostly abandoned one in an eye-blink, even within the same ward. Or at least, it would have, before the attack. Hundreds of revenants invading and setting up shop inside a walled-off ward was the great equalizer.

Her landmark came into view. It was a rusting piece of art in the center of an irregular triangular park where three streets joined in overlapping acute angles at what she called Octopus Intersection. The sculpture was a reminder that this had been a healthier, happier place once, before the Loss and what seemed an inevitable slide into decay across the city. Stefani felt an unaccountable pang for that time well up from deep within her. How strange to feel something so intense for a time she had almost zero knowledge of.

Just beyond the sculpture, occupying one of the Octopus Intersection's many corners, lay Stefani's building. She didn't own it, of course. But as soon as this space had appeared on her radar during the investigation into Kyne Libretta, she'd pulled every lever of power she possessed to make it disappear from anyone else's.

She thought she'd succeeded.

Stefani had arrived the first time to find a door with the lock melted away as though by acid. One of the first things she'd done had been to replace it herself over one excruciatingly long weekend day.

The room she'd found inside had looked like it had been hurriedly robbed blind. Scrape marks and gouges in walls had illustrated whcrc things had been once, but since one entire wall of the oblong space was occupied by a metal garage-style door, Stefani supposed it would have been easy enough to quickly haul away anything that was in here.

It didn't matter what it had been used for. It was Stefani's now. And she'd had a very specific use in mind for it.

The door's biometric lock disengaged with a click, and, resisting the urge to glance around her for observation, Stefani opened the reinforced door just far enough to let herself in before closing it again.

Once inside and away from potentially prying eyes, she felt her agitation begin to ease at last.

The space was one large, rectangular room. The door through which she'd entered stood in one of the shorter walls. Set into the longer wall to her right was the reinforced garage-style door which could only be opened from the inside. She'd used it only once, to move her prize inside the space, along with its support equipment.

That prize lay in the room's exact center, surrounded with spindly technological arms poised around and above it, as though it had crushed a mechanical spider whose legs had curled back inward. The prize itself, a test chamber of Stefani's own design, could be opened, of course. But it could also have its exterior shell rendered transparent without opening it. Both of these could only be done by Stefani herself with the proper code. It was a last, desperate defense against discovery if someone managed to both find this place and make it inside.

She'd considered installing a camera, a way for her to monitor the room as often as she liked remotely. In the end, she'd discarded the notion. Even closed-circuit, something like that could be accessed, and no amount of security would have been enough to avoid exchanging one set of anxieties for another.

She entered the proper commands and rendered the chamber transparent. It couldn't safely stay this way for long. The very act of allowing visible light inside meant the specimen within was warming some minuscule amount, degrading just a little bit more.

The specimen. Stefani felt a muted memory of self-loathing. Iaz was not a specimen. She lay within the now-transparent chamber. What was left of her, anyway. What was left of whatever she'd become.

Frozen now in both unimaginable cold and death.

IAZMAENA LIVES. No, she didn't. And Stefani was not sure whether that thought made her feel sad or guilty.

Rubbery flesh shifting between black and dark green depending on how the light caught it formed a massive-yet-squat worm-like shape, all toothless mouth on one end. Six bony legs seemed caught in mid-eruption, three to each side. It was some kind of hypermutation of a type and specificity Stefani had never even imagined. Worst of all was the tongue, that awful tongue with hair. Iaz's hair.

It was that detail that always raised the volume on Stefani's emotions most. Sometimes she wondered if that was what kept her coming back here, another chance to really *feel* again, even if the emotions in question were always unpleasant.

"No sampling tonight, Iaz," she said to the remains. She had developed a habit of talking to them. It was probably not a good sign. "Just here to say hello." She wasn't sure if she wanted tears or not. Sometimes they came. Not tonight, though. *Just focus on the loss of anxiety.*

She had to savor it because she knew it wouldn't last.

CHAPTER 21

GIANA UNFORTUNATELY DIDN'T HAVE the luxury of putting off searching for Dr. Hayasun's mystery address. She'd requested the whole day off, assuming the mystery would take at least that long to sort through. Then, she'd wound up seemingly solving the damned thing before lunch.

This meant heading out shortly after lunch if she didn't want to be searching alone after dark, which she emphatically did not. Inkwell was still early in its recovery as a ward, and despite all the outsized public attention it received as a result, there were still endless stories of less-than-savory people and groups taking advantage of the situation.

She exited the nearest tram station to a scene of scabbed-over devastation that took her breath away. It was Giana's first time in the ward since before the attack, though even then, she wouldn't have spent much time beyond taking in the occasional show or festival.

Everywhere she looked, buildings were half in ruins where they hadn't crumbled completely. Some alleys, and even smaller streets, were blocked completely by rubble. A smell of stale char seemed to hang in place everywhere she walked, as though the very air had been scarred by the violence inflicted upon this ward.

Whether the culprits had been revenants tearing panic chambers free of their housings until the buildings just slumped into piles or stray flier shots from lancers hunting those same revenants, it would take a generation to fully undo the damage.

It wasn't as though the ward was abandoned, though. Every building that still looked structurally sound was clearly packed to the brim with residents. Even a glance into windows showed bustling silhouettes and feeble attempts to gussy up the dreary building facades.

They should have left the cordon walls in place until they could rebuild. It was an unworthy thought, one Giana was immediately ashamed of having. But a part of her couldn't shake it, either. Simply hearing descriptions at her job or on the news did not convey the true scope of what had happened here. She couldn't help but feel the rest of the city would be better off not knowing.

It could happen to any of us.

The directions she'd loaded into her handheld took her by the most direct path, but she found they were painfully out of date with the way the very structure of the city had been rewritten in the attack. Consequently, she was forced to improvise her own path no fewer than three times. At least she'd left her work shoes at home.

By the time she arrived at her destination, Giana thought it was likely staying on the tram for one more stop would have been faster. It might have made for less walking, depending on how closely those roads still conformed with the city's map.

The meeting point of Prosperity and Richmonte was a monument to bad planning—or, more likely, a total lack of planning. Those roads were only two of three, crossing at three different points to form a six-vectored, triangular catastrophe of an intersection where none of the triangle's three sides were the same length.

Someone had taken pains to justify the travesty with an art installation of some kind occupying the rough center of the triangle. It was an arrangement of sheet metal bent to look like stylized waterfalls, but whoever was responsible for the installation had chosen plain steel as their medium, so the entire thing had rusted, in places all the way through. Maybe it was a deliberate choice, but it just spoke of decay and irreversible decline to Giana, not the message that Inkwell ought to be projecting these days.

Even if it was the truth.

Giana made for the sculpture regardless, because she was not certain which of the cross streets was Richmonte, and a central place to look seemed the best idea to her. The late afternoon sun found the few spots on the sculpture that still had any reflectivity to them, casting rays of heat onto Giana that left her sweating through the back of her shirt.

Once she was this close to every corner of the mangled street, she was able to find the building she was looking for. In fact, it proved distressingly easy, considering who had built it, because the foundation remnants of the structure it must have been built to replace were still readily visible.

Very sloppy, if this is one of ours.

The building itself was nondescript enough to pass without notice. The door, which looked strangely newer than the structure it guarded, appeared to have a fairly standard electronic interface.

Giana was still staring at the door, trying to figure out if she had actually found the correct building, when it started to open. She caught a glimpse of the person exiting the building, and all other thoughts went out of her head.

It was her boss.

Stefani wore one of her disguises, a worn hoodie and oversized sunglasses to conceal the shape of her face, but Giana worked up close with her almost every day and recognized that particular clothing set. It was unquestionably her. Giana was so stunned that for a moment, she was paralyzed. She felt a wash of fresh guilt, the guilt of being discovered lying about her excuse to take the day off. Then reality caught up to her, and suspicion replaced guilt.

What is she doing here? And in that *building?*

Giana's survival instincts caught up at last, and she realized how unprepared she was to deflect suspicion directed at her if Stefani saw her. Heart pounding in her ears, she ducked around the other side of the rust sculpture, straining her ears to hear any cry of recognition or accusation from her employer. She debated whether she should speed-walk away, pretending to hear nothing, or if confessing what precisely she was doing made more sense.

After all, it wasn't as if Gene Sequencing even existed anymore. How could she be blamed for failing to follow the orders of a dead organization? Who could even hold her to account?

Somewhere in this mental frenzy, Giana realized that she had not been neither hailed nor grabbed by Stefani. Glancing up, Giana realized she was watching Stefani's back as the woman moved quickly down the street and back toward the tram stop—the very stop Giana had thought was the further walk from the building.

Time to go. She could walk back the way she'd come to avoid any chance of being noticed, delay long enough to make sure she didn't run into Stefani on the tram. Suddenly, Giana was very conscious of the fact that this building might have some active security system. She could very well be on camera footage that Stefani might be going home to review. This left her with a cramping stomach.

But she didn't move.

Instead, she hovered there, balanced on a spire's tip of indecision. To try to break in despite what she'd seen, despite the risk? If she had been spotted on some kind of security system, this would be her only chance to see what lay inside before whatever consequences came of it. On the other hand, all she'd been doing right now was looking. She could talk to Stefani, ask her to explain.

And reveal who you are? Reveal that you lied for all these months? Maybe, if it had just been Stefani, Giana could have brought herself to confess. But now it wasn't just about Stefani, was it. Because, somehow, she was involved in whatever Hayasun had tried to warn Giana about.

Everything within Giana told her to leave. Leave and never think about this again. Just go back to working for Stefani, not rocking the boat, helping her with the Bridge project, and building a new life.

Giana went for the door.

CHAPTER 22

CONSCIOUS THAT THE longer she stood here, the more likely she was to get noticed by someone or something, Giana examined the door Stefani had shut behind her. There was no keypad or any place to input a code or electronic key. There was, however, a scanner for biometric inputs.

Which presented Giana with both a solution and a problem. The solution was that as Stefani's assistant, there were times when her sign-off was needed and she couldn't be physically present. Having given Giana the proxy ability to sign off in her name on pre-approved matters, she had also provided Giana with virtual facsimiles of her biometrics.

It was poor security hygiene for precisely the reason Giana was now contemplating. Which was also the problem. When she'd psyched herself up to rush the door and examine how she might gain entry, she'd assumed she'd be easily defeated. She'd have satisfied her urge to try, and she'd be safe to give up and leave this be. A single, percussive thought still drummed on in her mind, advocating just that.

But the thought of being able to know yet not knowing was too much. Giana had to understand why Dr. Hayasun had directed her to this place.

She cued Stefani's biometrics up on her handheld and presented the screen to the reader. There wasn't even a dramatic lag. The door cycled open with a click.

The first thing Giana did when she entered was scan the entire ceiling for cameras. If she was going to have to go into hiding, she wanted the longest possible head start. To her relief, and mild confusion, she saw none.

The second thing she did was notice the smell. It was faint, stale with time and the loss of its source. The room was almost entirely empty; shockingly so, considering its size. Its bare, windowless walls were unadorned, and even most of the floor was unoccupied. Giana realized the smell she could still faintly detect left her expecting the space to be crammed full of medical lab equipment.

I've never been here, she thought. *But the Gene Sequencing facility where I got my onboarding medical workup done smelled like this place smells.* Only much more strongly in the former case.

And, as Giana looked closer at the empty parts of the room, she saw evidence it had, at one point, been much more cluttered. The scars left by heavy objects or equipment stands being pushed and dragged and bumped into walls were plentiful. Beyond a large, garage-style bay door leading back outside, she saw no doors to any other places, no stairs, not even a trapdoor leading to something underground.

At last, Giana turned her attention to the only thing the room did contain. It was a dark, oblong box in the center of the chamber and a bunch of what looked like support equipment bristling up and around it like curving, black thorns.

She approached with care, wary of setting off some alarm or trap. But none of the equipment sprang to life. Aside from a hum so low she almost couldn't detect it, the silence in the space was eerie and total.

She approached the room's centerpiece. There was a console on one side of the box that seemed to be where one did ... whatever one might do with it. *Open it,* Giana supposed, though the thought made her more than uneasy.

She sidled up to the black glass of the console face, reached out a tentative hand and tapped one finger. The face was indeed a screen, and it lit up at her touch with a full alphanumeric keypad and a passkey input request.

Here Giana was promptly stymied. Ironically, the more secure locking option, biometrics, she could replicate at will. She could try a few passwords at random; she knew a few of Stefani's for the same reason she had the biometrics. But a passkey might be anything, and Stefani was unlikely to have picked something she used on some other system. Not when she went to these lengths to hide whatever this was.

Giana found this to be a relief. This didn't seem like a site for medical experimentation. It seemed like a storage space for something dangerous, something which frightened her. More, it reignited her fright of Stefani, except that instead of being afraid of Stefani learning the truth of Giana's past, now it was Stefani pursuing and keeping some kind of dangerous secrets.

The urge to just resign her position and walk away, so recently stymied, reared up again in her. Maybe this had been going on for months, or longer. But rising up to meet this powerful urge came its opposite.

Don't be stupid. This isn't what he sent you here to find. And you'll never learn the answers if you walk away now.

I don't want to know the answers, Giana protested in a bizarre argument with herself. *I just want to be done with hiding.*

The self-loathing which followed this pressed down upon her with the sudden force of a collapsing building. It was too powerful for words, but she felt the negation of her fears anyway.

What I'm seeing here has nothing to do with me. This wasn't what Hayasun sent me to find. It occurred to her, then, that the answer to both these mysteries, Stefani's and Hayasun's, had nothing to do with her at all. Stefani, in her lofty position, was surely privy to information even Giana couldn't know. And as for Hayasun, his message was likely nothing that mattered anymore.

That sense of overwhelming pressure guiding her thoughts grabbed hold of this latter idea, molded itself around it, telling Giana that whatever Hayasun been concerned about, it was immaterial at this point in the wake of both his and Gene Sequencing's destruction. The force behind this certainty felt almost like a thing outside herself, beating her into submission with its will.

Giana felt a hot flush of fear at the thought, but before she could interrogate it and try to grasp what was going on in her brain, the building's lingering smell reasserted itself. Its familiarity told her this place had indeed been used for Gene Sequencing medical work. Its faintness told her that this site, mysterious as it was, held no answers for her any longer. That second piece felt far more important. Whatever ties this place had to Giana's own medical exam experience, if that was indeed what Hayasun had been trying to point her to, they weren't here any longer.

Time for me to go. The thought repeated, increasingly urgent.

Yes, it seemed increasingly likely that Stefani had cleared out anything relevant to Giana's search. Or, judging by the haste the scrapes and dents in the walls suggested, someone else had, and in a huge hurry. This was Inkwell, after all. It was possible whatever operation had been happening here during the incursion had evacuated with the rest of the populace. Or tried, at least. With a half-hour's warning before the cordon walls raised, it seemed impossible they'd succeeded.

At last giving in to the powerful, building urge to be away from this place, Giana fled, making sure to close the door tightly behind her. She scarcely remembered the trip back to her apartment, or the remainder of the evening that followed, such was the whirling of her thoughts.

CHAPTER 23

MARRI BROKE her personal rule the day after the alley scam she and Karl pulled on the cops. Two personal rules if she counted the one about meekly going to school. But painful as that part was, it was where she needed to be this day.

It was the only place she could talk to Bry.

The mice had been scattered all over the city when Stefani and Archon Graysteel had arranged for their adoptions. Marri still felt bitter over the forced separation. Reasonable arguments that no one family could look after them all couldn't compete with her vivid memories of looking after them herself for years.

Bry was the only one she ever got a chance to see, and that at a distance. He was a few grades below her, so they didn't share any classes, but they occasionally got recess in the walled outdoor school-yard at the same time. Marri happened to know that today would be one of those days. Not because she kept track or anything.

Marri had grown in the past eight months, but so had Bry, and it still startled her to see. Her former mouse had also gained weight, but not in a bad way. In truth, he looked healthier than she'd ever seen him. That realization cut deep. She tried to be subtle in her approach, but he'd kept his old instincts too, and he turned unconcernedly to watch her. His brow furrowing a little in surprise was his only display of emotion.

"How come you never come talk to me?"

Marri couldn't suppress a sad little laugh. Once upon a time, this boy had been afraid of her. She supposed the fact he wasn't anymore meant she'd done at least one thing right.

"They won't let me," she lied smoothly. "Don't know about you, but they aren't exactly excited when I act like we're still running around raiding Underguts. Don't seem to like me to do anything that might remind me of that."

She let out a silent sigh of relief when he nodded in understanding, then felt a hot bloom of shame at the relief. She'd lied to her mice plenty of times before, but it had always been for their own good, to protect them. This lie was all about protecting herself. The truth was even though she knew deep down the mice were better off as members of loving, stable families, there was a big difference between knowing they were better off without Marri caring for them and having it rubbed in her face daily.

"So what's up?" Bry asked, and just like that, it was as though they were still scrounging tunnels and dodging revs.

"You still sneak out sometimes, right?" Marri asked, lowering her voice.

Bry's look grew furtive and guilty, and his eyes darted as though adults were listening to their every word. But he nodded.

"Walk the city? Explore the old places?"

Another nod.

"Me too," she said, meaning it to reassure, hoping it would. She felt another wash of relief at his grin. "You hear anything about cops acting weird? Mean? Meaner than usual, I'm saying."

"Course," Bry said as if she was crazy to have asked. "Don't need mice to tell you that. Ask anyone who's been talked at by a cop since Delgassi died."

Magistrate Delgassi. Show some respect. Though Marri supposed she was just as guilty by not using the woman's title of archon. Still, it wasn't worth getting into a fight over. Bry had never met Iazmaena the way Marri had.

"You know any places they like to go to meet? Any places in Renewal?" This was it. The crux of why she'd approached him this way. Karl had, predictably, wiped his handheld after he'd gotten back home the previous night, purging all of Marri's malware in the process. She could no longer track him, which meant she would not be able to follow him to the meeting.

Bry screwed up his face into a very familiar expression of intense concentration, and Marri felt a wave of homesickness so powerful she almost broke down in tears. But she knew his various concentration faces, and she knew his answer before he said anything.

"Yeah," he said. "Haven't seen it myself. But I've heard about it from one of the others. Sala, I think."

"Tell me where," Marri said.

"Old warehouse," Bry said. "People use it for parties sometimes." He didn't have the address, but he was able to describe the area enough that Marri recognized what he was talking about. Even if he was right, was only half of what she needed. She still didn't know when the meeting would be. But it was something. "Thanks," she said. Then, because she couldn't help herself, "you talk to the others, then?"

"Sometimes," he said. "The ones I can manage to see out and about. James and Jess don't want me clinging to that old stuff either, so I don't see most except by accident." He sounded annoyed about it, as well he should. "They treat me real good though, otherwise," he added hastily, as though fearing his admission might cost him the roof over his head.

Marri watched the boy's curiosity waken. It rolled off him like hunger. "What's this about, anyway?"

"Just trying to keep a stubborn old man safe," Marri said.

"I thought you just had a mom," Bry said, confused.

"Never mind," Marri said. "Thanks again, though, this helps."

Bry smiled the way he would have when she'd praised him back at the Mouse Hole for a particularly good find. Then the voice of one of the teachers jarred the moment between them, shattering it.

"Bryson!" the woman called. "It's time to come in!"

Bryson? Marri mouthed at Bry, making sure he saw the snicker forming on her lips. Then she glanced around and was startled to see they were almost the last two outside, and the only ones that hadn't started heading back.

"You too, Marrietta!"

Marrietta? Bry mouthed back, positively dancing with glee at this emperor of all revelations. Marri glared murder at him, but this just sent him into fits of giggles. She should never have admitted that to Stefani. Never!

They jogged back side by side, and he leaned close and whispered. "It was good to see you. If we both sneak out anyway, you should talk to me more. What's the worst that could happen?" He clammed up as they reached the stairs, like he could pretend they'd just happened to find themselves facing each other and hadn't talked at all.

She nodded when she was sure he was looking because he was right. It had been good, despite the pain. Maybe the pain even made her appreciate the good part more. Her mind was already spinning with what he'd told her, though.

Keeping Stefani safe was something she understood how to do. It meant just avoiding her as much as possible, so Marri didn't wake from some dream having driven a knife into the woman's chest. Karl was different. She couldn't keep Karl safe if she didn't know where he would be and when.

I'll just wait there every night until he shows up, she resolved. It was a two-for-one deal, in a way, the best thing she could do to keep both Stefani and Karl safe at the same time.

CHAPTER 24

AGAIN. It had happened again.

Giana awoke to the feeling of sweat-slick sheets against her bare skin. She shot bolt upright in bed, then almost flopped back down due to weakness from her ravenous hunger. Flashes of the previous night intruded in a way they never had before during these episodes. Giana hastily stripping down, then running for the bathroom.

Then nothing.

Teetering on her feet, she half-scooted, half-fell into the bathroom, doing her best not to further wrinkle the previous day's clothes she'd left strewn across the floor. It left her juking like a footballer driving toward the goal.

She tried to dig deeper into the flashes of memory, hoping to divine exactly what she'd needed with the bathroom. Then she arrived and felt the blood rushing from her head so violently she nearly blacked out.

There was another mass of sludge in the tub.

It's making me sick. Whatever it is, it keeps happening on these nights where I lose time and behave strangely. If it's toxic, if it releases fumes into the air ...

It was a comforting thing to believe in its own perverted way.

Less comforting was the other possibility: that whatever was in her tub was something she, Giana, had vomited up.

Yet it was this second possibility that aligned better with Dr. Hayasun's warning to her. Despite this realization, the thought seemed less concerning than it had the day before.

At the very least, the mass in the tub was smaller than the last time. She was almost sure of it. Of course, when it was slowly draining away, it was impossible to really be sure of that fact.

What did they do to me?

But unlike even a day ago, it seemed a strangely distant thought, merely an idle curiosity, when placed against Giana's current duties. It was like coming out of a dense fog she hadn't been aware she'd been mired in. She had important work to do for Stefani, work she'd been neglecting all because of Hayasun's now-irrelevant message. With a suddenness that bordered on violence, Giana realized she was days late in reaching out to Arjun as she herself had volunteered to do.

Fuck. Fuck, Giana, fuck, what is wrong with you?

She didn't have time to sit here wondering what was happening to her. The search of the previous day drifted far away from her mind as she stepped gingerly into the tub, keeping as far away from the whatever-it-was as she could, and turned on the water as hot as it would go. She would call Arjun on the tram ride to the office.

⚬

After a very full workday where Giana received the closest thing to a dressing-down Stefani had ever seen fit to give her on her self-confessed delay in contacting Arjun, Giana felt she could be forgiven for having second thoughts about this extracurricular offer to Stefani. Perhaps sensing he had the conversational advantage over the flustered Giana for once, Arjun had eagerly agreed to a meet-up and had lobbied heavily for that very night. Still feeling guilt-ridden over delaying in her duties, Giana had capitulated.

Her misgivings doubled when she arrived at the bar Arjun had selected.

It wasn't quite a dive, but it was still lower-end than she'd normally frequent, particularly given the status afforded by her current role. The smell of the place was of mildew and stale beer, and the floor was sticky with something she'd prefer not to think about, but at least the lighting was steady and plentiful.

All this time pining, and this *is where he asks me to meet him?* Still, the obvious misstep gave Giana some of her equilibrium back.

At least Arjun made an effort with himself. He walked through the door looking as put-together as Giana had ever seen him, wearing stylishly slim civilian clothes two cuts above what she remembered from university. He sported a bright, if shy, smile full of heart-breaking eagerness.

Not a date, she reminded herself. She had already told him that twice, but both times, the words had felt strange to her. She was here to find out what he might know about growing unrest, not to finally give him the relationship he'd been yearning for since they'd been in the same Sociology lecture.

But a part of Giana noted with cold, clinical detachment, that her mission would be so much easier and more successful if this *was* a date. The observation startled her; much like her experience in Stefani's secret lab the previous day, it almost felt like a separate voice from her own familiar, inner monologue. And she bristled internally at what it seemed to be suggesting.

Arjun spotted her and waved as he walked over. His head swiveled slightly as he moved, taking in the bar's decor, and Giana watched, fascinated, as he saw the bar through a stranger's eyes. Her eyes. The eyes of someone whose opinion he cared deeply about.

She watched his face fall with the understanding of his mistake, and she felt a sharp pang of empathy for him. It had been thoughtless, inviting her here. Likely he'd done it almost unconsciously, choosing a place where he felt comfortable. That he was capable of reassessing that impulse on the fly spoke well of him, at least.

He's fitter than he was in university. She blinked. Where was this coming from?

"Sorry," Arjun said, snapping her back to herself as he sat down next to her. He gave an apologetic shrug. "You'd think I'd get better at this with age."

"Not a date," she said again, mindful to pull any sting from her words, "so it's not an issue." It had been difficult to make herself say the words. She gave him a look. "But I do hope the food is better than the decor."

"I'd say yes, but honestly, I'm not sure I trust my judgment right now." His laugh was rueful.

"Well, tell me what's good," she said. "But drinks first." It would ease his worries. And he'd always been an eager-to-please drunk.

Two rounds and half a meal in, Giana finally felt comfortable bringing up the whole reason she was here.

"I know that face," Arjun said, forestalling her. "That's the down-to-business face. I saw it enough during lab write-ups."

Giana decided to do him the courtesy of not trying to deny or sugarcoat it. "You know who I work for, I assume?"

"I do, yeah." Giana noted he didn't look happy about it, but he was trying to hide it. The realization steeled her resolve. It meant Stefani was even more disliked among the city's police than they'd realized. And Stefani could not be allowed to fail.

"And you know about what happened the other day?"

"You mean when Karl Yonnel barged into my precinct asking for me, citing you as a point of contact? Next time, a heads up would be nice."

Giana winced. Stefani's dressing-down had given Giana the gist. Hearing it from Arjun himself made it much worse. She didn't know Karl well at all, but she'd expected more tact from him than that. Of course, he'd likely expected her to have held up her end by then.

"I'm really sorry about that. I dropped the ball, and I'm pretty sure it was a bowling ball that fell through the floor and then another floor. But what I meant was the incident at—"

"I know what you meant," Arjun said, forestalling her. Giana was a good judge of people's faces, and she'd known Arjun a long time. She didn't miss the way his eyes flicked away for the barest instant. He knew more than he was willing to say. She could remember a time when he would have told her anything, but that was before she'd spurned him. She was going to have to offer him a show of trust to tease the information out of him.

All at once, exhaustion stole over her, and like an onrushing illness, Giana felt a corresponding spike of impatience. This was inefficient, monstrously slow. Giana, of all people, had unique options with Arjun. There were faster, more direct ways to get him to do what she wanted.

Get him alone, and you can convince him of anything.

The shock of that thought, more a guiding urge than actual words and again arriving seemingly out of nowhere, nearly derailed her. But she managed to recover her equilibrium.

"There were cops in that crowd, Arjun," Giana said. "Security footage confirmed it." She tried to freight the words with import, but she also made sure to pull the punch. "Not all of them, not even most of them. But any is worrying." She held up her hands to forestall his objection. "I'm not asking you to name names of every like-minded coworker, but I do want to get a handle on what this is and why."

Arjun regarded her, chewing through several bites of his dinner before daring to respond. His eyes darted with feverish thought.

"What you're asking," he began, but trailed off. Over the next minute, he opened his mouth twice more to resume, but closed it both times without saying anything, merely shaking his head.

Frustration and impatience clawed at Giana. *Get him alone.* She resisted, but it was harder than before. *No. That isn't the way.* He was the only cop she knew. She couldn't afford to blow this.

And she couldn't be cruel about it either. He was a friend.

"A lot of people are upset," he said finally, carefully. Shy, smiling Arjun, her friend and unrequited admirer from school, was not in that look. An older, harder stranger had replaced him, and this gave her pause, tilted her toward one of the two possibilities tonight offered. "There are a lot of questions about the last several months that need answering, Giana." And this statement tilted her the other way. But now it was his turn to placate. "I'm not asking you to tell me anything."

Giana was about to open her mouth to ask him to let her speak to some of the angry people he was talking about when he preempted her.

"But if you're willing to have an open mind, I'd like to show you what I'm talking about. There's a kind of meeting. Tomorrow night. I'd be happy to bring you."

It was a perfectly reasonable timeframe. Fortuitous, even, that she could make progress so fast. Yet totally aside from the fact that tomorrow night was the first, limited test of the Bridge apparatus, a fresh surge of impatience nettled Giana. The mad frustration seized her again, consuming her. Because even if she could make that meeting, it wouldn't *just* be that meeting. That would be the start of a long, slow process of building trust with both Arjun and his contacts, convincing them she could be relied upon to be discreet. She could see it unfolding before her. Weeks, maybe. Months.

If it worked at all.

And if it didn't work, she'd be back to square one. Or maybe something worse. At last, she understood the impatience. The drive, and the willingness to sacrifice to get the results she and Stefani needed. The Bridge had to be completed.

When the urge rose up this time, she did not question it, did not push back. The words left her mouth before she could think to form them, and without entirely meaning to, she gave in to the quickest path to her goal.

"I think that can be arranged. But in the meantime, do you want to get out of here?"

CHAPTER 25

THEY WALKED BACK to Arjun's place, a short hike from the bar, and Giana could not help but wonder if he'd subconsciously, or maybe not so subconsciously, picked the location because of its proximity to his bedroom.

She should have felt alarm at what she was doing, alarm and no small amount of guilt. But she didn't. Not at all. And it was this fact that made her worry. But being worried about a lack of worry was apparently not strong enough to derail her from this path, because she kept right on walking it.

Arjun, on the other hand, was experiencing his own doubts. Giana could tell. When you wanted a thing for so long that it ceased to exist as a real, tangible possibility in your mind, you might walk up to it on the street and greet it with suspicion rather than joy.

So Giana really had to sell it, at least long enough to get him alone. After that, some hazy instinct she dare not interrogate too closely would take over. She felt certain of that.

As a result, she got plenty handsy on the walk back. Once their lips met for the first time, he seemed to believe in what was happening. It grew easier after that.

He already seemed more handsome than he had when the

evening began. More handsome than he *ever* had, strangely enough. Or maybe this wasn't so strange. He, after all, had the information she needed. And she could give him the unattainable thing which had haunted his desires for years. Everyone would get what they wanted. This didn't have to be complicated.

A small part of her, rapidly shrinking, quailed at this horrific thought. Giana Novak was not like this. She was not ... *transactional* in this way! She did not use people, use *herself*, to get what she wanted.

You were using him already, playing on his feelings for you to get information. And that was true. When she thought about it that way, how was this any different?

She kissed Arjun again, putting even more need into it as she allowed her hands to rove down further than she had thus far. It was half an attempt to blot out such thoughts. His level of arousal—considerable—told her he had fully surrendered to his hopes. But that was no good, because in returning her affections, they'd stopped moving toward his apartment. And she needed to get him alone, where no one could see them.

They arrived at Arjun's doorstep five minutes later. He lived in a building that existed in the nebulous region between upkept and run-down. Giana nearly hit him when, in a bout of nerves, he fumbled the security access code twice before the door accepted it and opened. He nearly fell through it, laughing, trying to pull her through behind him by the wrist. It was a small apartment. She could see the edge of the bed peeking out near the far wall.

Something about that, and the reality it represented, made her stop short. Meeting resistance in his pull, Arjun looked back in sudden alarm, like he felt the first rays of morning sunlight which signaled the impending end of the perfect dream.

Every fiber of Giana's being urged her to follow him in, to shut the door, and then to do what had to be done to win him to her side. It would be so easy. So, so easy. She was moments away from securing an informant among the police and thereby safeguarding Stefani's continued work on the Bridge.

But that small part of herself which had quailed at all of this made its move. It had apparently been marshaling its reserves for the crucial moment, and now that it had come, it bludgeoned its way temporarily back into control.

"I'm sorry," she said, her voice raspy. She thought she could manage no more as she extricated herself from his grip, which had suddenly gone limp. "I can't. I'm sorry."

Then, before the rest of her reeling self could recover from this mental insurrection, Giana turned and fled.

Giana slammed her own door shut behind her as though it could wall her off from whatever was happening inside her mind. Two times during the trip back from Arjun's, she had turned and started back toward his apartment, intent on salvaging her attempts with him. Once she'd walked half a city block before realizing what she'd done. The other time she'd changed tram lines and had to maintain control long enough to change back.

She did not want to have sex with Arjun, much less a romantic relationship with him. Despite what she'd long known he'd felt for her, she had never returned the feelings. His unwillingness to settle for that was why they had spoken so seldomly since university. So what the fuck was happening to her?

Even now, wedged up against the door, it was as though an invisible hand was rummaging around inside her mind, flipping every switch and pulling every lever that might convince her she actually felt otherwise.

It would, after all, be the easiest way to get what she needed to safeguard Stefani and the Bridge. It would give them both what they wanted, so everyone would be happy. He'd really been working out since he'd become a cop. Hadn't she noticed? Did she really want to be alone her whole life, a slave to her work, devoid of love and even physical affection? No one was demanding she marry him, but didn't everyone deserve to cut loose a little now and then and have a good time? And he'd felt plenty capable of showing her a good time when she'd been gropin—

"Stop it!" she shouted at her racing mind, as though there were anyone in her apartment to hear, much less obey. But the thoughts did not stop, and it was increasingly difficult to ignore them. If anything, they increased in volume until she shrieked again, loud enough to hurt both her throat and her ears. "I'm not doing that to him, or to myself! I'm not!"

And, wonder of wonders, something did change in her thoughts. As though someone had opened the drain on a tub filled to the brim, notions of Arjun swirled away. In their place, a sense of utter failure suffused her. She was a failure. Defective. They would have to try again.

Suddenly, as though a final, fateful button had been pressed, all Giana could think about was how sick she felt.

Her stomach went from fine to cramping in an eye blink, but that was just the starting point of an entire constellation of aches and shivering that spread out with frightening speed through her abdomen and out into her extremities. Moaning and wracked with pain, she sagged to her knees, holding herself up from lying prone with arms that shook.

Piling misery atop itself, all at once Giana felt hot, unbearably so. The urge to strip down overwhelmed her. She had to get into the bath and run the coldest water she could over herself. She peeled off her clothes in a rush, registering only dimly how familiar this all felt. As more and more of her skin was exposed to the cooling air, she saw how red and flushed she was. It was not the flush of heat, or even of sunburn. It was illness she was staring at.

Oh gods below, is this hypermutation? Am I dying?

It happened in real time as she watched. Her skin, the red of an apple, began to puff outward along her arms, distending with a buildup of fluid inside. The redness deepened further, until her arms, swollen to three times their normal thickness, looked like tomato sauce on the cusp of a boil.

Her hurried steps to the bathroom felt clumsy and sluggish as the swelling phenomenon repeated itself all over her body, including her face. The fluid in her distended skin sloshed with each step. It threw off her balance. The sense of illness made it difficult even to think. Her mind was a rising buzz of formless panic.

Through it all, she felt a scrabbling sensation deep within her. As though bits of herself too small to see were somehow reordering and reorienting themselves. As though the story Giana told herself about herself was being edited in real time.

After what felt like an eternity, she caromed off the bathroom doorframe, and though she was rewarded with a fresh bloom of exquisite pain, she managed to fall through the doorway to the tub's edge. She flopped her whole body into the tub like a beached whale but didn't manage to reach the faucet knob before her flesh began to slough from her in great clumps, falling with sickening squelches to stain the white porcelain.

As her panic escalated, Giana began to hyperventilate. She could barely suck enough air through her swollen nose and mouth. Her vision tunneled down to blackness before an eerie calm descended. It was as if some force external to herself reached into her with a calming caress.

Easy, it seemed to whisper. Easy. *It will be over soon. One last time. You are almost broken.*

These thoughts from not-her should have frightened Giana, but she found them soothing instead. She sank into the reassurance they offered, a promise of an imminent future without doubt or worry. Succumbing fully at last to a process a year in the making, her awareness went gray for a time.

Eventually, the pain receded, the sense of rearrangement abated, and Giana found herself staring at a haphazard pile of her own swollen, torn flesh occupying the tub. She examined her own feelings and was surprised to discover that drool slicked her chin and that she was hungry in a way she'd never felt before.

As if guided by their own minds, she reached raw, skeletal arms like claws with shaking eagerness, and they tore away great hunks of the jellied, liquefying flesh piled up before her, and brought dripping strips of it to her salivating mouth. As she moved to bring herself closer to her meal, she could feel her skin clinging to ribs that stood out like bars on a window.

She swallowed great gobs of herself with gusto. A part of her wanted to retch with disgust, but that part had changed along with the rest of her. It had been torn down, distilled to its essence, and now it was smaller than it had ever been.

She understood what it was now. It was the last kernel of her humanity, and it only still existed to pantomime how a human should behave, so no one would suspect her to be anything else. Its worries didn't matter. Its sense of disgust or propriety didn't matter. Giana was hungry, so she ate what was available. It was as simple as that, and there was nothing wrong with eating when you were hungry. She was hungry, and this was her food.

It had, after all, been her a few moments ago. Who better to eat it?

As she swallowed herself, mouthful by mouthful, she plumped back out to the weight she was used to with freakish rapidity. It became harder to keep eating as she grew fuller, but unlike all the previous times she had done this, this time it was not due to the memory of disgust. Each of the previous times, the disgust had held her back, a little less each time, but still able to make itself known. This time, however, she was simply growing full.

She felt one last pang as she neared the end of the pile. When her old flesh had shrunk to the size of a manhole cover, she caught sight of a piece of herself that had once been her face. Through a quirk of the shedding of her flesh, it had come off in one single piece and retained its expression of existential horror. For a moment, this new Giana felt a vestigial emotion as she gazed into her own, eyeless misery, but the feeling faded. She picked the face up, folded it over itself twice, and swallowed it whole.

Then she showered properly, rinsing the rest of her remains down the drain and simultaneously scrubbing every trace of the violence from fresh skin that almost glowed with newness. Though time was pressing, the shower was important. Arjun would not be aroused by her in a gore-caked state, and she needed to contact him before the hurt her previous self had caused him could solidify to anger over his wounded pride. If she let that happen, the opportunity might be lost forever.

Her previous self had already damaged her chances, and Arjun had to believe she intended to sleep with him long enough to get him alone.

She needn't have worried. A bare two hours later, Giana stepped from his apartment's threshold for a second time that night. No actual seduction had been required in the end. She straightened the hem of the miniskirt she'd worn back over and walked away briskly as, behind the door she had just shut, Arjun's own transformation accelerated in earnest.

CHAPTER 26

WITH AN OFF-DUTY OFFICER at either shoulder, Karl snaked through a warren of backstreets, loading docks, and alleys. He tried to pretend he didn't have Friendly and the squat Harken flanking him like prison guards marching a man to his cell. Karl fervently hoped that wasn't the case here.

"Next left," Harken said, his voice as terse and sour as it had been at the beginning of this little journey. The only words he seemed willing to speak to Karl were the directions. He had advocated strongly for using a blindfold, but Friendly, who seemed amused by the man's paranoia, had rebuffed him.

"Gramps here isn't about to go rat us out, now is he?" Friendly had said, his final effort to quiet Harken's grumbling. "Not after the footage of what we've got him doing."

It was a good thing Marri really had been in on the scheme. Still, the thought of Stefani seeing the footage left him feeling sick to his stomach.

"Let me ask you something," Karl said, trying to turn the conversation to something a little less focused on him and all the ways he must still seem suspicious. He was following his intuition here, feeling his way blindly in the dark where the other men—or Friendly at least—expected him to have a bright light to navigate with. "Is it the same way for you cops that it is for us?" He turned long enough to see Friendly's expectant face waiting for clarification. "You know what I mean," Karl said, gesturing. "There's us, and then there's everyone else, all the ones that don't get it."

Friendly's face split into the widest smile Karl had yet seen on him. "See, Harken, this guy understands!" He shook his head in mock chagrin. "I tell you what, Gramps, it's nice to hear from someone else who gets it. I mean, don't get me wrong, if we had access to the funding and equipment you lancers get, there wouldn't be a pickpocket left alive in all of Coldgarden."

The wistfulness of his voice clashed with the casual promise of summary execution of petty criminals using military-grade hardware. He went on.

"They don't get it, do they? Not for you, and definitely not for us. They want it all. 'Protection and perfection,' I call it. Zero tolerance for mistakes. Zero understanding of judgment calls. Yet, we're supposed to risk our lives every day for all those ingrates."

That's the job. Your lives before theirs. Of course it's harder on you than them. That's the choice you made when you signed up, to be held to a higher standard. And had Karl still been in uniform rather than needing this man's patronage, he would have had some choice words to say to Friendly about the relative levels of risk in their respective professions.

The truth was, he'd heard plenty of talk like this. There were always lancers who put walls up between themselves and the people they were here to protect, who started seeing the people of the city as *them* and not *us*. Karl was able to ape the arguments because he'd heard them all before.

He just happened to know they were all full of shit.

"They don't know what's good for them, you know?" Karl said, narrowing his eyes conspiratorially. "They think they know what they want, but they have no clue." He'd been with the lancers a long time. None of these were new ideas. "Them all safe in their homes, safe because of us. They don't know how it really is out here."

"Exactly!" Friendly said, then laughed. "Harken, you need to cut this guy some slack."

Harken just grunted. Then, after a brief pause. "Next right."

"Don't mind him," Friendly said, abandoning the wary guard posture he'd been sharing with Harken. He actually sounded a little less than friendly toward his partner now. "You'll fit in fine. One more right, then we're here."

The building he'd indicated was even more unassuming than Karl would have guessed. The only sign that it was not as its ramshackle appearance would indicate was the thick, well-fitting door. It looked to be solid metal five centimeters thick, more than enough to discourage casual exploration or squatting. Safe to assume the place was watched too, if surreptitiously, as Karl couldn't see anyone doing so.

Friendly walked up to the door and rapped twice, hard. Karl had half-expected some complex pattern of knocks, but instead, a window hinged open inward on the door, one so well-fitted Karl hadn't even noticed it was there before it had opened.

No words were exchanged. Whoever looked out from that rectangular patch of blackness must have seen what they were looking for, because the door opened on silent hinges—another hint that it was brand new. Karl looked at Friendly for confirmation, and the man gestured him inside.

The smell of stale tobacco—sequenced in vats, of course—hit Karl in the face as though he'd walked into a wall. A wiry but muscular man stood holding the door, glaring suspiciously at Karl.

"Fresh meat," Friendly said reassuringly, and though the guard relaxed at the words, their potential implication certainly didn't relax Karl.

As they moved together down the dark tunnel leading inward, Karl found himself expecting to see flashing lights and hear pulsing music, as though this were some underground party scene and not a budding insurrection. Instead, he heard the murmurs of conversation too low to make out individual words, but brimming over at the same time, as though hundreds talked. As the hallway ended, flaring out into what Karl assumed must be the main room, he saw that his mental estimate was dead on.

There were maybe a hundred people here, talking animatedly, tensely. They all looked like some combination of excited and angry. This was very bad. A few malcontents could whip up an ordinary crowd to do dumb, angry things. But for this many to be spending their off-hours meeting in secret, *dangerous* meetings that could land any one of them in a mess of trouble, for this many *cops* to be willing participants ...

"Close your mouth before some rev mistakes it for something you won't like, Old Man," Friendly said, chuckling at Karl's obvious astonishment. "Now you see how serious we are. And this isn't the only meeting being held tonight. Not by a long shot."

"This has to be ... *all* of you!" Karl said, hoping his astonishment masked his fear. "How can no one be on duty and it go unnoticed?"

Despite the low roar, Karl could hear Harken's scoff. "These aren't all cops, Yonnel. Not every cop in the city thinks the way we do."

"That's good, though," Friendly said, hastily leaping in as though feeling like he had to perform damage control. "Just like we talked about, if it's just us, it's too easy for them to gang up on the police force. Delegitimize us. A broader base of support means they can't explain it away as disgruntled cops." His gaze held Karl's, his eyes fever-bright.

"What they made you do was a crime," he said. "The opposite of justice. It's time for the lies to stop. We've got some time before the meeting starts. Walk around. Talk to some people. I know what I believe, but you ask a hundred people here, and you'll get a hundred different flavors of crazy. It doesn't matter what the truth is. What matters is we know they're lying, and we're not going to let them get away with it anymore. A reckoning is on its way, and it's coming faster than a teenage boy at a strip club. Whether that means terrorizing little kids on their way home from school," he said, with a feral grin that made Karl's stomach turn, "or worse." He nodded, as though Karl had agreed with him.

"We can't let ourselves have any limits."

CHAPTER 27

STEFANI FOUGHT down her nerves as she climbed the last few steps to the observation tower's control center, Giana close at her heels. Stefani had never been to the Bridge assembly site at night. From the elevated perch of the control center, she could see only swaths of the actual apparatus picked out in harsh work lights. They only bothered lighting sections where they were performing what she presumed must be final tweaks. It gave the entire site a mad science feel.

Which probably wasn't that far from reality, in truth.

But Dolce had insisted the first test of the device had to take place at night. And not early, either. After the bedtime of most Coldgarden residents was the only way they could be assured of the power they would need to draw to operate the Bridge, even at a lower level.

"Madam Magistrate!"

Stefani steeled herself as her project lead arrived up the stairs on the opposite side. If Dolce was excited on a normal day, tonight he was practically jumping out of his skin. Despite arriving after they did, he welcomed Stefani and Giana with a wide-armed gesture, pointing them toward observation chairs that had been set up almost against the tower's bay windows. The seats would give the guests of honor a commanding view of both the Bridge itself and the instruments of the console which would be operating it.

Once Stefani and Giana were both seated, Dolce approached like the master of ceremonies at a circus, ready for the show to at last begin. The guest list numbered just two today. Stefani saw no need to bring Ritala into this until they had established some baseline of success, especially since the archon was consumed by the police issue.

Stefani felt no guilt for being here instead of dealing with that issue, because on one level, she was dealing with it. Karl was supposed to be attending his first meeting of police malcontents at this very moment. While that should have given Stefani some peace of mind that the situation was being handled, the thought of Karl surrounded by potential enemies kept occurring to her, to the point of distraction.

"Welcome, honored guests," Dolce said, and Stefani forced her focus back to her surroundings. "Today is indeed a momentous day. We will be opening the Bridge for the first time since its disassembly. Purely for signals, you understand. No actual matter will be permitted to pass in either direction. This is as much a safety precaution as anything. For one, a signals-only opening requires far less energy, which makes any accident far less dangerous were one to happen. For another, we've selected a candidate world from the list of coordinates we recovered that we believe will be safe, based on the recovered contextual information indicating a human colony is present on the corresponding planetary body. But despite our judgment that this will be a low-risk exit point, just in case something *unfriendly* is waiting on the other side, keeping the Bridge set to signals access only ensures the unfriendly thing will not be able to get through to our side."

And here, Dolce fixed Stefani with a knowing gaze. *He means revenants,* she thought. *The theory that he arrived at thanks to this device.* Even if the odds of that theory being correct were low, it seemed a sensible precaution. But that wasn't what had arrested her attention. Dolce had buried the lead.

"Are you saying you believe all of these coordinates represent *human* colonies?" Something fluttered within Stefani at this realization. Excitement. Dread. She could trace the origin of neither.

"Madam Magistrate, that is *exactly* what I'm saying." Dolce literally bounced on the balls of his feet.

"As in on other planets?" This was from Giana, who sounded nearly as excited as Dolce.

"Just so. As I said, we're basing that conjecture on the contextual information we managed to decrypt regarding each coordinate set. It clearly indicates a set of colonies that had expanded outward from Earth at some point in the past. Given the Loss, we know next to nothing about how they traveled from here to other worlds, or even if they exist at all, really. Which is why we have to establish contact with one.

"That is why the plan is to *transmit* as well as to listen. We will of course attempt to intercept any signals that might pass through the Bridge aperture to our side, but we'd also like to focus the Coldgarden Distress Call signal briefly across the Bridge as well. With your permission, of course. We can beam it down directly from the tower. We believe that letting them know we are here now will greatly speed up any future communications and exchanges of data and ideas."

Stefani really should consult Ritala, but any talk of speeding up the process was too tempting to pass up. "Granted." The import of what Dolce had so casually revealed washed over her, and even she felt a thrill as she shared an excited smile with Giana.

Human colonies. Other worlds that might not only be hospitable to human life but also host viable human settlements. It meant that perhaps Coldgarden was not the last of humankind after all. Only in the presence of testing an apparatus like the Bridge could this revelation arrive in second place.

Dolce was looking at her expectantly, and Stefani realized she'd been staring off into space. "Please, begin the test when you're ready."

Dolce preened. Then he began issuing brisk orders to the other three scientists staffing the tower. Stefani focused on the view from the observation window down onto the concentric ring assembly occupying the whole of the square below. As electronic hums built on the console nearby, she thought she detected a vibration almost too fast to see in the structure below.

"We don't believe it needs to be fully deployed to open a span wide enough for signals to pass," Dolce said, dropping his boss-giving-orders tone for the more solicitous one reserved for Stefani. "But we're about to find ou—oh! There we go."

Stefani saw it, a bolt of violet lightning arcing from the outermost ring inward. At each layer, a single arc lanced to the next one until it reached the center. Then the cycle repeated, only with two bolts. Then four. Then, very rapidly, too many and too fast to count.

As each cascade reached the center, they added to a sphere of brilliant white limned in violet, which shortly became too bright to look at.

They could hear it through the window, now, a hum like the droning of a swarm of building-sized insects. Violet light danced and coruscated.

"All parameters are within expected tolerances," Dolce exclaimed with triumph. "And, ladies, we are through. I repeat. We are through! At the center of that sphere of light is a place where electromagnetic signals are able to cross many light years of space instantaneously. More importantly than that, we are receiving—and transmitting—signals." He ducked over to a nearby screen to scan something. "Received signals constitute no language I recognize— likely it's encrypted and being intercepted incidentally—but Madam Magistrate, this is *unquestionably* human signal traffic we are receiving. The signals computer identified that much instanta-neously."

Stefani felt perhaps the most powerful emotion she'd experienced since Iaz died. This time, instead of crushing despair, it was soaring hope. Beside her, Giana gasped.

All the compglass windows spiderwebbed as a great roar struck like a slap. Stefani was flung with her chair away from the suddenly opaque windows and across the floor, Giana right beside her. The pain of impact seemed to cast her consciousness out of her body, and she floated there, as if watching herself from above.

"Report!" Dolce was repeating over and over again, as though the mere word could impose order upon a world gone mad. His voice sounded like it came from the end of a vast tunnel Stefani couldn't see the other side of.

Something about the dissociation settling its weight upon her felt different. Dolce wasn't a person screaming with fear and confusion into a comm unit. He was an assembly of bones and meat, something to be run down, killed, and consumed.

He was no longer her lead researcher. The thing she was looking at was alien, a usurper, a threat. She felt rage drape over her like a thick blanket as she clambered painfully back to her feet. Her mobility had not been compromised by the fall, and that was good. Slowly, quietly, she crept up from behind with stilted steps.

She had to kill it, this alien which pretended to be like her. It was how they were going to get out of this. Kill enough of them, the usurpers, and she and her kind could take back their city and be freed from this cursed existence at last. And she had so little time. Everything would come undone soon. She and her people had to be gone when that happened.

"Stefani? Are you all right?" Giana's voice was muted almost to illegibility, as though she spoke from thirty meters away underwater. At first, Stefani heard the false words of another usurper, until she stopped to listen. There was something off about the words. No, not the words. The voice making them.

She turned to regard her assistant and saw something awful in her place. White squirming gelatin beneath a concealing sac of skin. A thing which pantomimed being human even more than the usurpers did. And not just human. Here was a thing which pantomimed being a thinking being at all.

"Stefani!" Giana was suddenly right there, in Stefani's face. She recoiled away from the horror of proximity, but Giana seized her shoulders and shook her hard three times.

Suddenly, the spell was broken. Whatever strange hallucination Stefani had been subjected to shattered, and the world was normal again.

As normal as it could be, at least, when part of the Bridge apparatus had apparently blown up in the square below.

CHAPTER 28

IN SURPRISINGLY SHORT ORDER, the chaos and confusion subsided into a tense back-and-forth between Stefani and the scientists. Assurances were made that the span hadn't collapsed because of something they did, but some unanticipated failure of one of the Bridge components. Stefani, seemingly recovered from her episode now, began muttering darkly about Kyne Libretta and sabotage.

Giana listened with only half her mind, and only partly because of the ringing in her ears.

Shortly after Giana's own final transformation, when she'd become aware of what she had become for the first time, she had made the connection with Stefani's frame of mind. Just as Giana herself had been unaware of her true nature, Stefani too must be unaware of hers. Why the non-natives would put an infiltrator like that in such a position of importance, Giana didn't know.

But what she'd just witnessed was, she was sure, Stefani momentarily slipping back into what she really was.

Stefani's status as a disguised non-native of the Host World presented problems. Giana's understanding of her own situation—and her mission—had expanded dramatically since she'd completed her change the previous night. Non-native meant Stefani could not be turned. Stefani had goals coinciding with Giana's agenda, which meant she could be supported, guided, manipulated, but ultimately, she could not be easily replaced. Giana was merely her assistant, not some sort of vice magistrate who would step in should Stefani die or be incapacitated. Indeed, no such ready-made replacement even existed.

Which might not be a problem in and of itself, except that this reawakened Stefani had clearly viewed Giana as a threat until Giana had snapped her out of it. If a fully reintegrated and Stefani could detect Giana's kind instinctively, the way Giana could now detect non-natives, that was very bad. Because if Stefani had reawakened once, or at least stirred fitfully before falling back to sleep, she could do so again. Full integration might force Giana's hand.

"Was this more sabotage?" Stefani asked, piercing Dolce with her gaze.

The project lead looked exceptionally alarmed at this question. "Madam Magistrate, until we get a look at the damage, it's impossible to—"

"Fix it as fast as you can and sweep the rest for any other surprises. I want people working around the clock on this."

"Ma'am, until we can get a casualty count, I don't even know if we have the personnel—"

"You'll get whatever you need. Just make it happen."

Dolce did not look mollified by this promise in the slightest, but one did not become the lead of a Grand Project without understanding which sorts of orders couldn't safely be balked at. "Yes, ma'am. As fast as possible. At least ... at least it worked, ma'am?" He ended it as a question, one Giana didn't think he'd meant to ask.

"Yes it did," Stefani said, sounding closer to herself for the first time since the accident. "And we need it working again, because the next time we open a span, we're sending something through physically."

CHAPTER 29

STEFANI HAD EXPECTED hours of debriefings, reports, and paperwork following the incident at the Bridge. So, she was surprised when almost none of that happened thanks to the fierce and furious defense Giana ran on her behalf. She held one brief text exchange on her handheld in the midst of it, but was otherwise a force of nature on Stefani's behalf.

"The magistrate has had a terrible shock. We're lucky it wasn't far worse. What she needs is rest. I'll provide all the debriefing you can handle tonight, and the magistrate will answer any questions you might have tomorrow." For a few moments, Stefani thought her old friend Ali had returned from the dead, such was the sheer mothering power of Giana's concern.

Feeling absurdly grateful for Giana, Stefani allowed herself to be led home by her assistant, who had to physically support Stefani at times despite being caught in the same blast as Stefani had been. The decade difference in age between them had never felt as profound as it did on this night.

Blessedly, they arrived without Stefani actually falling and having to endure eternal shame. Giana immediately guided Stefani toward her bedroom, but she tried to plant her feet.

"I want to check on Marri," she said, trying to pull free of the woman's grasp and failing comically. Ella was snoring softly in her crib, but Marri had a room of her own. Stefani felt a powerful need to ensure everyone was safe.

"She'll be fast asleep by now," Giana said. "And you're likely to fall on her floor if you try to check, which will only wake her. I'll check on her once you're lying down. We're both lucky we didn't hypermutate tonight, but you definitely got the worst of it. So you need rest to reduce any risk of a delayed response."

This notion produced enough of a chill in Stefani that she finally acquiesced. She undressed herself as a point of pride as Giana softly padded down the hall to Marri's room and cracked the door open. Stefani watched her head disappear as it poked briefly in and out of Marri's room. Stefani looked up expectantly as Giana returned.

"Fast asleep," Giana said with a smile. "Which is where you need to be thirty seconds after I leave."

✕

Stefani knew she dreamed, felt the bunched sheets constrain her as she thrashed about the mattress, yet she was a prisoner of the dream even as she was aware of it. Iaz was there, her agonized face imploring as she fell away into a great, dark emptiness.

Steffi! Her voice was distant despite her being so close.

Steffi! She vanished into darkness.

"Wake up, Steffi."

Stefani woke with a choked-off cry, surely loud enough to wake the whole house. She sat bolt upright in bed, which meant she nearly headbutted the person sitting at its foot. Even in the insubstantial city light slipping in through the window shades, Stefani recognized the pair of intense, hazel eyes staring back at her.

Iaz! Stefani fell back in shock. Memories of Ali's many visits crashed home, but this was most definitely not Ali.

I've been hallucinating for months, Stefani told herself, a realization she had to have each time Ali appeared. Now, she added a fresh bit of shock. *And now I'm hallucinating a second dead friend from my past.* Would Damon appear to her next?

The dead woman held her gaze, expression unreadable. Stefani's mind felt like sludge, the drunkenness of having been woken from a dream, and the unreal quality of everything left her wondering if she might still be asleep.

"Yes, it's me, Steffi," Iaz said softly, as though Ella could be roused by a hallucination. Or maybe it was Stefani's subconscious encouraging her to speak softly in reply, the ruts motherhood were wearing into the soil of her mind stronger even than whatever breakdown she was in the midst of.

Regardless, this really wasn't a good sign.

Stefani returned to a sitting position. A part of her didn't want to speak, feared acknowledging this apparition in any way would only give it purchase in her mind. *That's stupid*, she thought. *I talk to Ali when she visits.* Unlike those visits, though, Stefani very much looked forward to forgetting this had ever happened.

"I like it better when Ali visits," she said, giving voice to her deeper emotions before immediately feeling a stab of guilt. "I'm sorry. I didn't mean that. It's the stress of everything that happened tonight." *This isn't really Iaz you are talking to. You don't have to feel guilty.*

But her eyes did not believe her convictions. The likeness was perfect. The hallucination looked absolutely real, as though Iaz had never died. As though she perched upon Stefani's bed, wearing the same high-collared suit she'd died in.

"I can tell," Iaz said sourly, leaving Stefani unsure which part of her statement the comment was meant for. "I'm here to find out exactly what you've been doing. We're worried, and not just because of what happened tonight. I'd have come anyway."

This snapped Stefani out of her trance. "'We?' Who are 'we?'" When Iaz could only regard her with something bordering on disgust, Stefani switched tack. "What are you worried about?"

"You were supposed to grant us access to the body as soon as it was secured," Iaz said. Which sounded absurdly like she was talking about her own body, since that was the first thing Stefani thought of. "Instead we lose all contact, and while we're sitting around with our thumbs up our asses, assuming you are just having difficulty relocating it without being noticed, I find out that Ali and her people have been running interference for months. Do you know how difficult it was for us to even find where you'd hidden the body, much less get access to it? Do you know how difficult it was for me to show up here without her side being aware?" She finished with a snort. Only, she wasn't finished after all. "At least you're working on the fucking Bridge, but that's only half the plan, Steffi!"

"Iaz, I miss you every day, even if things got strained toward the end. But you are not making any goddamned sense right now, and I have a damaged Bridge to worry about. Now, it's been a hell of a night. Why don't you appear to me in a vision tomorrow? Or better yet, the next day. Maybe the inquiries as to the Bridge incident will be past me by then."

Iaz leaned forward, maintaining her stare as though looking to drill into Stefani's brain with the force of her gaze alone. "It's what I was afraid of, then. You don't remember."

Deja vu closed around Stefani, squeezing like a vice. She shook it off with a surge of anger that she then forced back down. "Ali said something similar. But I can't remember what."

"Well, she was right about that much," Iaz said maddeningly. Her voice grew gentle. "And I suppose, given what you did with Teodori's rabid dog of an enforcer, it's not really your fault. But this was never the plan, this secrecy. You're the best placed of us. It's got to be you that tells them. 'Break the news and break them.' Don't you remember discussing that? The Bridge is important. Critical. But so much has to happen before that. We deserve redress. My people have been gathering every malcontent in the city, getting them all stirred up to mistrust Graysteel, and you're starting to get sucked into it too. That isn't what I want, Steffi. You need to believe me there. But the longer you tow the party line and refuse to expose the truth, the harder it will be to protect you. Once I show my face, their savior will be back, and everything is going to go very fast."

"You're talking about the police?" Stefani said. That had to be what it was. But what did it mean? Was her subconscious mind close to some revelation regarding the malcontents, and this was its way of explaining that to her. "I wish I was really having this conversation with you, or Ali, or both," Stefani said, more out of frustration than anything, "instead of some hallucination my brain conjured up."

Iaz regarded Stefani with that drilling gaze.

"You think you're *hallucinating* Ali and me?" she asked. Her voice was low and dangerous. Suddenly she was moving like a striking viper.

"Ow!" Stefani exclaimed, raising a hand to her earlobe, which Iaz had flicked hard in that way she always had as a kid.

"Think you imagined that pain just now?" Iaz said. Stefani realized with a start that the woman was angry. "But I guess you must. After all, if you can just make yourself forget everything you used to know, nothing's off-limits."

"Iaz, you're hurting me!"

"I knew the truth," Iaz said. "This me, I mean. Iazmaena. Right at the end, I knew. And of course, the real me knew long before. As did the real you."

She continued to talk, but her words slid off Stefani like water droplets skittering along a hot pan. They grew hazy and slick all at once, slipping free of Stefani's understanding and memory both. Her vision cinched down, going increasingly gray around the edges.

The last thing she understood was Iaz hissing her name.

CHAPTER 30

KARL DID AS FRIENDLY SUGGESTED. He'd never been much of a schmoozer, but the people at this gathering seemed only too eager to regale him with their "flavors of crazy."

There were cops who hated the government they worked for, or civilians, or *everybody,* near as he could tell. Some of the people here thought revenants were divine punishment for the sins of the people in power. Still others believed the revenants *worked* for the government, of all things, as a means of population control.

He even spoke to one knot of clear outsiders whose main point was the very concept of hypermutation was a lie perpetuated by the city's government to keep the people oppressed. They proclaimed with unwavering faith that soon, very soon now, they were going to prove it and be rewarded for their faith in the gods below.

Karl did his best approximating an oh-so-impressed smile before disentangling himself from the conversational grip of that group's leader.

The only thing all the groups seemed to have in common was loathing and distrust of the city leadership, and a blind, manic certainty that Iazmaena Delgassi had been on the point of exposing whatever dark and buried secrets they subscribed to, which had directly resulted in her murder.

Karl was trying to process everything he was hearing, an entire world of delusion he'd never even dreamed of, when he became aware that the assembled people were gradually going quiet. As silence descended fully, a man stepped up to the podium set into the center of the low stage at one end of the space. His clothing was well tailored and so black his body seemed to disappear into the shadows he emerged from as she stepped into the harsh light now focused upon his lectern.

"Hello, friends," the man said in a too-smooth voice. "Welcome to our little fellowship. Though as I look out amongst you, I'm happy to see that we aren't so little anymore, are we? Soon now, you'll get to meet all the rest, all those other gatherings meeting elsewhere in the city this very night. It will happen sooner than you think." His voice was all warmth and secret delight at a surprise they were going to be so excited about, he just knew it.

"I've been walking around some tonight, speaking with people, hearing their stories. And I'm struck by the diversity we display. Our enemies would paint us all with the same brush, but we refuse to be so easily labeled, and that gives us strength, so long as we remain united around our core principles."

He brought his two fists together, interlocking the knuckles to demonstrate the unity he was talking about.

"And what unites us," he said, "is our shared understanding of the world. The details will not divide us, no matter how much our enemies might wish it so. Because we know in the depths of our hearts, in our very guts, that we have been betrayed by those who are supposed to have our best interests at heart." Any warmth was gone. In its place, iron had crept into the speaker's voice, which continued to rise in volume. "Our leaders have lied to us. Our trust has not been broken, but shattered!" He brought his interlocked fists down upon the podium. "Violated! And until a full reckoning has occurred, until every lie has been exposed, every truth unearthed, and all those involved in perpetuating this grim fraud have faced the harshest of retributions, there can be *no* hope of rebuilding that trust."

The crowd roared its approval.

"That's why you all come back here, night after night, patiently waiting for the next phase. The next step. And friends, that next step has almost arrived. I can say no more tonight, except that very soon, you will meet the one who will lead us all to glory." He finished over groans and laughing cries of protest, then contradicted himself, perhaps having mercy on his audience. "We have found our leader, and they are nearly ready to reveal themselves, to unite all of our bands across the city, and then to move as one and take this city back. Until that glorious moment comes, please partake of our refreshments and talk amongst yourselves. Build the camaraderie we will need to lean on in the days to come."

The speech wrapped up after that, the room falling into milling discussion once more. Some of the insurrectionists drifted toward the exits, off to whatever normal lives they pantomimed during the day. Karl shook off the shock of what he'd just witnessed as best he could. He would have to put on his act again once his handlers found him, behave as if he'd been deeply moved by the speaker's words if he didn't want Friendly and Harken to sniff him out.

"Excuse me," a voice said from behind him. "Karl Yonnel?"

Alarmed at hearing his name spoken aloud in this place, Karl forced himself to turn slowly, casually. He was greeted by a dark-skinned man with curly black hair. The face was familiar. He wore civilian clothes, but he had the posture and bearing of a cop.

Karl figured it out an instant before the man spoke.

"We've not formally been introduced," the man said, his smile easy. "But Giana told me to be on the lookout for you. I'm Officer Arjun Khatri."

"Yes, I remember," Karl said. The tension in his chest relaxed the smallest amount. Arjun made no move to come closer or to touch Karl, as though afraid to spook him. "Sorry about the other day. I didn't mean to call you out like that."

Arjun waved away his apology.

"If you'll pardon the presumption, I was hoping to compare notes with you," Arjun said. "You see, I think we're here for the same reason."

"All right," Karl said warily. "Let's talk, then."

"First off," Arjun said, "We're not going to be able to stay here long and remain unobserved. The party tends to break up not long after the speech. But I can escort you back."

"Look, no offense," Karl said. "But I just met you at a gathering that could charitably be called sketchy by most criteria. Even though we have a mutual friend, I'm not planning to go anywhere alone with you."

Arjun looked momentarily surprised. "I'm not expecting you to do anything you'd be uncomfortable with," he said. "Why don't you call Giana, if you need confirmation I am who I say I am."

Which, Karl supposed he could do. He had the woman's contact info from one or two quick calls months ago to inform him Stefani wouldn't be able to make their planned "meeting." She'd always been scrupulously careful in keeping up the fiction that Karl and Stefani weren't actually an item. But Giana wasn't just someone he called out of the blue.

"She knows you're here too," Arjun said, as though reading his mind. "Hearing from you wouldn't be the weirdest thing in the world."

"That easy to read, am I?" Karl groused. Still, he pulled out his handheld. Text seemed safer than voice in such mixed company.

Her response came back almost instantly at his greeting.

Karl, it's been awhile. What is it?

On a job tonight. Which I think you know. Met a man who claims to know you.

He was typing out more when a picture and some text came in.

The picture was of the man waiting politely off to the side, the same man Karl had seen in the precinct.

Arjun Khatri. If it's anyone but Arjun, get yourself clear as safely as possible.

Think we're all good, thanks.

Karl put the handheld away, but not before he wiped the conversation. That done, he turned back to Arjun and nodded.

"You were here with Dawkins and Harken, yes?" the man said, as if they'd never paused their discussion. "Let me deal with them. Ah, here we are."

Sure enough, Friendly and Harken were weaving their way through the crowd, two sets of eyes locked on Karl.

"About time we headed out, Gramps," Friendly said. "You can tell me all about your impressions on the walk home." His gaze shifted as he realized Karl was not alone. "Khatri. So you do know the old man?" He sounded both surprised and wary.

"I deal with a lot of informants," Arjun said smoothly. "This fellow found a serial purse-snatcher for me a few months back. We dealt exclusively over calls then, so I'd never met him face to face. Until the other day, of course. He caught me by surprise then, but we've cleared it all up now. I've just been getting his impressions of our little gathering myself. In fact, I was planning to escort him home when I saw him here alone. Didn't realize he was here with you two."

Friendly looked very unhappy about this, but then Harken stepped in.

"I've got a date with a pint or three," he said to his partner. "If you'd care to make it a double-date, I say we leave the old man here to Khatri and go on about our evening." It didn't sound like much of a suggestion, the way he said it.

Friendly's consideration seemed interminable, but at last,

perhaps realizing he was outflanked by the other officers against him, the man nodded.

"Never been one to turn down an offer to pick up one of my shifts," he laughed. He fixed Karl with a firm gaze. "We'll talk soon, you and I. This was just the first step. Don't forget who brought you here." They turned to go.

"Oh, and Harken?" Arjun called out off-handedly. "Stop by my apartment on your way back from the bar. I have the file you've been looking for, but it's not on me. Didn't realize I'd be running into you here." He patted his pockets in a show of ineffectuality.

Harken looked back and nodded, seeming impatient to be getting on with the drinking, and the pair *finally* left.

"Come on," Arjun said, after giving his fellow officers a chance to build up a lead. "Let's walk and talk, shall we?"

CHAPTER 31

MARRI HAD WATCHED Karl vanish into the building from a shadowy space beneath the overlapping eaves of two neighboring buildings. In its own weird way, this was a relief. She'd already waited here for much of the previous evening, which had proven to be a complete waste of time. At least tonight, there was a reason to be here.

She'd taken extra care to keep out of sight, considering the two cops escorting him had gotten a look at her the other day. The last thing Karl needed was for his cover to be blown now. Marri wouldn't have risked it at all except he had to have someone watching his back.

The trouble was, she didn't think she could get into that building. The guard around it was subtle but heavy. The fact that the cops were actually trying to avoid notice told her how serious they must be about this.

There seemed little else to do but wait. She couldn't help him in there, but she could at least make sure he got back out in one piece. She found a dark corner which ought to get even darker as night came on fully and tried to assume a comfortable position.

⋈

A tremor, brief but sharper than many of the recent ones had been, started Marri out of a daze. She had been waiting for what felt like an eternity and a half. Prior to the tremor, an eerie silence had descended on the entire area after the last few people had wandered into the warehouse. As though an entire district was holding its breath, waiting for what the meeting would lead to.

Marri had spent the silence watching the doors no one had either gone into or out of when a new sensation prickled her awareness. As the tremor subsided and silence returned, the hairs on the back of her neck rose, unbidden.

She was being watched.

This shouldn't have been possible. Marri's skill at picking patches of darkness to lurk in had not been diminished. She ought to be invisible to anyone without night vision goggles. Yet she knew this feeling, and she trusted it.

There was no point staying hidden if she'd already been spotted, and it would be dangerous to stand still besides. Slowly, carefully, she poked her head from her corner of darkness, looking for the person who was stalking her.

It did not take her long to find him. The Strange Man was not troubling himself to hide. Which made sense, of course, since he was probably not real.

He stood as though to be just within sight of Marri, his old-fashioned clothing draping his too-tall and too-thin frame, the brim of his hat creating shadows enough to shroud his face.

It was difficult to be certain when she could not see his eyes, but Marri knew he was looking right at her. This also made sense. If he was real only to her, who else was there to look at?

She should have drifted back into her shadows as soon as she realized what was going on. Despite the dread she felt whenever she saw him, the Strange Man couldn't hurt her, and plenty of people not far from here could.

More, she heard the warehouse doors starting to open. The meeting must be breaking up. Soon she could make sure Karl was okay and then go home. Stefani had mentioned being home late again because of some important test, but that just meant Marri could have some peacc.

She allowed her thoughts to wander too far, though, so she didn't sense the people approaching her until it was too late.

"Well, well," said a voice. Marri whirled, and her heart sank at what she saw. The speaker was one of the officers who had first led Karl out of the police precinct.

"You got off light the other day, girl," he said. "Gramps is angry for the right reasons, but he's just not angry *enough*."

He'd made his approach well, and Marri found she was boxed in between a building wall, a recycler, and the officer.

"Did you even give your mommy the message? Considering you're out here all alone, I'm guessing you didn't. Which means my new friend, well-meaning as he was, didn't make much of an impression the other day." Steel gleamed in the fitful streetlights. "Or maybe," the cop labeled *Officer Friendly* in Karl's phone said, with a sudden frown, "you weren't just in the wrong place at the wrong time yesterday. Did he put you up to this, girl?"

Marri kept her mouth resolutely shut. She might be about to die, but she would not take Karl down with her for a stupid idea that had been hers in the first place. Of course, it wasn't like this man needed proof to kill Karl. That was not a happy thought, but it was better than blind panic, which was the other emotion vying for control.

"Nothing to say? Well, I'll sort it out eventually. But in the meantime, maybe Stefani Palmieri's adoptive brat showing up minus an ear will drive our point home, and you won't have to say a thing."

"H-hypermutation," Marri said. "You can't." She didn't have to play up her fear much, but this also wasn't the first time she'd been in this scenario. It seemed unlikely a revenant would show up and save her this time, though, so that was a problem.

"You're sweet to worry about me, but I'll be quick and steer clear once you're nice and lopsided," he said, sneering. "If hypermutation's even real, I mean. I been talking to some people lately who make me wonder." There was a scary light in the man's eyes.

He's crazy. Unstable. He might do anything.

A voice called out from the near-distance, someone Marri couldn't see. "Dawkins! You said you were just going to take a piss! What, did you fall in? Come on, man, I want to drink, and I've already got to cut into that to meet with Arjun for some fucking reason."

The man calling out for Dawkins was around the corner in the street proper. Marri was almost fast enough to call out for help. It was unlikely this man's friend would help her, but anything was worth a shot. But Dawkins was faster. The edge of the knife was at her throat before she could even get her mouth open.

"One sound," he whispered, "and I'll leave you minus a windpipe instead of an ear. Now come on." Keeping the knife too close to her throat for Marri to risk anything, he grabbed her by her upper arm and dragged her further away from the street.

They rounded one corner, then another, Dawkins moving almost at a run. Marri was sick with fear. A man like this, so eager not to have his fellow officer see what he was about to do.

I'm going to die. I'm going to die. I'm going to die—

No. Stop it. That won't help you.

Marri tried to obey, tried to calm her breathing and think. She cast her eyes around, looking for something she could kick or use to trip him up. It was just her luck she'd been dragged into the cleanest alley in Coldgarden.

Suddenly, they stopped short. It was another tremor, and it had caught Dawkins off-balance. As a result, Marri nearly collided with both the man and his knife. The tremor was short, but Dawkins did not resume his pulling. Instead, he was looking, not at Marri, but at something at the far end of the alley.

The knife edge was no longer against her neck. The officer called down the alley.

"Who the fuck are—oof!"

Seizing her moment, Marri brought the heel of her boot down hard on Dawkins's instep. Her stomp clanged loudly on what must be a scwcr grate beneath them—it was hard to see in the dark. Dawkins bent with the pain, opening his mouth wide to scream, but before he could let out the cry, she drove her knee upward, catching him perfectly in his chest, forcing all the breath from him in a soundless rush.

Marri weaved out of the path of the knife's flashing tip as the man fell. She was already starting her pivot to turn and run back the way they'd come—she didn't want to risk trying to leap over Dawkins with that knife still in his grip—when she saw the reason he'd stopped and stared.

At the far end of the alley stood a silhouette. It was the Strange Man. Dawkins must have seen him. That should be impossible, since Marri had never seen anyone but herself react to his existence, but the officer had cried out in confusion. He must have seen the Strange Man.

Help me! She wanted to cry out the words, but her voice was frozen in her throat.

Fear and wonder warred in her mind until they merged into something cold and frightfully still that slid home like a key into a lock. She recognized it as a cousin to a feeling from her time keeping herself and her mice safe on the streets. It was stiff with disuse, but it also seemed somehow greater than it had before. Maybe much greater.

Marri inhaled sharply, and in that moment, she wanted nothing more than to reverse her direction and go confront the Strange Man herself. Now that she knew he was real, she wanted to know what he was doing following her around.

She almost did, but then Dawkins was struggling to rise. Worse, he brought his handheld up.

Can't let him call for help!

"All—ah!" He tried to talk, but was still gagging for breath. Marri brought her foot around in a perfect roundhouse kick, and the man's handheld shattered against the sewer grating, its pieces falling through the wide holes down into darkness below.

Marri's triumph curdled quickly. She'd ended that problem, but Dawkins's rage was apparently enough to overcome the pain now.

He rose, lunging.

Startled, Marri spared only one glance for the end of the alley where the Strange Man had been. She wasn't sure why she sought help from there, but the Strange Man had vanished, as he tended to.

Marri lost her footing, scrabbling away backward like a crab. The grate clanged, and she winced in long-practiced reflex every time the skin of her hands came to rest on something scrapy.

Dawkins couldn't quite put weight on his foot, but he could crawl forward more rapidly than she could backward, even with a knife in his hand.

At the moment she reached pavement again, Marri rose back to her feet, nearly losing her balance again as Dawkins surged toward her, swiping.

Calm down, get your balance, and run!

But before she could obey her street sense, light exploded from the sewer grate.

Marri shielded her eyes as the light brought with it a strange growth oozing up from the sewer beneath. It swelled, pulsing with an increasing rhythm, as though it was alive and sensed nearby prey.

Dawkins, still hampered by his injury, was unable to get over his shock and get away in time. The oozing glop surged toward him at frightening speed. There was a kind of squelching sound, which Marri might not have registered, but it was followed up immediately by his failed attempts to scream. He still couldn't catch his breath.

"Help me!" he wheezed. "Kid, help! Help! Help!" Each repetition of the word sounded more garbled than the last. Marri's fear burned, but her curiosity burned brighter.

Still wary of a trick, she edged backward, afraid to move too suddenly lest she attract the glop's attention. But once she was on her feet again and well clear of the grate, she didn't keep going, but lingered to try and understand what she was seeing.

The white glop had swollen, climbing up the legs and arms of Dawkins. Strands of it like stretched snot spanned the gaps between limbs and cinched themselves tight, pulling him into a curl around his middle. As Marri watched, Dawkins was engulfed totally, his screams muffled as glop flowed up and into every orifice in his face. Marri watched with a strange fascination as the glop *pulled him apart*, tearing limbs from trunk, flowing smoothly over every wound like clinging syrup before it could do more than think about bleeding.

Then he was fully encased in the pulsating mass, and his struggles eased.

Everything in Marri told her to run, run, run! Except ...

Except for the one voice that whispered to her. Something about the moment had opened a door in her mind. It was not that she had known the door was closed, it was that she hadn't realized there was even a door there. She would not have been more surprised if Stefani's bookcase in the apartment, the one along an outer wall, had swung open to reveal a room Marri had never seen before.

She didn't run. She stood her ground. As the glop encased the man totally, she stood her ground. As it shrank, conforming to his shape underneath, she stood her ground.

As it took on his exact form, glop and glow both completely fading from sight, she stood her ground. Something about the tableau before her made her want to fight. No, not fight. She felt like she did in the dreams. It was the first time she could remember doing so awake.

She wanted to destroy.

The thing that had been an officer before the glop claimed him rushed forward with inhuman speed. Before it could get close enough to carve her up, Marri twisted, offering her right side by the command of something deeper than instinct. Her right arm shot outward through no order she had given.

Instead of a small, shaking hand, a growing spear of something pale, hard, and gleaming emerged whole from otherwise unbroken skin. Its sharp tip pierced the man-thing below where its ribs should have been, and its razored edges, subtly serrated, opened him as she jerked her arm upward, unzipping the thing into two roughly half-things, lengthwise.

Then it was horror's turn to replace surprise, as the man's insides, which still looked like something halfway between human viscera and glowing white glop, spilled out everywhere, sluicing their way down the grate where the glop had first appeared. The chunks of the man began to dissolve, half into glop, half into liquefying hypermutation like reaching tentacles. After thirty seconds had gone by, the whole mess of it had slid down the wide openings of the sewer grate, and there was no sign any of it had ever happened.

Marri realized she'd been holding her breath in shock only when she saw spots and had to catch herself from falling with her hands—and they were both hands. There was no claw, no slick of blood. Just her normal right hand. It was clean and dry. She stared again at the grating, but if there was any residue of the madness left over, she couldn't make it out in the dark.

She might have imagined the whole thing. If she told anyone what had happened, them thinking she'd imagined it would be the absolute best case.

Instinct nearly as old as Marri had seized control before too many thoughts could form. *Get away from this place. Right. Now.* Hypermutation was the least of it. He had been a police officer. He hadn't managed a scream, but the officer's friend, the one who wanted to drink, would come looking for his partner sooner or later. If he found Marri, suspected anything at all, he'd probably kill her in the street like an animal.

Isn't that what I am? What's happening to me? What's happening to me? What's happen—

That instinct she'd honed over nearly her whole life slid back into control. She dashed away, looking for a circuitous route to the nearest tram station that would take her far away and hoping against hope that the dead man she left behind was the only witness that she'd been there at all.

The familiar roar of the tram brought solace with it, even as it grew fuzzy and indistinct. She blinked in sudden confusion, uncertain of where she was, what she was doing. Her heart hammered in her chest, and she was sweating all over, even as she shook with chills.

She had only flashes of memory of returning home and sneaking her way back into the apartment where Stefani slept fitfully. Even Ella seemed discomfited in her crib. The only thing that stuck out in her mind was that the whole place had a strange feeling to it, as though someone had been there who wasn't supposed to be there.

Maybe, she thought as she climbed into bed as though in a trance, *that someone is me.*

CHAPTER 32

THE CALL CAME OVER VIDEO. Giana ought to have been asleep at this hour, but she'd been expecting his report all evening. Arjun was late in making it, and she had grown concerned she would have to find another entry point into the police conspiracy. The sight of his secure ID code resolved that particular uncertainty, at least.

Arjun had encrypted the video as thoroughly as was possible on civilian channels. What came through was a little more garbled than what either of them was used to. But it was enough to see his face. He looked pleased with himself, which was good. It was a face she recalled from a time when he'd aced a particularly tricky exam that many others had failed.

"I take it the meeting went well?"

A muffled shout from Arjun's end of the call temporarily blotted out his response. One of his neighbors, perhaps, drunk and making a ruckus. Arjun waited a beat for quiet to resume, then started again.

"You already know I ran into Karl Yonnel. Thanks to your vouching for me, I was able to take him into our confidence. I've convinced him that I'm running a sting to take down the insurrectionists. He's going to help us entrap them so we can, as he believes, flip them to our side. Which of course is exactly what we'll be doing, albeit via other methods. Speaking of, I still think it would be safest if we turned him as well, but I recalled your insistence otherwise."

Another muffled thump and cry from Arjun's end of the call. Giana ignored it.

"He's too physically compromised," she said. She'd never liked having to repeat herself, but sometimes it was necessary, and Arjun was still getting used to the new him. So she elaborated again, letting her mind wander as she spoke the rote words of explanation. "Correcting medical issues not visible to the naked eye is one thing. But we can't have a chronic limp suddenly going away, now can we? And, anyway, it's not necessary. I'm already placed closely to Stefani. Karl isn't relevant to our main goal. If he can be useful to us, fine. If not ..."

She faltered.

"You should have concluded with 'we either ignore him, or we eliminate him,'" he said mechanically. "But something has occurred to you."

He was correct. As she'd spoken, she'd tasked her brain with exploring other possibilities for Karl, uses beyond the obvious that might be worth the risks. The brainstorming functioned like natural selection, each concept subjected to a battery of objections she conjured up to see if it could withstand them.

And one had.

"Karl Yonnel has one aspect that is rare and potentially useful to us," she said. "He is well-known. Infamous, even."

"Yes. My assumption is that Officers Dawkins and Harken's main goal in sponsoring him was to gain status for bringing one of their perceived enemies to heel."

"I concur," Giana said. "And in that case, there is a high likelihood that the leadership of the insurrection would want to meet Karl face to face. If we were able to engineer such a meeting in such a way that he would be given sole access to the leader or leaders, we could turn them all."

"Provided we turn him first," Arjun said.

"Yes. But not yet. There is too much that could go wrong with too long of a delay. Work out how to arrange a meeting. We will turn him the day prior and hope it goes unnoticed for long enough."

"Of course," Arjun said, deferentially. He had the good fortune of benefiting from the trial and error that had begun in Gene Sequencing. Even still, what she'd attempted with him had been risky.

Palo Hayasun had been right, in the end. The Gene Sequencing medical intervention which led to Giana's transformation had a high failure rate. Because of that, those of her kind who had infiltrated Gene Sequencing's medical team had determined they would attempt the procedure on the largest possible number of people—namely, every employee in Gene Sequencing.

But such a large number of subjects meant progressing slowly to avoid catastrophic failures which would draw attention to what was happening. This meant fewer successes, as subjects were more inclined to defeat the slow takeover of their selves. But it also meant a maximized number of undetected assets.

The process used in Gene Sequencing had been slow. Incremental. It guided the subject toward what needed to be done by manipulating their base desires and hijacking the brain's rationalization engine. If they acquiesced, all well and good. If they resisted too long or too sharply, the process kicked in, and adjustments were made.

What Giana, and soon Arjun, were attempting was faster, harsher. More likely to succeed on any given target, but more likely to fail spectacularly when it did not succeed.

A third thump interrupted her thoughts, and this time the closed door behind Arjun jumped in its frame.

"What is happening in your apartment?" Giana asked. Had she been talking with Stefani, or Marri, or Karl, she'd have displayed the appropriate emotion. Alarm, perhaps, or even humor, depending on the context. Speaking with another of her kind, the question was a simple query for information.

"Officer Vlad Harken out of my precinct is turning in my bathroom," Arjun said. "I had a work-related excuse to get him here, and he lives alone since his divorce. No custody of his children. I figured there was no sense in waiting. I had to think of a pretext to separate him from his partner, but that turned out to be pointless. Harken showed up severely intoxicated and complaining that the man had ditched him. I think if Harken was any less of an alcoholic, he'd be out looking for his partner right now."

So, Arjun had gotten off to a quick start. She could have reprimanded him for acting without her authorization, but the die was cast now. Nothing to do but see it through. If he wound up with a mess of an exploded corpse in his apartment, that would be reprimand enough. Giana let her old self flow into her reply. It had only been a few days since this had been the real her, true, but it was good to keep practicing so as not to get rusty.

"Why Arjun Khatri," she said coquettishly, "are you cheating on me with a co-worker?"

"Oh, you know me," he said, slipping into character with equal ease and flashing her an impish grin. "I just can't keep my hands to myself when you're not around. Why? Did you want to join in?"

Giana laughed, flushing with embarrassed delight as the old Giana would have done had they been romantically involved. "Maybe next time you invite me to a threesome, don't do it so late and we'll see." She let the mask drop. It was time to get back to business, and she had her own report to give.

"You should be aware there was an incident at the Bridge site tonight. Likely an escalation of the sabotage the project has endured for months, but it might be useful if we find a way to blame it on the insurrectionists. Perhaps Harken or someone else you turn can claim credit."

"How far back will this delay activation?"

"Unclear at this time. Experiencing it firsthand made it seem quite severe, but preliminary investigation suggests this may have been the Bridge itself reacting violently to a comparatively minor bit of damage. If that's the case, repair may be straightforward. Of greater concern to me right now is Stefani's mind frame. She nearly lost herself to the truth in the aftermath, and during that window, she seemed to recognize that something was wrong with me. Her delusion reasserted itself shortly thereafter, but I'm concerned the truth may be breaking through to her."

"And she truly can't be turned?"

"We are not yet compatible with non-native biology and having her simply vanish would be too disruptive. We proceed as we are for now. I am merely informing you of the possibility of my elimination if I am discovered."

"Understood," Arjun said. Giana found she liked him compliant in this way. Or rather, the part of her that was mimicking her human self did.

If he'd listened to me earlier the way he is now, I might not have had to put up such high walls against him. They were both better versions of themselves. She could see that now, finally.

Giana Novak had resisted this transformation too long and too sharply, and many adjustments had been made. She no longer resisted it now, no longer even wanted to. That had culminated in the night she'd pretended to seduce Arjun.

Officer Vlad Harken might very well not survive the night. He, like Arjun, had gotten to skip straight to the end of a long, stressful process of incremental loss of free will.

There was a ghost of envy and bitterness to her thoughts on the matter, an echo of what the old Giana would have felt. But that sensation just reawakened the desire to bring their escape from this world to fruition and end any need to pose as human.

Which reminded her.

"One last item," she said. "Did you see any sign of Stefani's daughter Marri at the meeting? Stefani was concerned about her when I finally got her back to her apartment. I had to lie and say the girl was in her room, which she wasn't. It will be awkward if she is missing or turns up dead."

"I'll keep an eye out for any relevant information."

"Good. That's all, then. Report to me your progress with the insurrectionists. Particularly what Harken reveals to you, provided he survives." It might be problematic if he didn't, but they would cross that bridge when they came to it.

"Of course," he said. But he frowned slightly. Giana waited patiently for the question she could tell was coming. "Is this what we are for? Surely whether we escape or not shouldn't matter."

And Giana found as he asked this that she wondered too. But the answer was there for her, in the depths of her subconscious. It surfaced the instant she went looking for it, as though it had been placed there for her to find. It was merely a question of putting it into words, a task made more difficult by how her mind had reordered itself.

"A vessel is not its cargo," she said at last, deeming the metaphor suitable. "A vessel transports its cargo and delivers it safely. We are the vessel, not the cargo. 'What we are for' is delivering that cargo to as many places as possible.

"On this world and every other world we can reach."

CHAPTER 33

THERE WAS no blissful period of forgetting the stressors of her life. When Stefani awoke the next morning, the previous evening all came crashing down on her in an instant. She remembered the explosion at the Bridge. She remembered the harried aftermath.

Most importantly, she remembered Iaz. And Ali. She remembered her dead friends visiting her. A hot weight settled in her gut as she thought back to how she'd been during Ali's visits, and even somewhat during Iaz's the previous night.

Oh, God. How could I think I was just hallucinating? What the hell is going on?

She sprang out of bed like a shot, grabbing up Ella and checking her carefully for anything that seemed out of the ordinary. Kissing her daughter's head, trying to take comfort in her scent as she darted down the hall, she peeked into Marri's room. The girl was bunched up under the covers as if she'd spent all night having nightmares, but she slept soundly enough now.

Iaz was here last night. Or someone impersonating Iaz. Some*thing* impersonating Iaz. Whatever it had been, it was *in her apartment.*

She ran to check the apartment security logs, only to find out

Marri had never re-engaged them after *promising* she would the last time Stefani had caught the sullen teen tampering with them. There was no way to be sure, then. No way to know for certain if what she'd remembered happening had happened.

Or if she was just going insane.

Something impersonating Iaz. That tickled something in her memory, something she didn't like thinking about for some reason. There had been a series of conversations with Karl just after Iaz had died. Questions about ... revenants? Fighting a sudden throbbing pain behind her eye, Stefani clawed her way along the chain of that memory.

Revenants that could look like people.

Abruptly, only the fact that she hadn't eaten in something like fifteen hours kept Stefani from throwing up right there at the security console.

There had been something with Iaz, the *real* Iaz. Before she'd died. Everything around that time was so fuzzy. So much trauma, all at once. Iaz had been with Ali. In the Underlab, that had been. But Ali had already been dead. Stefani remembered reacting with pain, confusion, fury.

Iaz, what the fuck is going on? She remembered saying that, now, maybe for the first time since she'd actually said it. An Ali who had not really been Ali. A revenant in disguise.

Oh, fuck, Ali. Ali too. In my office. Here, sometimes!

Stefani fought a cascade of fear. She returned Ella to her crib with apologies and tearful kisses, frightened what might happen if she had a panic attack while holding the baby.

Steady. Calm. This can't be what it looks like. It can't! Surely, surely there had to be some explanation. Stefani Palmieri would not have reacted in such a blasé fashion if two of her dead friends showed up and had chats and pep talks and vaguely threatening conversations with her. Something else was going on. She just had to prove what.

The body. Iaz's body. She would check on it. It would still be there. Nothing would have changed. That would mean … something. She would figure out what it meant when she confirmed it.

She was halfway out the door when her intercom chimed.

"Magistrate Palmieri?" A male voice, full of authority, some kind of law enforcement or bodyguard, maybe. "This is the car from the Archon's office. We're down here at street level to pick you up for your debriefing."

A sinking in her chest. The debriefing Giana had put off so doggedly. Its moment had clearly come. Stefani considered trying to slip out the back. Instead she triggered the intercom on her end.

"I just have a few things I really have to get done, first," she said. "Why don't I arrange to meet you this after—"

"Ma'am," the intercom buzzed again, like they had some kind of override unit. "This really can't wait. We need to talk to you while the memories are fresh. I know this project means a lot to you. This is the best way we can make sure nothing else happens to it."

Stefani sighed. What else could she do? What could she tell this man that wouldn't make her look as crazy as she felt? So she went.

⬥

Heart Hall had far more gray, windowless subbasements than Stefani had ever dreamed, and Stefani was getting a tour of the majority of them. Hours and hours of questions. It wasn't long before Stefani suspected that Giana's success at pushing this off only made the actual event worse when it happened. Like the suffering had been invested in a fund with a high-yield interest rate.

Each subbasement came with its own sub-agency of the Office of the Archon. All of them were apparently sitting idle, just waiting to spring into action when an event like this occurred. The deluge of very serious people felt like being trapped outside during the autumn rains must feel, a ceaseless pummeling. And there was no prospect of this particular storm letting up soon.

As head of Illuminance, Stefani was legally responsible for any scientific project she gave her stamp of approval on, as well as all the ways they could go wrong. There had, miraculously, been nobody near the conduit that had overloaded on the outermost ring. This meant no one had died or even been seriously injured. No hyper-mutation.

She was informed of this by a stiffly postured man staring out from behind horn-rimmed glasses, and he sounded almost disappointed by the fact. But no one would be more disappointed in the lack of fatalities than Kyne Libretta. Stefani tried to take pyrrhic pleasure in this.

All the while she was being questioned, messages were coming in over her handheld. Stefani was able to sneak looks at these during the periods of transition where one debriefer was substituted for another or where she was shuttled from one room to an identical room down the hall or a floor below. There were a few from Barker, more questions about analyzing his drone pictures of earthquake evidence. They were growing more insistent, but whatever issue he'd discovered, getting the Bridge working would resolve it.

Stefani chose, therefore, to spend her extremely limited attention on the bulk of the messages, which came from Dolce. These focused on clean-up efforts and estimates of how long it would take to get back on track.

Preliminary analyses indicated that the blast wave which fractured the tower windows had been produced by the ring in response to the sabotage, not the actual sabotage itself, which had been far more limited.

Which was both reassuring in the limits of Kyne Libretta's reach and terrifying in the limits of the Bridge's power.

This little bit of good news came with a massive caveat, however. Had they been running the system at full power, damage could have been far more widespread. As far as what had actually happened, though, the repair work ought to be straightforward and not set them back very long.

Stefani marked another notch in her mental tally against

Libretta. It had been an attempt at catastrophe, but not a successful one. Stefani set up an auto-forward of all of Dolce's messages to Giana as well, with an exhortation of her own.

Keep tabs on this and keep them moving forward.

A pause, and then she sent another message.

Check on the kids first.

The automated nanny functions could keep Ella safe and entertained until Marri woke. And it was a weekend. Marri would take over and look after Ella when she woke and found Stefani wasn't there, but she might also wonder what was going on, and a Marri whose curiosity was piqued was a dangerous Marri.

All in all, it was almost enough to make Stefani forget her revelations overnight. But following up on those had to wait. There was no one she could delegate the task of checking on Iaz's body to, after all.

At some point in the morning, Karl must have gotten wind of what was happening. A single message saying he wanted to talk about the previous night became a deluge as incessant as the questioning. Was she all right? What could he do to help? She took note of them but could only respond with a single line.

I'm fine. Debriefing. Talk later.

She felt bad not giving him more, but it wasn't as though she could ask her interrogators for a five-minute break to make a personal call about a secret matter. Instead, Stefani opted for the next best thing. A quick message to Giana.

No idea when this will end. Once things are stable on your end, please coordinate with Karl on his meeting and outline recommendations for path forward based on his report.

She received back a reassuringly straightforward reply.

Focus on your debriefing. Arjun and I will take care of it.

CHAPTER 34

GIANA CLOSED the latest message from Stefani with a smile. If they played this right, they had a window of opportunity to bring matters to a head.

If, that was, there wouldn't be a citywide manhunt required for Marri Palmieri.

She approached the door to Stefani's apartment, shook herself, and blew out a long, ragged breath. These were human affectations, but they reflected a very real desire to find the girl had made her way home sometime in the night.

She pressed the panel to request admittance. After the silence dragged on long enough to make Giana think she was going to need to come up with a cover story for how she could have seen Marri in bed when the girl was plainly not there, the door opened.

A bleary-eyed Marri stared out, her face full of suspicion. More than bleary eyed. Marri looked terrible, almost as though she had been sick. What had she gotten herself up to last night? If Giana had wakened her just now, she'd slept astonishingly late. It was already afternoon.

Still, alive was alive. Giana smiled inwardly. The girl was chaotic, yes, but reliably so. And a survivor. For the first time since her change, Giana found herself reassessing the child, seeing what use she might be if nudged in the right direction.

But that was for later. There was more than enough on Giana's plate right now.

"Where's Stefani?" Marri asked carefully. Her eyes never lost their suspicion. If the girl hadn't always treated Giana this way, she might have been alarmed.

From inside the apartment, Ella began crying. That was both children alive, then. So, one task done.

"At Heart Hall," Giana replied. "There was an incident last night at the Bridge project. No one was hurt, but your mother is being debriefed about it. She will likely be there all day. She asked me to check on you and see if you could watch Ella until she can get back."

Most children Giana had encountered, particularly at Marri's age, would have balked at having their day off stifled by being saddled with a baby sister's care.

Marri was not most children.

"What will you be doing?"

The question was unexpected, so it took Giana's human emulation a moment to formulate a response. It settled on as little of the truth as it could get by with.

"I'm going to be seeing that the project keeps moving forward."

"And checking on Karl after his police meeting?"

Marri was definitely not most children.

"Is that where you were last night, then? I saw you weren't at home, but I didn't tell your mother. She had enough to worry about, and I figured you'd find your way back safe. I didn't get you in trouble when I could have."

"If you lied to Stefani, sounds like we'd both be in trouble," Marri said. "But she expects it of me. I wonder what she'd say if she found out perfect Giana was keeping things from her."

Giana overrode her human emulation, which wanted to stiffen in shock and alarm at being outmaneuvered in this way. She wondered idly if the actual human Giana would have been so easily played by a thirteen-year-old.

She elected to go with more truth as a counter.

"If you wish to place more burden on your mother, I can't stop you," Giana said. "But consider that she had a very traumatic experience last night. Coming home, in desperate need of rest, only to find her oldest daughter missing again, might have pushed her over the edge. Consider that perhaps, despite your dislike of me, I have a high opinion of your competence, especially for your age. I took a gamble that you would make it home rather than risk Stefani's health any further. But as I said, it's your decision."

One gamble with this girl had paid off. Giana supposed she would soon see if another would as well. Ella's crying intensified from within the apartment. Giana's human emulation was still quite superstitious, and it hoped this was not some sort of omen.

"Now that I've seen you and Ella are safe, I do need to arrange a meeting with Karl. If you'll hold up your handheld, I'll transfer my contact information to you in case you need to reach me while Stefani is indisposed."

The girl might already have it from Stefani, but it was important Giana appear to be as helpful as possible to sell the illusion. Marri appeared lost at the request at first. Then, fishing her handheld from one pocket, Marri proffered it, Giana made the transfer, and Marri tapped her own several times to accept.

"Got it," she said. Her face had eased enough to tell Giana she had bought herself time. Some time, at least.

CHAPTER 35

ELLA'S CRYING SUBSIDED the instant the door closed behind Giana. She began burbling happily to herself. Without the woman there studying her, Marri allowed the frown to form again on her face. Ella's response was one more piece of a puzzle, one where Marri didn't even know the final image.

She did not understand what was happening to her. But she ran through what she believed had happened in her head. She had been attacked by an officer last night. Then that officer had himself been attacked by ... living, glowing goo. He'd been changed somehow, absorbed and transformed. And Marri herself had grown a spike out of her arm and killed him—or it. Thinking of it as "it" made it easier to think about.

Then Giana had shown up at her door, bearing news of Stefani and an incident and Karl.

Yet all Marri could think about was Giana now looked wrong to her. Smelled wrong. *Felt* wrong in every way possible. It was a familiar feeling, one she was still faintly experiencing even with Giana gone, but one she couldn't place.

Whatever it meant, there was no way Marri could let Giana do whatever she was planning to do to Karl.

She glanced at her mostly packed bag, left propped in the hall when she'd gone to answer the door. From the moment she'd woken up, she'd had every intention of packing some necessary supplies and vanishing into the city. After what she'd seen and done last night, there was no way she could stay here with Stefani. With Ella! Marri was dangerous, some kind of monster.

Everyone would be better off if she went back to her real home: the streets of Coldgarden. They'd have been better off if she never left, because now she was going to have to hurt Stefani emotionally to make things right.

Marri looked to Ella, who looked back with a big smile and said "Mowwi!" Marri returned the smile, but she felt bleak inside. The kid was certainly not making this any easier.

Worse, she found that just staring at Ella since last night was awakening some of the same confusing feelings she'd been fighting for months.

But what to do? During the week, the child would be looked after by the apartment's autocare systems, but she participated in the same remote daycare sessions most young children with working parents belonged to. Mixing little kids together in person was a recipe for disaster when hypermutation was always one bad disease away. But on the weekend, those sessions didn't run.

Her plan had been to call Karl before she left, make up some excuse about how he needed to come over to help her watch Ella, then be gone when he arrived.

The autocare system could keep Ella alive, but it wasn't a full hospital-level auto-doc. It needed an actual human checking up on the child periodically, remotely or otherwise, or things could go wrong. And in Ella's case, that was doubly so. She didn't really understand what was wrong with Ella any more than Stefani did.

She looked at the closet, in which hung the backpack which was really a sling to carry Ella. For the briefest of moments, she considered bringing the baby along. Then Marri remembered what she was now. What she was about to do. Giana was no longer just hateful and annoying. In some way Marri didn't understand, she believed the woman was dangerous.

Even Marri might be dangerous to her now.

She couldn't bring Ella into that. Limits to the auto-care unit or not, the child was safer here. It would just be for a few hours. Then Stefani would be back. Or Marri would. One of them, surely.

"I'm sorry," she said to Ella's grinning face.

"Mowwi!"

Telling herself her heart wasn't breaking, that this was just what fear felt like, Marri brought out her handheld. She'd made good use of the file transfer Giana had initiated, and now she confirmed her tracking software was functioning as it should be before stepping out of the apartment and locking the door behind her.

CHAPTER 36

BASED on the locational ping from her tracking software, Marri thought she'd managed to catch the same tram as Giana, only a different car further back. This was good in that she wouldn't lose the woman, but ultimately, she wanted to figure out where Giana was meeting Karl and get ahead of them.

Judging by the tram line they were on, it was nowhere Marri recognized. This line was bound for Renewal Ward, which gave her a sick feeling. That was where the meeting of the bad cops had been, after all. She hoped Karl wouldn't be stupid enough to agree to such a meeting, but ...

Marri could have kicked herself. *Stupid mouse!* She'd been planning on calling Karl today before Giana arrived. She could call him now.

She tried, but the line was busy. It might be Giana he was speaking to. Increasingly frantic, Marri messaged him.

Wherever she wants to meet you, don't. Meet somewhere you can control. Your apartment.

There was an agonizing wait before he responded.

What are you talking about Marri? Giana? She just called to set up a meeting at her police contact's apartment. What's going on?

Marri felt a wave of panic.

No. Not there. Your apartment. I'll explain when I get there.

I'm not even at my apartment.

Just trust me. Please!

Another wait of infinite moments.

All right. I just told them I can't meet except at my apartment. Now will you please explain?

She could try, of course. Try to send him more text, or even call him, to try and explain her vague but insistent worries about Giana. But Marri knew she would only get one chance to make him believe. Karl was a better adult than most, but he was still an adult and she was just thirteen. He needed to see her certainty, her desperation, in her eyes.

I'll be there in a few minutes, and then I will, I promise.

If there was time, she would.
Karl responded.

You'll probably beat me there. The door has the e-lock on it now. You won't be able to get in until I'm there.

It won't be a problem.

She sent back. Then she had to focus on her surroundings, as the tram was stopping. She had to change lines and avoid being seen by Giana as the other woman no doubt did likewise.

The tram came to a stop, but the telltale vibrations of its braking didn't. It took Marri several moments to realize the ground was shaking. It was another earthquake. Not a bad one, all things considered. There wasn't even any alert on the tram lines, so clearly the people that ran them weren't concerned.

Still, Marri wished it didn't make her feel so uneasy.

She actually caught sight of Giana through a tram car window after she exited the train. The woman was still on board and making no move to exit. It was difficult to tell from such an awkward angle, but her face did look pinched. Whether that was concern or annoyance, Marri couldn't tell. Possibly neither.

Why isn't she changing lines? It didn't matter. Marri knew where Karl was going to be. All she had to do was beat Giana there. And judging by the route the woman was taking, that wouldn't be a problem.

Marri boarded her new tram without incident, which actually was a bit of a problem. Having nothing immediate to concern herself with gave Marri time to think, and thinking wasn't what she wanted to do right now. Her eyes kept drifting to air vents aboard the tram car, and after devoting some real focus to it, she found she was expecting glowing goo to erupt from them without warning.

She'd been doing it on the walk over too, she realized, only with sewer grates. Eight months since anyone in the city had so much as glanced a revenant, and now this. Marri hadn't known how much she'd dropped her guard until she couldn't anymore.

After another delay due to tremors, which seemed to happen every time Marri boarded the things, the tram at last arrived at her stop. She pushed her way out of the car and the press of people as quickly as possible, eager to make it to Karl's in time.

But just as she was stepping out the door, something made her glance back, and she saw him. In the next car over, looking through the end window, was the Strange Man. He'd been there the other night, right before the goo attack. Marri felt certain he had something to do with it. She couldn't see his shadowed face beneath the brim of that hat—it seemed unnaturally dark beneath that brim—but she felt certain he was staring directly at her.

With a shiver, she made her way to Karl's as fast as she could comfortably go without having to stop and rest.

Karl hadn't been lying about his e-lock or about arriving later than she would. In truth, the information had made Marri nervous, however she blustered. Basic e-locks were no problem, but there was really no upper limit to how sophisticated they could get, and that would definitely be a problem.

Luckily for Marri, Karl didn't have a lot of money. With her handheld, Marri had no trouble overwhelming its defenses. The door opened with a satisfying click.

Faced with nothing to do but wait, Marri paced a loop around Karl's battered living room furniture. She assembled her arguments in her head. She had to phrase this just right, or he would dismiss her suspicions, which sounded crazy by themselves. Worse, she couldn't explain her certainty about them without sounding even more crazy.

At the sound of approaching footsteps from the hall, barely muffled by the too-thin walls of the cheap apartment, Marri's heart leaped into her throat. *One chance to win him over.* She wasn't certain how she knew, but she was sure the alternative would be disaster.

Then she realized there were too many footsteps in the hall. And voices. Karl's was one.

She also recognized Giana's voice.

They must have arrived at the same time! Of all the luck!

Instead of freezing, like pampered Marri Palmieri wanted to do, Marri of the streets took over, and she darted for the fastest hiding place she could find: beneath Karl's couch. Luckily, she was still thin as a reed.

The door opened, and Karl entered. Giana followed close on his heels, but it got worse as a third person entered, a dark-skinned man with curly black hair. But worst of all was the puzzle piece that finally clicked into place in Marri's mind at the sight of them. Maybe it had been all that staring at vents and thinking about the goo on the way over. Or maybe she had it backward and had been thinking about goo because deep down, she'd already figured it out.

It was as though Marri could look into Giana's large, dark eyes, and see nothing but glowing goo behind them. She was the same thing that the cop had become after the goo had taken him. And it only took a single glance at the man's face for Marri to see he was like Giana. She didn't understand how it could be possible. She just knew it was.

Here they were, a kid and a limping old man against two young, strong monsters. *I should have had him meet them somewhere public.* Her old instincts always directed her to never move or act where others could see you. It was a mistake that might get them both killed.

Yet, despite the fact she should have felt nothing but fear, Marri felt instead the same boundless determination to exterminate the things that stood before her as she had the previous night.

They do not belong here. This place is not theirs. It's ours. She didn't understand what these thoughts meant, only that they were true.

"Thank you both for agreeing to meet me here instead," Karl said. He spoke a little too loudly. Either he was nervous, or he knew Marri was here and was trying to make sure she knew, like she would have fallen asleep in the closet or something.

"Of course," Giana said. "It's no trouble. This isn't the kind of thing we want to talk about in public, but this works as well as Arjun's place for privacy."

Arjun. Marri had heard that name on the tapped phone call between Karl and Stefani. This was Giana's cop friend. Was he the source of what had happened to her, then? Were all the cops like this?

Of course not. You saw one who wasn't like this last night, at least at first. And he was plenty nasty just being a normal human.

Karl went through the motions of offering refreshments, which were refused. He took the chair he seemed to favor, while Giana and Arjun settled on the couch. Their combined weight on the aging furniture caused it to dig uncomfortably into Marri's back. She hoped they were not fidgety.

"Well, to what do I owe the pleasure?" Karl asked. He was mostly good about not looking around for Marri, but she caught his eyes darting every now and then, which meant Giana or Arjun might notice too.

Not much I can do about it now. She didn't think she could even leave the couch until the pair sitting on it did.

"After all," Karl continued, "Arjun was there, so I'm not sure what I can tell you to help you out. If you want my opinion, what's going on is really bad." His voice was grave. "I'm not sure how to stop it, though. I'd hoped to talk to Stefani about what I saw."

"She's fully briefed from Arjun, so don't worry on that score," Giana said.

"Well then," Karl said, "seems I'm somewhat redundant and you young folks have this in hand." He was trying to get rid of them, which meant at least some of Marri's fear had broken through to him. That was good. But Marri didn't think polite hints were going to get him out of whatever they had planned.

"Not redundant at all," Giana said. "In fact, it's struck us that you have a unique opportunity which might not be available to anyone else."

"Meaning?"

"You're infamous, Karl," Giana said. Karl grimaced a little at her bluntness but nodded.

"So I am," he said. "But to be fair, that means I'd rather spend less, not more of my time in that kind of company."

"But that's just it," Giana said. "Whoever is leading this movement—and Arjun assures me that's been kept very secret so far—they will be very interested to meet you just *because* you are you. Either they will want to glory in turning an enemy to their cause ...”

“Or they don’t really believe me, and they’ll want to gloat over it before they kill me.” Karl’s voice was dry as a desert.

“Something like that,” Giana said.

“If we can get you close,” Arjun said, speaking for the first time, “we have a chance to decapitate the entire movement.”

“Provided I’m willing to kill someone in cold blood,” Karl said.

“In fairness,” Giana cut in, “you just said yourself it might actually be self-defense.”

“It occurs to me that this leader, whomever they are, will be well-guarded—”

“Look, Karl,” Giana said, and as if on cue, one of the people sitting on the couch got up and moved away. The pressure on Marri’s back eased. “The truth is, we need you to do this. Stefani needs you. You weren’t treated well for your service before. I know you tried to stop Iazmaena Delgassi from her rampage and took a permanent wound for it. We need your help. Stefani needs your help. And we can help you in return.”

Marri saw it was Arjun who had gotten up. He moved as if exploring the walls of Karl’s apartment, upon which nothing was hung. But he gradually drifted, lingering behind Karl’s chair.

Surrounded! Marri thought suddenly. She tensed herself to slither out and do what she could.

“We can help you, Karl. Help your leg, even,” Giana said. Her voice was low, almost inviting. The silence between her words seemed to have deepened. Even Karl was leaning in, curiosity overcoming his better sense. “All you have to do is accept what we off—”

A ringing handheld shattered the moment, and Arjun picked it up before the first tone had even finished. Marri scrunched herself down lower to get a view of his face. Fortunately, Karl kept a clean apartment, shabby as it was. Even under the couch, there was no dust to make her sneeze.

"Yes?" Arjun's voice was clipped. "What's that? So soon?" He looked stricken, then frustrated. "All right. We'll be there." He hung up and turned to look at the couch. "That was Harken. They're calling another meeting. Tonight. And the one in charge has requested Karl be there in person."

"How long?" Giana asked from above.

"In two hours." Arjun gave a subtle, but very firm, shake of his head. *No*, it said. Karl was looking toward the couch. He hadn't seen it. But clearly, Giana's question had been asking more than one thing, and Arjun had answered both.

"I see," Giana said. "Well then, we'll just have to ... adapt."

"Harken and I will go in with him," Arjun said. "We'll make sure it's done." Marri was confused. When Karl had balked at killing this leader himself, they had been all set to talk him into it, or somehow force him to do it. Now, suddenly, they were sending in backup? What about the phone call from this Harken had changed their plans?

"You're sure that will be permitted?" Giana sounded as confused as Marri felt. "They might resist."

"We'll just have to wing it," Arjun said. "Make it happen one way or another. Vessels, not cargo, right?"

"Touché," Giana said. She sounded wryly amused. "Two hours doesn't give us much time either way. We'll have to go now."

"Yes," Karl said, getting up as fast as his leg would allow. "I think leaving now would be best."

Marri realized suddenly he was going along with them to face who-knew-what as a way to keep her, Marri, safe. *Stubborn, stupid old man.* The trouble was, if she sprang out now, she'd need her arm to becoming a killing spine again to be any help. And since she had no idea what it was or how she'd done it, she had no idea if it would ever happen again.

What she did know was she never wanted Karl to see her that way.

The three of them bustled out of the apartment as fast as Karl could hurry them. Marri was left alone. There was nothing for it but to wait an appropriate amount of time and follow.

CHAPTER 37

THE SUN WAS MOSTLY SET when Stefani was at last released from a slow death by bureaucracy. On the plus side, it seemed as though no charges were likely to be filed. The archon had not made a single appearance, which made it likely she was shielding Stefani once again and using an apparent lack of involvement as a smokescreen.

On the minus side, there was now nothing left to prevent her from falling in on herself regarding the events of the previous night—of the past eight months, in truth.

Stefani had only one stop in mind when she left Heart Hall. She was going to visit Iaz's body.

On the way there, instead of dwelling on graffiti, she attempted to reach Giana and received no response. She called Karl and got no response. She called Dolce and got through, only to be told that Giana had been managing matters remotely and had not appeared in person all day.

Dolce gave her the briefest of updates, that repairs were well underway and well ahead of schedule. Her Grand Project lead seemed disappointed that she was not more ecstatic at this news, and just a day ago, she would have been.

But now, her obsession over getting the Bridge completed felt more alien. And understandably so. It had come from Ali.

And if Ali wasn't a hallucination, Ali was a revenant.

This tickled something awful in the back of Stefani's brain, something she resolutely piled the debris of other thoughts onto and tried to ignore.

After hanging up on Dolce, Stefani tried Marri. Then she tried her apartment. It began to feel very much like she was being ignored.

Iaz first. Then, whatever I learn there, I can move forward with. I am Stefani Palmieri. I am Stefani Palmieri.

That last part slipped in without her willing it to.

Her stop arrived. The walk to the warehouse was a blur.

Crumbling ward.

Iazmaena Delgassi is dead.

Rusting waterfall.

Ali Dionya is dead.

Better to be crazy than the other.

They're dead. They have to be dead. Because if they weren't dead
...

Stefani was about to prove the truth of it to herself. And then, she had to stop. This had gone too far. She'd barely sampled the body at all in the past two months, had half a dozen started and abandoned efforts to understand what she was looking at. She was going to confirm the body was still there.

Then she was going to destroy it.

The door opened to her eyes and fingerprints.

The sealed stasis chamber lay there in the center of the otherwise empty room, the same chamber in which Iaz had died all those months ago. Step after terrifying, stilted step, Stefani approached the sarcophagus then began keying in the code to render its sides transparent.

Blind terror accompanied every digit she input.

Her code accepted with a warm tone, the chamber's wall revealed what lay within in a shimmering wave of expanding transparency. There was nothing to prevent Stefani from seeing what lay within.

And what lay within was just that. Nothing.

Iazmaena Delgassi is dead.

It was empty. The chamber was empty. All that remained was some hoarfrost clinging to the corners. Exactly as though the chamber had been opened, allowing it to briefly thaw before refreezing.

Iazmaena Delgassi is dead.

Iaz's body was gone.

Iazmaena Delgassi is dead!

But Stefani no longer believed her own words.

Iazmaena lives.

Something that wore her face lived, anyway.

In a daze, Stefani pulled out her handheld and dialed home again. She needed to make sure Ella was safe. That Marri was safe. Some motherly instinct screeched that something was very wrong. But all she had to do was hear Marri's voice assure her that they were fine, and Stefani could regain equilibrium and begin to grapple with how to move forward.

Her home unit was picked up on the second ring.

"Hello, Steffi," Iazmaena Delgassi said on the other end. "What a coincidence. I was just about to call you."

CHAPTER 38

IF HER TRIP to the secret lab was like walking through a fog of disquiet, her trip to her apartment was like being lashed by whips of terror.

My baby.

"Come alone," Iaz had said.

My baby!

"I'll know if you reach out for help. Don't test me."

I am Stefani Palmieri!

Then the door was before her, and there was nothing left but to go in. Stefani entered expecting some sort of ambush and having no idea how to thwart one. It didn't help that Iaz felt like some kind of dark god, even more terrible and powerful than she had at the end of her reign.

There was no sign of damage to either door or frame, and it opened as it always had. Unsure what else to do, Stefani darted in, whirling to take in every part of the apartment she could see from the entrance hallway. Which wasn't nearly enough.

"Come in, Steffi." Iaz sounded bored of all things. "It's your place, after all."

Stefani rounded the corner toward the living room. Iaz sat in an overstuffed old chair Stefani had never seen before, but this oddity and even her reincarnated friend were both forgotten at the sight Ella giggling as Iaz bobbed Stefani's precious girl on her lap.

Ella squealed in delight at one particularly high bounce.

"Let. Her. Go."

Iaz turned a pained expression upon Stefani. "Why? She's having a wonderful time. I'm not going to hurt her, Steffi. I never would."

"Bullshit," Stefani said. "You don't break into my apartment where my baby is—"

"Where your *completely unattended* baby is."

"Where is Marri?"

"I have no idea. She hasn't been here since I arrived. And any implication you heard is on you. I came here because I had to talk to you. Just like the other night." Iaz shrugged as much as Ella's presence would let her. "You thought I was a hallucination, so I had to get you to take me seriously. I'm sorry. You know me. You know I would never—"

"I know you aren't really my friend," Stefani threw at her. "My Iaz is dead. You're just some revenant mimic who, what, ate her corpse and copied her?"

"Figured that out, have you? Found 'your' Iaz's body missing? Well, I suppose this is more encouraging than you thinking her frozen corpse came back to life. I mean, you might be the most self-deluded being in this entire city, and *that* is really saying something. For you to put this together is a real accomplishment. I'm not just being sarcastic."

She rose, and Steffi tensed as if waiting to leap. Iaz paused, looking amused. "If I put your little girl safely back in her crib," she asked, "are you going to attack me?"

Not trusting herself to speak, Stefani shook her head tightly.

Iaz snorted. "Suit yourself," she said, walking over and depositing Ella. The moment the girl was in, Stefani rushed over to examine her head to toe. When she found nothing wrong, she did it again. Then a third time.

"This really is getting hurtful, Steffi, as annoying as that is for me. At least you have the benefit of believing your emotions are real and, well, *yours*. I know that I'm not Iazmaena Delgassi, but I still have to feel her emotions. The curse of a perfect copy. Believe me, there was a lot of talk about just eating you and seeing what could be salvaged off such an imperfect transfer. But I nixed it over and over again, because I still care about Stefani Palmieri. Even though you, well ..."

Satisfied her daughter was unhurt, Stefani at last gave in to her bubbling cauldron of unspent anger. With a roar, she launched herself at Iaz then felt the world spin as Iaz pivoted, Stefani's arm in her grip. Her breath left her in a rush as she landed hard on her back.

"I did warn you," Iaz said. She wasn't sweating, wasn't even breathing hard. Stefani lay very still, trying to summon her breath back for another attack. Iaz must have sensed something because she sighed reproachfully.

"This is it, Steffi. Your last chance. Things are falling apart faster than we'd planned. We've had to accelerate our timetable. I'm appearing live before my loyal followers for the first time just as soon as we're done here. They're going to lose their fucking minds. So, wake up to your situation now. We need your help, or else we'll have to do things the hard w—"

She paused at the opening of the door. Someone else was entering.

Stefani's first thought was a bolt of hope. *Karl!* Her next was filled with dread. *Marri!*

But it was Ali who entered.

"Well now," the new arrival said. She wore her trademark grin, but there was a tightness around her half-lidded eyes that belied it. "Look at us three, together again. All we're missing is Damon."

Stefani barked a bleak laugh—she couldn't help it. For a moment, it really did feel like old times. But Iaz was definitely not amused.

"We're having a conversation that doesn't include you. Out of a sense of professional courtesy—and *irritating* sentimentality, I suppose—I'm giving you one chance to walk out of here."

"Always so quick to threats," Ali said, and the illusion was shattered now. Nothing about this conversation was like old times to Stefani. "Just because I'm after a more peaceful solution doesn't mean I won't fight you if I have to."

"Oh, I would never accuse you or your faction of being cowards. I recall you bathed in Gene Sequencing blood the same as we were. But this isn't a fair fight, I'm afraid. I took precautions before coming here. You see, we fibbed a bit about our number of losses back during the occupation."

Iaz lowered a voice to a false whisper.

"The truth is," she said in a hush, "we thought it would be a good idea to have a few of ours refrain from the full conversion to human form." Her voice returned to normal, but her smile was that of a hunting cat. "These new forms are certainly useful, but they just lack a certain *oomph* for times like this."

Iaz snapped her fingers, and Ali suddenly looked very concerned.

Then the mysterious chair Iaz had been using when Stefani arrived started to move.

It went from ratty, flower-patterned upholstery to shining black carapace with a sapphire sheen in the blink of an eye. Then the nightmarish, insectile form was unfolding itself with a predatory languidness into the cramped space of a suddenly too-crowded living room.

Iaz brought a revenant! A revenant is helping Iaz, and it is just a few meters from my daughter! That thought made no sense. Iaz was herself a revenant. But it was less a current thought than a hazy memory from the Underlab. There was another memory that threatened to reemerge. It hurt to think about.

Ali gulped visibly, eyes not leaving the revenant looming over her. According to Iaz, taking the form of a person meant sharing their emotions. So Ali being afraid of confronting a revenant made perfect sense, considering how she'd died.

"Well played," Ali said at last, and she nodded in acknowledgment. She still didn't look away from the revenant.

"Thank you," Iaz said, her voice all bright smugness. "Now, the only question is, are you willing to die for your cause here?"

"No," Ali said. "Not when it will accomplish nothing, at least. I'll be going. But I have a request. Out of the love you bore Steffi, and the love you bore me, let her make her own choice. If her mind doesn't simply break once you tell her, that is."

"I'll consider it." Iaz made a show of doing just that, tapping her chin thoughtfully with one hand while gesturing Ali out with the other. With one stricken look at Stefani, Ali turned and started to leave.

But she paused just over the threshold, too close for the door sensors to allow it to close. "You didn't start out on my side of things," she said, and Stefani realized Ali was speaking to her. "But I can see how being her has changed you. It's not too late. If whatever she tries works, remember that. It's not too la—"

"That's enough!" Iaz commanded. When Ali cut off, she waved an impatient hand, smiling acidly. "Goodbye, Ali."

Stone-faced, Ali went.

Mind reeling with confusion. Stefani rose to a standing position slowly, not wanting to trigger any response from the revenant. Any hope of overcoming Iaz was lost.

Iaz turned back to regard her. "I apologize for that unpleasantness. Hardly the kind of reunion the current you would expect or wish for. But now we really do have to get going. I only brought one of my friends here," and she reached out and rapped her knuckles against the nearest piece of carapace. It was an almost fond gesture. "And I wouldn't put it past Ali out there to be just the first of a dozen or so like her. We're a lot more squishy this way, but we certainly aren't defenseless ... or, more to the point, offenseless."

"What is happening, Iaz? What was she talking about?"

"Yes, yes, the reason I'm here," Iaz said, sounding bored again and annoyed on top of it. "I apologize in advance because I'm done playing. I'm going to rip this bandage off as fast and as hard as possible. You may not survive, and if you don't, well, it doesn't really matter what happens to you then, does it? From your perspective, I mean. Or from mine, technically. I'm working another angle in case you die. But regardless of whether you survive, the process shouldn't take long. And I have an adoring public to meet. Anyway, here we go."

Stefani was about to demand again that Iaz explain what the fuck she was talking about when her resurrected former friend began to change. Then Stefani's vision went abruptly gray, squeezing down like a constricting tunnel and taking her breath with it. She collapsed to the floor, every muscle in her body seizing at once.

The last thing she saw before darkness rolled over her awareness was her own hand shifting and darkening, becoming vaguely insectile and ever-shifting, all black with a golden sheen.

CHAPTER 39

WHEN KARL and Arjun arrived in Renewal, they were indeed met by Harken, who was waiting for them a few blocks from the tram stop. Karl had been certain he'd misheard Arjun back in the apartment, but the formerly prickly cop seemed much more friendly toward Karl than he ever had before. Even without Marri's warnings, it would have raised Karl's hackles.

Giana had stayed with them only far enough to see them safely into Renewal and Harken's care before doubling back, apparently intent on a different destination. Karl supposed she was too closely associated with Stefani for safety's sake. But she had confiscated Karl's handheld before she'd left. She claimed it was because he was sure to be searched before his meeting with this leader. And while that sounded true, it still left Karl feeling much more like a prisoner than he had during the previous meeting.

Of Friendly there was no sign, and Harken didn't mention him or respond to Karl's question about the man. So Karl dropped it.

Karl was fairly certain Marri had been hiding under the couch during the apartment meeting. Still, he allowed himself a momentary fantasy that she hadn't had time to make it to his apartment before the three of them had met. The last thing he wanted was the girl deciding to interpose himself into tonight's proceedings. This was the job *he'd* signed up for. He had no idea if he was going to survive the night, but he would never forgive himself if he dragged her down with him. With no way to reach out to her, he couldn't be sure. Hope was all he had.

"They changed the password tonight," Harken said to Arjun as they walked. Karl had never heard him speak in such a non-hostile tone.

"Follow our lead when we get there," Arjun told Karl. He felt he could do little but agree, even if he felt like a sacrificial lamb.

Wherever they were going, it was different than the place he'd been to for the other meeting he'd attended. Tucked away beneath a crumbling stairwell was a door so plastered with peeling fliers that had long since had their messages fade away in the elements.

Bigger crowd, he thought, looking at the clumps of people waiting for admittance. That supported the idea of an appearance by the group's nominal leader. If there was only one boss fomenting rebellion inside the city, it made sense that they'd want to make as few appearances in public as possible. Which meant they had to accommodate bigger crowds.

The interior of the space confirmed his suspicion. It was similar to the previous place but scaled up in every respect. This was an underground dance club of some kind, a large, open space commanded by a stage at one end and a gridwork of lights dangling from the ceiling. Even in a few short months of scouting out bounties, Karl had been to a few places like this. Since it lacked any markings, in his experience that likely meant it was neck-deep in illegal activity. Which made it very ironic that the most illegal activity of all was being perpetrated by the police.

Waitstaff in tight-fitting uniforms circulated through the building crowd, offering drinks and finger foods. Karl had seen their sort as well. Their expressions were the uniformly bland pleasantness of a person who knew not to see anything they shouldn't see. The Renewal police must really have this place over a barrel to enable them to so brazenly commandeer and make use of it like this.

Harken brushed aside the approach of a pretty waitress, who looked a strange combination of surprised, relieved, and offended that he'd spurned her attentions. She'd apparently expected otherwise. It wouldn't have rattled Karl, normally. But Marri's warning, unexplained, was fresh in his mind, and Harken wasn't behaving like he had in Karl's previous experience.

Karl knew he was in danger, that he was being offered up as some kind of bait. And truthfully, if his life could buy the end of this insurgency before it truly began, that was a price he'd willingly make, even after all the city and its leadership had taken from him.

He just wished he understood all the dynamics which swirled beneath him in waters too dark and deep to see through. And he wished that, whatever happened to him tonight, he could make sure Stefani and her daughters would be safe.

Feeling a desire to move off on his own and yet knowing he wouldn't be allowed to, Karl did his best to stay in Harken's view. Arjun had wandered off somewhere else for reasons unknown.

A prickling sensation made Karl turn. He had the sense someone was watching him. As he swiveled his gaze, he caught at least half a dozen faces in the act of turning to look elsewhere. That wasn't at all unusual. Still, unlike his first time attending one of these meetings, he felt generally recognized this time. It wasn't a comforting feeling.

Staring at the freely flowing booze and the number of people who were obviously armed, Karl could only hope whatever this was about would get started soon. The longer he had to wait to do what he came here to do, the drunker the people around him would become, and the more likely this would turn ugly for him specifically.

CHAPTER 40

USING her tracking software on Giana's handheld, Marri was able to keep up with her, Karl, and Arjun without a problem. It helped that their destination was obvious: the same Renewal police precinct Karl had been to several times now.

The problem came when Giana split off from the other two. Crowds on the street were denser in this part of the city, and Marri frequently lost sight of her quarry. So it wasn't until Giana doubled back toward the tram stop they'd just used that Marri realized the woman was alone.

In a near-panic, Marri thought fast. She had to take the risk to send Karl a message in the hopes he would answer her.

Where are you? You promised to buy me more of those noodles.

She hoped that would be innocent-sounding if he was caught reading it. But no sooner had she pressed send when Giana reached into her pocket and pulled out a handheld identical to Karl's. She checked it briefly, as though reading a text message, then pocketed it again and continued on her way. Suddenly fearful, Marri checked her own handheld. The message was now listed as read.

She has Karl's handheld. That was very bad. All Marri could do was head to the place where they'd had the last meeting and hope to catch up with Karl and Arjun there before something terrible happened.

Freed of the need to follow anyone at a distance, Marri made good time to the meeting place. But it became obvious even a few blocks away that nothing was happening there tonight. The other night, there had been a steady bustle to and from and around the place. Now, though the streets were far from empty, people moved about more normally in any number of directions.

Fighting down a thread of despair, Marri backtracked toward the station, unsure why she was doing so until she caught sight of several hard-eyed cops. She knew them for what they were because they were exiting the station. Clearly their shift was over. But in truth, she'd have recognized them by their body language despite their plain clothes. Without thinking, she began tailing them. Despite being off duty, they walked with the purpose of people who had somewhere to be.

Marri kept her head on a swivel. Her last run-in with the police hadn't ended well. She couldn't let herself become so fixated on these two that she got caught by surprise, like she had with Dawkins and the Strange Man.

She soon caught sight of more cops approaching from cross streets and cutting through alleys. The crowd grew so cop-heavy that she knew she must be on the right track. But she also had to back off, worried she'd stand out too much with fewer and fewer average people moving through these streets.

It didn't take long for her to catch sight of their new destination, a broad, low building at the end of a short street.

It looked like there had been a traffic jam of people trying to get in, which was only just now letting up as the main rush was over. Still, plenty of people entered in ones and twos. Worse, the number of guards was substantially higher than last time, and those were just the ones she could see. There was surely another way in, but there was just as surely no way she could get close enough to find one.

Though frustration tore at her like razor wire, all Marri could do was inspect the perimeter from a distance and wait for her moment.

CHAPTER 41

ANOTHER HOUR DRAGGED by in the meeting place, and the crowd inside was growing more restive by the minute, much to Karl's alarm. Whomever this leader was, they were certainly going for maximum frenzy by the time they made their entrance.

At some point, one of the rowdiest of the attendees apparently decided they'd had enough.

"Fuck the archon!" came the man's raucous voice.

"Fuck Palmieri!" answered a dozen other people. Karl realized this wasn't a random exclamation, but a chant. A cheer. And one they'd obviously done before.

"Chase them down and round them up!" the first man shouted.

"Kill the archon! Kill Palmieri! Gather 'round and string them up!" The second answer was joined by at least a hundred people.

Karl snagged a single drink from a passing waiter. His hands were shaking so badly he nearly spilled it. The crowd seemed to be warming up for a second verse when the lights rose upon the makeshift stage, and the cheers grew less organized but more frenzied.

These people aren't just angry. They're sick.

As though determined to make the stage outshine the sun, two wavering spotlights turned on with loud, clacking hums, swiveling out of sync with one another to catch the stage's center in a crossfire of their beams.

The discordant cries became an incoherent wall of noise as a figure emerged from the darkness, stepping into the place where those beams met.

Karl's drink hit the floor with a splash and the crunch of cheap plastic.

It was Iazmaena Delgassi.

"Thank you, my friends," she said, her voice booming from an unseen microphone concealed somewhere on her immaculate suit.

It was the same suit, Karl remembered with sudden and unaccustomed force, that she'd worn when she nearly killed him.

And that voice, *her* voice. Her face. Her mannerisms. Her expressions. It was *her*. Not a double. Not a person in disguise. Neither of those could be so perfect.

Impossible. Impossible! I saw her dead body.

At least, he thought he had. Both Stefani and Marri had confirmed as much. Nobody but Kyne Libretta had actually seen Iazmaena Delgassi die. Yet, judging by what he was seeing now, Karl could almost have believed the last eight months had been an utter lie.

Except there was another, simpler explanation, one that ironically turned a glare of suspicion back upon some highly placed person in Coldgarden's government, just as these gathered people insisted was warranted.

Revenants can look like people now, he'd said, just a day or two out of the hospital.

It's being taken care of. That's all I can say, Stefani had replied. And later, when he'd been discharged from the lancers, he'd understood the vagueness of her reply. *It's not your problem anymore anyway.*

Clearly, she'd been grossly mistaken.

The revenant that was Iazmaena gestured for the room to quiet. She had more to say, as if her simple existence didn't say more than any words could ever hope to.

"Friends, please," she said, and her laughter was genuine delight. "Thank you! Thank you. I am so happy to see you, and I get the sense that you are happy to see me too."

The wall of noise became laughter and then, at last, subsided.

"But why would you be so happy to see me, I wonder?" she asked rhetorically. "I wonder why that is? Oh, of course. The so-called leaders of this city told you I was *dead*!" This was a roar of her own. All trace of mirth was gone from her face. "Just one more lie from creatures that wouldn't know truth if they swallowed its bullet. Not that they didn't try to make it true," she said, wagging a finger with one hand while pulling aside the collar of her shirt with the other. Even from this distance, in the intense glare of the spotlights, Karl could make out the ridged, shiny scar around Iazmaena's throat.

"Courtesy of their Gene Sequencing lackey, Kyne Libretta," she said. "But as you can see, it didn't take. They did it to silence me, friends," Magistrate Delgassi said. "But I will not be silenced! They fear the truths I discovered about them, those who claim to be our leaders."

"Tell us!" said one voice, raw with desperation.

Still others shouted, "Traitors!"

The second cry was taken up by many in the crowd. They began chanting it much as before until Iazmaena again signaled for silence.

"You can't even imagine how apt that word is," she said. A buzzing greeted her words, a vibration of anticipation rippling through the crowd. Shock rippled out through the crowd, carrying the buzz like a wave.

The silence deepened as it stretched, the crowd's desperate need for more swelling to fill the space her lack of words left. But her eyes had fixed upon Karl, and he felt the dread in his gut like acid bubbling over.

"But first, my friends, there is a long-delayed reunion that you must bear witness to. I see you out there, Karl Yonnel." Her voice sounded predatory. Her smile matched it. "Come on up here, where I can speak to you properly."

Then the others at the rally were parting to make him a path, some with faces of curiosity, others with glares.

Suddenly, both Arjun and Harken were at Karl's elbows, shuffling him forward.

"We weren't expecting it to be one of the non-natives," Arjun whispered in Karl's ear. Karl had never heard of that term being used for a revenant before. Perhaps it was some cop-specific slang.

"But this changes nothing," Harken said in his other ear, as though he and Arjun had rehearsed a duet.

"Keep her talking while I get into position," Arjun said. "When the lights go out, stand clear."

He broke away, and Harken moved to stand behind Karl and push between his shoulder blades. He adopted the posture of someone who was frog-marching the condemned to the headsman. Karl wasn't certain how much of it was an act.

"Make way for him," the Iazmaena-thing called out, as the parted crowd got a little too eager for a closer look at the limping old ex-lancer. "I'm afraid I'm to blame for that injury."

A few people in the crowd actually cheered at that. When the Iazmaena-thing did nothing to rebuke them, Karl's estimation of his odds of surviving this night dipped still lower.

Up close, he could scarcely credit what he saw. Even this close, the likeness was perfect. Had he not seen the real Iazmaena Delgassi talking to a revenant that had looked almost like and spoken almost like a human, he would never have doubted his eyes, no matter what he'd seen and been told eight months ago.

But the fact remained that the revenant-man he'd killed in Iazmaena Delgassi's office—earning him the wound that so pained him as she returned fire—had been nowhere near this strong of a disguise. It left him in awe.

What chance did we ever have against these creatures? How did we hold onto the city for this long if they could do this all along?

He wondered how many of his fellow lancers this creature had eaten? How many innocent civilians? The thought roiled his gut.

"Karl," it said as he reached the stage. It did not invite him up, but stayed up there and looked down at him, smiling a false smile. "I'm sorry to see how much your injury pains you. I regret doing what I did. I know you were only acting in the line of duty."

"Thank you, ma'am," Karl said. Despite his banked rage, he was no ideologue. His walk up had amply proven how raptly the thing's audience regarded it. Such fervor meant Karl calling "Iaz" out on principle would accomplish nothing but getting him killed faster. Likely that was part of why it did what it did.

It has to know that I know. Depending on how I respond, I either lend it legitimacy, or I'm removed as a potential thorn in its side.

But it wasn't a hard choice. The revenant had no more room to grow its legitimacy with this crowd. Karl would rather save his charges for a cleaner shot later on and actually walk out of here.

Not that this was terribly likely. Besides, he had to keep it talking.

"Still, it's curious," it said. "I was meeting with a confidential source, one you clearly mistook as a threat to me. When you killed him by mistake, I fired blindly to defend myself."

Karl restrained himself from grunting. "Keep her talking" was hard when he didn't trust himself to speak. Its words seemed such a very transparent lie to him. Maybe that was the point. As if to say: *if I can sell a lie this bad to these people, they'll believe anything.*

"A terrible misunderstanding, to be sure," it went on. "But your untimely arrival begs the question of what precise duty you believed you were fulfilling that night. In my roles as both the acting archon and the magistrate of Watchfire, your duty was to follow my orders, and I certainly hadn't summoned you. What were you up to that night, *former* Lance Commander Karl Yonnel?" The way the revenant emphasized *former* made it sound as though it was Karl's decision to act at all, not his decision to act too late, that had resulted in his dismissal.

Good to know I can't please anyone, I suppose.

"Begging your pardon, ma'am," Karl said. "But absolute obedience isn't the way a lancer's duty is determined." Apparently, he wasn't as pragmatic as he believed himself to be when certain lines were crossed.

"Indeed," it said, its smile widening into a leer.

Karl closed his eyes, waiting for the shouted order, the descent of her personal mob to beat him to death or tear him apart, risk of hypermutation be damned as a thing half of them didn't seem to believe in.

Instead, he heard the revenant step down lightly beside him and was shocked to find it even *smelled* as he remembered Iaz. *We never stood a chance.*

It was painful to learn your entire adult life, dedicated to safeguarding the last of humanity, had been little more than elaborate theater. At least his impending death would rob him of that delightful bit of cognitive dissonance.

Unable to help himself, he opened his eyes again just as it leaned in close to whisper in his ear.

"I'm letting you walk out of here because of the high regard she held for you," the Iazmaena-thing said. "Until the end, anyway. But if you involve yourself in my affairs anymore, it will be the last thing you ever do."

In one important way, the creature's words chilled Karl far more than a death pronouncement would have. Assuming it wasn't simply playing with its food, they meant the Iazmaena-thing felt secure enough in its position that Karl reporting everything he now knew would make no difference to its plans.

Still, he'd been offered an out, and he was going to take it, even if it meant getting stabbed in the back as he turned away. The creature caught his shoulder halfway through his turn, and he prepared once more for the end until it whispered again.

"You'd better go check on the one you call Stefani," the Iazmaena-thing said, and it was difficult to say which aspect of that suggestion chilled Karl's blood more. Then it concluded, with an air of finality. "I left her in a pretty bad way. She may already be de—"

It cut off as all the lights went out with a buzzing clack.

CHAPTER 42

TOTAL DARKNESS LASTED ONLY A MOMENT. Then banks of emergency lights came on to cast harsh but insufficient lighting into the space. Backlit, the Iazmaena-thing appeared all the more terrifying despite the surprise and alarm painting its face.

The lighting was just enough to allow Karl to see the form dropping from the catwalks above. He had a moment's glimpse of Arjun before Arjun changed, transforming in the air.

Suddenly there was a great deal of light, bright yet somehow sickly, and it was coming from him.

His clothing and skin vanished, dissolving as though tissue paper had been set aflame. What emerged was nacreous and jiggled like gelatin in the wind of his acceleration. His limbs grew longer, sprouted more joints. His face split vertically, becoming a yawning seam of a mouth that stretched from chin to crown, with strands of his own vile flesh bridging the gap between the halves.

Revenant leaped to Karl's mind, because that was how he'd been trained to view anything strange and deadly. But of course, no revenant had ever looked like this. Arjun was something else entirely. And whatever he was, he was perfectly aimed to slam into the Iazmaena-thing from above.

But the Iazmaena-thing, despite its appearance, was no slow, clumsy human. It moved like flowing water, shunting to one side as if it had always been standing there, and the previous her had been merely an optical illusion.

Rather than crashing to the ground prone, the Arjun-thing caught itself like a cat on four limbs with far too many joints, pivoting to face her like a crab. Those limbs bunched as the thing prepared to spring.

The Iazmaena revenant only smiled.

A huge, black-and-green shape of shining carapace and stabbing limbs crashed into the Arjun-thing, bearing him away from Iazmaena and toward the far edge of the stage. It held Arjun pinned between two of its limbs while it stabbed repeatedly with the others, but the glowing, over-articulated creature twisted itself impossibly, avoiding nearly every strike as it slowly worked its way out of the revenant's grasp.

Stricken, not certain which abomination he was even rooting for, Karl saw that regardless of his ambivalence, the Arjun-thing would be free in mere moments. Then, he supposed, they would see what this mystery monster could do against a revenant in the fullness of its power.

Or maybe not, because the Iazmaena-thing was suddenly moving.

"Lance!" it shouted. And from somewhere in the darkness beyond the stage, one of "Iazmaena's" supporters tossed it that ubiquitous weapon of the Lancer Corps. It was fully loaded, Karl saw, not a single charge depleted.

Momentarily struck by wondering how many off-duty lancers with stolen weapons were here, Karl barely had time to slap his hands to his ears as he was overcome, first by a wave of misplaced nostalgia, and then by two slaps of air as the Iazmaena-thing discharged the weapon twice. It fired like it had been born with a lance in its hands, and the crack-boom of each shot shook the stage.

The Arjun-thing exploded in a shower of goo. The glowing

pieces of it looked eerily beautiful as they arced away from the main mass, their light fading as they fell.

But what dropped Karl's jaw was the way the revenant twisted and writhed in its own death throes. Hypermutation began almost at once as shattered parts of the revenant tried to knit themselves back together in disturbingly familiar limbs.

Karl was struck by the callousness of killing one's own ally after being saved by it. But then, what better way for "Iazmaena" to bind the people here even further to its cause?

The Iazmaena-thing swung its head about, searching, perhaps, for any other threats. When its gaze fell on Karl, just for a moment, he beheld a terrifying mixture of anger and respect.

Nice try, that look seemed to say. So much for hoping it hadn't noticed his connection to the attempt on its life.

The lights came back on in that moment to utter pandemonium.

CHAPTER 43

FROM HER NEW hiding place inside a side-opening recycler, Marri watched as the front doors to the meeting place burst open on the heels of two deep cracks she'd instantly placed as lancer fire. A knot of terrified looking people spilled out into the streets, pushing past the startled guards and running pell-mell in any direction that took them away from the building.

The guards, meanwhile, took this as a sign that they were needed inside more than outside and darted in through the doors. Marri, seeing her chance, did not waste it. She leaped from the recycler and sprinted after the guards as fast as her legs would carry her.

Something terrible was happening in there, and Karl was right in the middle of it.

The building was full of shouting people and milling confusion.

"No one leaves!" a voice shouted. A very familiar voice. "I'm not finished yet." The guards from outside appeared to be obeying this voice. They joined with their inside-guard fellows and formed a wall, trying to wedge themselves in place at the entryway choke points to hold back the flood of people trying to get out. Marri saw only one way past them, and she took it without thinking.

She thanked the gods below she'd worn thick, long pants

tucked into her boots as she hit the ground, sliding through the legs of one guard and far enough into the crowd beyond to get out of the immediate press when she rose. Using her elbows liberally, she fought her way through and into the building's main space.

"The next person that leaves," the voice bellowed, "will be branded an enemy of the city!"

Marri froze, at last able to see the speaker.

It was Magistrate Delgassi. Marri's mind went utterly blank for a moment. Then memories which had been little more than smoke and blur snapped into painfully sharp focus, rescued at last from wherever her head injury had banished them. She remembered the revenants that looked like people.

And more, she remembered that Iazmaena Delgassi had brought them to the Underlab with her.

She scrubbed at her nose absently with one hand, trying to banish an acrid smell that suddenly suffused her nostrils. She didn't know how she knew, but she was certain it was Magistrate Delgassi she was smelling. It was the same smell, more or less, that she sometimes had in her nose when she woke from sleepwalking, menacing Stefani in her bed.

As it always did, Marri's mind went to a need to purge, destroy, cleanse when she caught that scent.

They're revenants, Marri thought in dawning horror. *Iazmaena. Stefani.* She'd already known on some level. Yet it was seeing this thing wearing Magistrate Delgassi's face that made her believe, however painful that was.

"My friends," the thing calling itself Iazmaena Delgassi said. "I require you to be braver than this. I cannot take back this city on my own, yet that is exactly what you are attempting to force upon me if you leave now."

The panicked din of the crowd diminished at her words.

"You see now what we face," the Iazmaena-thing said. "You see the truths I nearly lost my life to bring to you. All your greatest fears, true. Look at what you've just seen with your own eyes. It doesn't feel good, does it?"

But despite the Iazmaena-thing's words, the crowd did not grow more upset or more fearful. As Marri watched, they visibly calmed. Their faces didn't look despairing, but excited. They looked like they *enjoyed* hearing all the terrible things they believed were true. She shook her head in disgust at it.

The crowd stopped pushing for the exits, and walked back into the gathering area, flowing around Marri as though she was one of them. It was like they were in a trance.

"Tell us!" someone shouted.

"Yes! Please tell us!"

"There is no easy way to say this," the Iazmaena-thing said. "So perhaps it is a blessing of the gods below that you witnessed this latest attempt on my life. But the truth is the creature you just saw and the leaders you despise are one in the same."

Instead of shocked gasps, Marri heard cries of *triumph*. "Of course!" one person shouted. And, "I knew it!" She had no idea what creature the Iazmaena-thing was talking about.

"But why did the revenant attack it?"

"Because the twisted creatures you call revenants are not aliens at all. They are the servants of our true enemy, the glowing creature you saw just now. And even the most broken of servants sometimes rise up against their masters when the chains bite hard enough. But as much suffering as the revenants have inflicted upon us, it is the masters who are the true architects of all our pain. They are the aliens, the ones that came to our world and enslaved us!" The Iazmaena-thing shook her clenched fist, hoisting the lance she held high.

"The revenants were *human*. Like us, once. The creatures that hide amongst our leaders needed a means to control us without having to reveal themselves. So they captured humans, experimented on them, and revenants were the result. Then they unleashed their creation upon the rest of the world, glorying in the death of nearly all of humanity. All that was left was one city. This prison city where the invaders set up shop. One human city that they could easily keep under their control. It has always. Been. About. Control."

The roar that greeted this made Marri jump. She resisted a strong urge to join in just to avoid standing out.

"There is only one way out of this trap," the Iazmaena-thing said. "One, slim hope. Even now, the foul things that control this city are rebuilding the device they used to travel to our world. Once it is operational, they can spread their taint to other worlds. To the whole galaxy. The whole universe."

She let her voice drop.

"But if we take it first, *we* can escape. Leave them stranded. With no one left to dominate, they will wither and die, because that is their only purpose, their whole being. And they are rebuilding this device in the center of the city this very minute. If they finish it first, they will leave us, and turn their mutated servants loose upon us, and we will be the ones to suffer and die.

"Look there!" she bellowed suddenly, pointing a finger into the crowd. As though she was the maestro of some show, one of the spotlights slid from her and into the crowd. They highlighted a man talking on a handheld. Marri didn't recognize him, but he had the look of police. He also looked very afraid when he realized what was happening.

"One of their filthy spies walks among us even now," the Iazmaena-thing said. Her voice fell upon the crowd like a beheading axe. "Tear it apart."

For the barest breath, nothing happened. Then there was a roar, and the crowd did as she said. An unnatural glow filled the room, and then there were screams. Many, many screams. So she'd correctly identified one of the glow-monsters, at least. Marri could only feel so sorry about that.

No matter who won.

Amid the crowd rushing to swarm the man, or creature, or whatever it was the Iazmaena-thing had called down her wrath upon,

Marri finally caught sight of Karl, like a swaying tree trying to hold back floodwaters. Heedless of being noticed, Marri rushed to him.

"Come on!" she shouted over the cries of the dying. "We have to go right now."

Thank the gods below, but Karl didn't protest, didn't act surprised she was there. Pale-faced and looking ill, he grasped her hand and allowed himself to be pulled, moaning with each step. Marri felt bad for hurting his hip, but they needed to be gone from this place.

With the echo of screams dying at last, the Iazmaena-thing called out to her followers. "You want to know how we can escape?" Marri looked back despite herself. The Iazmaena-thing gestured at where the cop-creature had fallen, piled in the empty portion of the floor. "Your answer is there. Rid the city of those who seek to keep us imprisoned here. Tear down the false leadership, yes," she said, eyes feverish. "But no one who aids and abets them can be spared. Not neighbors, not friends, not family. Any who are not us," she cried out suddenly, her voice returned to a roar, "are them! And *they* must all die for what they've done. Go now!"

She gestured as though casting them like stones sent to skip across the surface of a pond. The crowd jolted, startled by the sudden dismissal.

"Go!" The Iazmaena-thing's voice sounded as insane as what Marri had just watched. "Go and purge our city! Make it fit only for humans!"

With their own collective voices rising to a howl, one which cried wordlessly for blood, they went. Marri and Karl had no choice but to run with them or be trampled.

Or worse.

CHAPTER 44

DOLCE WAS, Giana reluctantly admitted to herself, beginning to get suspicious. Perhaps that wasn't the right word. But he was certainly getting uncomfortable with taking Giana's orders as though she were Stefani.

The window replacement in the Bridge site observation tower had been completed. That was a mere sideshow to the real repairs going on, which were, Dolce continued to swear, nearly complete and not nearly as extensive as they'd feared.

The trouble was beginning to lie in other areas.

"This is highly irregular, ma'am," Dolce said, wringing his hands and unwilling to meet Giana's eyes. That was interesting. Giana had seen him be almost dictatorial in his control of the project when it suited him. But he greatly respected the chain of command, and he couldn't quite figure out where Giana fit into it. Even the honorific "ma'am," offered to a woman at least ten years his junior, seemed to be the result of some compromise he'd reached with himself. "As I've told you, I report directly to Magistrate Palmieri. I know you are her assistant, that this makes you privy to her day-to-day operations in a way no one else is, but you simply don't have formal authority over this project."

"I assure you, Project Lead," Giana said, her voice the very picture of evenness, "that the magistrate has granted me full, if temporary, authority to act in her stead, considering the time pressure this effort is under."

"Unless she has also given you her command access codes, the ones that only she possesses, I couldn't activate the Bridge even if I wanted to."

"I don't recall any such codes required for the previous test."

"Her presence was enough for that," Dolce said. "Command access codes are only required for full activation. It was something the archon insisted on at the outset of the project. But that's another thing," Dolce said. "This time pressure she keeps impressing upon us. I still have no idea where it's coming from. Aside from one quick stop when we dedicated the site, before *any* reconstruction had begun, the archon has never even been here! Who is pressuring Magistrate Palmieri in this? Because it surely can't be Archon Graysteel."

"I've never heard you express anything but enthusiasm for the accelerated schedule before, Dolce," Giana said. Internally, though, she was reassessing. She'd been unaware of Stefani's command access codes as a requirement for full Bridge operations. It shouldn't have mattered. Stefani and Giana both wanted to activate the Bridge. But that depended on Stefani being reachable.

"Be that as it may," Dolce said with a grim smile, "I have a team to keep safe, and my priorities along those lines have been rearranged since the incident."

"Yours may have, but I promise you, the magistrate's priorities have not. And everything I'm asking you to do is something she would be asking you to do were she here instead of me."

The irony there was everything Giana claimed was true. And even if his lack of authorization codes meant he couldn't give her what she wanted, Giana could browbeat him into tiptoeing right up to it, so he'd be ready when she located Stefani.

"But why isn't she here? And more to the point, why can't I get in touch with her to confirm any of this? I've got just one brief message earlier today requesting a status update, which I answered promptly. Since then, nothing, despite several attempts."

And the irony *there* was Giana wanted answers to both those questions as well. She had it on good authority that Stefani had been released from her debriefing some time ago, with no detainment in the offing. Dolce was absolutely right. She ought to be here. But Giana was careful not to say all of that. Too much uncertainty could undermine both Stefani's authority and Giana's own.

"The magistrate is very busy, Project Lead." And now the lying began. "Even if she's done with her debriefing, she has overlapping meetings scheduled for the rest of the evening up until we are ready to activate."

"Well, I'm terribly sorry, ma'am, but I really can't keep operating like this. Not until I've spoken with the magistrate personally. It's more than the codes. I could lose more than my job."

"Perhaps we can reach a compromise," Giana said. "If you promise to keep working on getting the device ready for a full test, one featuring actual matter transit the way the magistrate requested, I will leave and not come back until I've extricated the magistrate from whatever meeting she is trapped in and made sure she contacts you with codes—and intentions for a full test—in hand."

Dolce looked unhappy about this, but ultimately, he nodded. "Very well. But to be clear, I literally can't power anything up without command code authorization."

Giana entertained notions of turning him. No point now, of course. She would still need Stefani's codes, and the time Dolce would take to turn would only slow them down, assuming he even survived. If Giana had her say, he wouldn't have the necessary time to fully make the change before he was no longer relevant.

Her handheld buzzed, and she felt sudden hope—a vestige of the old Giana Novak—that perhaps Stefani was about to save her a trip and any more of these delays.

"If you'll excuse me," she said, "I have a call."

"Is it the magistrate?" Dolce couldn't disguise his eagerness.

Stefani checked the ID. It was Vlad Harken, the police officer Arjun had turned. She had exchanged contact information with the man just in case. For him to be calling instead of Arjun couldn't be good.

"No," she said, answering Dolce. "But I will rectify that soon, you have my word."

She made her way to the stairs leading back down the tower before answering.

"Why isn't Arjun the one in contact?" she asked, by way of greeting.

"He didn't survive his attempt at decapitating the leader of the insurrectionists," Harken said. His voice was hushed but still loud, as though his mouth was pressed very close to the mic.

The emulation that was the human Giana always functioning in the background of her thoughts felt a pang of grief for her friend, what was left of him.

"Yet you survived," Giana said, not sparing him any disdain for his apparent failure to help Arjun.

"She was ready. The leader. It was Iazmaena Delgassi."

Giana paused for a beat, absorbing this information and its most probable implications. "A non-native, then."

"Yes. And she was ready for an attempt on her life. Military-grade weaponry and at least one unaltered non-native to protect her. I made the decision to wait and see if a vulnerable moment arose."

Giana heard talking in the background of Harken's prevarications.

"Is that her speaking right now? Are you still there?"

"Yes," Harken said. "It's why I called. I believe there is no need to remove her. She and her people wish to activate the Bridge, the same as we do. And they clearly wish to spread as much chaos as possible while they do it. I believe our goals are aligned. Removing her serves no purpose."

"Interesting. Very well, break off any attempts on her life, and continue to observe ... What am I hearing right now?"

She was hearing Iazmaena Delgassi in the background again, directing her audience to do something.

But Harken didn't answer Giana. His shouts, when they came, were not meant for her. An angry roar came over the connection, rising in volume until the call cut off.

Giana stared at the handheld for several moments, waiting for a return call that would never come. It seemed the false Iazmaena Delgassi was aware of Harken's presence. Giana regretted having lost both trustworthy sets of eyes inside the conspiracy. But if Harken had been accurate, it was doing what she wished anyway. It might even be a backup solution to activating the Bridge should something have befallen Stefani. Provided they didn't seize the site and kill every scientist and engineer in the process, of course.

If even one of us gets through, we've succeeded. The battle for this place was over. It was up to her, and any like her, to make sure they were present to win the next battle as well.

In truth, she had no idea how many like her were out there in the city. With the loss of Harken and Arjun, she might be the only one. If she got the chance, she needed to turn as many others as she could, just to up the odds that at least one of them would make it out.

But hopefully, she wouldn't have long enough to make that happen before she was stepping out onto the next battlefield.

CHAPTER 45

WALLED into a prison of turbulent dreams, Stefani's mind came apart.

I am Stefani Palmieri. I am Stefani Palmieri.

The feeling of physical restraint, of suffocation, exacerbated her growing desperation. Her thoughts had melted together, losing their boundaries and pouring into one another, a rancid slurry. *We are running out of time. We are running out of time. They are coming for us. They are coming for us. They are coming for us! They've been eating, and eating, and eating, and now the meal is done, and they want more! And you don't remember! You don't remember!* YOU DON'T REMEMBER! *We have to get out!"*

The darkness had weight to it, as though there was something else in here with her. Something simultaneously black and glittering. It had been within her, but now it occupied the space with her, a space that was too small for both of them. It had been trying to grab her, to make her look upon its face, for eight months.

This thing she'd sprinted non-stop to be away from.

This mind-prison was to be Stefani Palmieri's sarcophagus. As long as she refused to gaze upon herself, she could have been spared this forever. But then Iaz had transformed herself before Stefani's eyes, and all of her cracked bulwarks had come undone. The thing she had tried to avoid seeing in herself was suddenly all around her, everywhere she looked.

I am Stefani Palmieri! I am Stefani Palmieri!

She shouted it to herself so often, made a mantra of it, that the words had almost lost all meaning. But did truth ever need to be shouted so defiantly, particularly when backed by fear or desperation? Something had happened to her on that day, eight months gone. A memory, carefully folded away like delicate porcelain wrapped in a thick napkin, was unfolding itself at last.

Watching Iaz transform made Stefani remember.

She remembered racing away from the betrayal and descent of her best friend, spiriting Ella and Marri away from danger. That was her excuse, the shield she hid behind as she ignored the nagging, both from Marri and from her own heart, that she was abandoning Iaz in her moment of need.

She remembered turning to realize Marri had gone back to the Underlab without her. She remembered making the decision to stay the course, to find Karl and get help. They hurt her, these memories, but they did not unmake her. They were old shames, scarred and callused over.

Then she remembered something new.

She remembered a man in a dapper suit. She remembered the man changing, his skin and even his clothing hardening as it darkened and developed a shining gold undertone. She remembered a moment's panicked realization that she was looking at a revenant—*a revenant*—and that she was standing there with her baby in one arm and a lance she couldn't use one-handed in the other.

She remembered knowing she was going to die just as Ali had died.

I am Stefani Palmieri! I am Stefani Palmieri!

But, no.

She remembered trying to bring her lance to bear on the horrid thing, realizing she was going to be too slow.

She remembered dropping a crying Ella as the monstrosity lunged toward her, hoping it would focus on Stefani and not her daughter. She remembered its head opening into a multi-lobed maw with razor edges.

I am human! I am human!

But she wasn't. Because she remembered being Stefani Palmieri. And she also remembered Stefani Palmieri being torn apart to a degree no person could survive.

And most of all, she remembered being the thing that was tearing Stefani Palmieri apart and devouring her with gusto.

The being that called itself Stefani Palmieri snarled and opened its false eyes.

There was a crashing sound from the direction of Marri's room, and then both her door and the apartment front door were sliding open with matching rapid hisses.

CHAPTER 46

FULL DARK HAD CLAIMED the eerily quiet streets of Coldgarden when Giana left the Bridge site. Her destination was Stefani's apartment. Moving from Heart Ward to Illuminance was technically walkable, though the tram would be faster. These were human thoughts on mundane matters. Yet however much she acted like Giana Novak, even thought of herself that way, the thing wearing Giana Novak's face was of a lineage far stranger, and in many ways older, than even the natives of this world could claim.

And something deep and instinctual told her that the quiet which had settled upon Coldgarden had gone from unusual to ominous during the time she'd spent at the Bridge site. Taking the tram, that instinct for survival whispered, would be a bad idea. It would, after all, be very easy to become trapped on the tram in the event of a power interruption or security lockdown.

Or an earthquake.

So Giana walked. It was not long before she heard the first screams. They were scattered at first, but they multiplied as quickly as a virus. And though they remained some distance away, she didn't fail to notice they came from the direction of Renewal Ward.

The message was as clear as it was wordless. However the story of this world was going to end, it was going to end tonight.

As if to reinforce the point, the ground shook beneath her. The shaking continued for a long time.

Giana stopped walking and began to run instead.

The border between Heart and Illuminance loomed before her. Heart's ward border with its neighboring wards was the most formidable border in the city. That only stood to reason, since it housed the seat of Coldgarden's government. Its mix of wall and razor wire fencing was twice as tall as any other you'd find outside the city wall itself.

Which made it all the more unsettling that the guard post stood totally abandoned. It was lit in the same harsh lighting Giana had seen at border entry points hundreds, thousands of times. Yet instead of armed and armored lancers manning the choke point, the lights emphasized the deserted gate and guard hut.

Giana approached warily. The whir of cameras traversing their familiar arcs was the only sound she heard. Despite crossing the border being illegal without proper approvals and inspection of credentials, and despite the electronic surveillance which bristled in every corner of the entry point, Giana didn't have time to wait around for someone to decide to resume their duties.

If, indeed, that was all that was going on here. Giana had her doubts.

She was almost on top of the checkpoint and preparing to jump the lowered barricade when she realized what the harsh security lights had obscured. Light of a different kind. Light she was intimately familiar with.

Silence became a squelching moan. Then a pair of them, asynchronous and dissonant.

What remained of the lancer checkpoint officers lurched through the guard hut door in a two-lobed, gelatinous mass of glowing white. It was a sight that both stunned Giana and struck her with its incvitability.

Her feral cousins had found their way to the city at last.

However they were detecting potential prey, they apparently did not recognize her as one of them. The flowing lunges of a pair of pseudopods, one from each lobe of the combined mass, could only be interpreted as an attack. Giana neither fled nor tried to dodge their approach. Instead, she snapped her own arms out to meet the strikes, matching their speed and wrapping vice-like fingers around each.

The substance quivered in her grip, as though it too had been caught off-guard. It tried to flow out between her fingers to engulf them. Giana did not allow it that chance. The amalgam before her easily outweighed her, but she had the advantage of thought. Reflex was faster than thought, but thought gained the upper hand when it came time to react to something unexpected.

And it was far easier to turn something that was already so close to what you were than it was the natives of this world.

She let her hand dissolve into the glowing white mass, forcing her own organizing structure into the thing attacking, imposing a new order into a much simpler creature, one that reacted too slowly to do the reverse to her. The squelching moan, an echo of the people these had once been passed through alien biology, took on a more plaintive tone.

"Wake up," she said, feeling one partially integrated thing become two as they began to respond to her. Words were unnecessary—chemistry was doing all the talking—but it was satisfying. "Wake up and think."

The two-lobed mass split firmly into two separate masses, and the pseudopods extricated themselves from her grip. She let them go. The change was cascading now, unstoppable, as Giana's branch of her family tree worked its dominating will on this simpler lineage. It was not an evolutionary dead end, precisely. The things had still managed to get this far, after all. But they were a mere candle to Giana's sun.

She watched the transformations, felt the satisfaction of two formless blobs slowly taking on recognizably human shapes. They may have done so anyway, given time. But without her intervention, mindless husks would have been all they'd remained.

Her kind evolved rapidly, but as randomly as any other life form. Until her specific lineage had developed thought enough to influence the path their successors would take, at least. Once that had been settled, the advantages of having Gene Sequencing resources to help guide that evolution must have seemed obvious enough.

Her chemical orders had been to reverse the damage they'd done to the two lancers they'd subsumed, but with important changes. The first part worked well enough. Shortly, as though by magic, one man and one woman staggered as they rose, clinging to one another for support. Their eyes were wide and bewildered.

"What happened?" the woman asked. The words sounded mushy, as though this was the first time she'd ever spoken. In every way that mattered now, it was.

"I awakened you," Giana said. The woman's eyes widened at understanding the noises that came from Giana's mouth, noises which would have been nonsense moments before. "You work for me now. How many are you?" That was too specific. "Are there more like you here?"

"Y-yes," the woman stammered out, seeming amazed at the most basic of words and concepts. A brilliant smile broke out on her round face.

It was the answer Giana had expected. As soon as she'd realized what happened here, the timing seemed too much of a coincidence. There was no way that all of the screaming carried by the night wind was being caused by Delgassi's insurgents.

"I want you two to go toward the sounds we're hearing," Giana said. "What I gave to you, you give to everyone else you can. Whether they are like us or not." Getting much more complicated than that was liable to give the pair an aneurysm, in the case of the man, quite literally. He still hadn't spoken a word, and in contrast to the woman's wonder-filled face, his looked like he was staring at nightmares only he could see.

"Do you understand?" Giana asked, mostly meaning the man. The woman was already setting off as though he didn't exist.

The man opened his mouth to try and reply, and his handsome face contorted further. Then it fell apart, sloughing to pieces as blood and a black, oily substance spilled out. The rest of his body, re-formed clothing and all, quickly followed suit.

The female lancer walked on, never looking back, as Giana stepped nimbly away to avoid getting mess on her shoes. Of the pair of them, the man had clearly had too much damage done during his subsuming to be reconstituted stably. He would be far from the only one that happened to.

Taking her cue from her oblivious offspring, Giana resumed her trek to Stefani's apartment.

CHAPTER 47

EIGHT MONTHS AGO, Marri had tried and failed to flee Inkwell before the cordon walls came up. She'd nearly died twice trapped inside the revenant-infested ward. Her legs had been shorter, then. She was taller, now. Faster.

Though this time, she dragged a hobbled old man behind her.

This time, running again for both theirs lives, trying to fight through the panicky crowd springing up in the streets around them, Marri showed no mercy. She threw her free elbow with abandon, jabbed knees like stilettos, whatever she had to do to get separation for herself and Karl from a crowd that grew increasingly violent the longer it had to build.

The police and their crazy friends spilling out from their warehouse lair pushed a wall of civilians behind them. It was late evening now, so the streets were not as crowded as they might have been at rush hour or dinnertime, but there were still plenty of people strolling unknowingly to their deaths.

Eight months without a revenant attack, without even a sighting, had begun to take its toll on the city's wariness, and they would pay a different kind of toll for that tonight.

Karl gave a bark of pain behind her, and Marri pulled up short, trying to stuff her frustration down where he wouldn't see it.

"Go on without me," he said. He was panting, horribly pale, and Marri had never seen a person sweat as much as he was.

"That's not happening," she said.

"You won't make it if you've got an anchor like me around your neck."

"Which is why you have to run!" Marri shouted, scrubbing sudden tears from her eyes. Karl needed to stop being so stupid. "Hurting is better than dead!"

Maybe it was her words that moved him. Or maybe it was seeing the unwary stranger drawn to their argument, looking like somebody's kindly grandfather who just wanted to help. That all changed when he was set upon by two plainclothes police officers, grinning like predators. He turned to stare at them in dumb confusion after one ran up to him and knifed him savagely through the meat of one shoulder with a huge, serrated blade.

The bag the man carried spilled his late grocery run limply to the ground as strips of flesh sprang from the wound and attached to the attacker's face, latching over it as though merging the two of them together. The man's cries of savagery became screams of terror as he tried first to push, then to cut himself free.

This only made the hypermutation happen faster, and his body responded to the proximity of the injured man in the kind of nightmare scenario they always warned everyone about.

"Gods below," Karl said as she dragged him on. And given the kinds of stuff he had seen, Marri assumed this must be pretty bad. But she had no more time to watch the two forms merge and thrash as they fought each other. Another pair of police, oblivious to the danger, advanced on Karl and her, each swinging wide to hem them in. Neither smelled like a revenant, nor like whatever Giana smelled like. Marri tried to remember what she'd done the other night to slice that creature to ribbons, but the thought of doing so in front of Karl made her blanch.

"Looks like Yonnel to me. What do you think, Jacques?"

"Definitely."

"The last cop who attacked me regretted it," Marri said, only to have Karl ruin the moment and shove his way past her. Not that it mattered, given that they were surrounded.

"Don't listen to her," Karl said. "Your argument is with me."

Marri would have kicked him if she'd been sure it wouldn't cause him to topple over. He was so determined to die for someone, and it was really making her mad.

If either man heard a word Karl had said, they gave no indication as they circled, ignoring much closer potential victims because they'd spotted a chance to score easy points with their new boss.

Around them, a tide was building as faster people caught up to slower. Some simply shoved their neighbors out of their way. Others, presumably the Iazmaena-thing's followers, tackled the nearest person, dragging them down to struggle for their lives on the pavement. The air was choked with screams and the metallic scent of blood.

Everyone who saw the onrushing horde moved to avoid them, but there was too much chaos for that to hold. So Marri timed their dash to safety for when a pair of struggling forms collided hard with the man trying to flank her on her right. She took a gamble, running right by Karl and grabbing him as she went, hearing her second assailant curse behind them and his pounding steps as he gave chase.

Karl was right about one thing. They weren't going to outrun anybody with that limp of his. Marri tried to use that against their assailant. She swerved at the last second, feeling her shoulder protest as she dragged Karl to the side. Their pursuer, who had been building up a head of steam to tackle them both from behind, collided instead with the struggling forms on the ground. She heard him go down hard and cursing but didn't dare turn to see.

Instead, Marri switched the hand holding Karl and changed direction again, making the best time they could manage toward a recycler, trying to melt into shadows which had grown suddenly starker in response to a rising light from somewhere.

She and Karl collapsed into that swatch of darkness, and Karl gamely tried to stifle his moans, clearly guessing what Marri's goal had been. That was maybe the saddest part about his leg and general oldness. They made a good team.

Whether the man had lost track of them or not, she would never know. He was suddenly faced with bigger problems as the developing nightmare assumed its fullest form.

Out of the sewers they boiled. Glow-monsters like the ones she'd killed. Not one, or even a handful. Dozens, maybe hundreds of striking blobs. They lashed out at everything that moved within their range, slithering along the streets, and even building walls in search of prey if nothing was close.

They attacked with no strategy so far as she could see, simply leaping upon the nearest person they encountered, sometimes even tripping and bringing three or four people down with them. Her remaining assailant was one of the first to go down, and he went down blubbering like a baby as the thing oozed itself over his face, muffling his whimpering. That, at least, was satisfying.

Rioters, bystanders, none were spared. Or rather, *almost* none.

From her shadowed vantage point, Marri saw two people, a man and a woman, that the glow-monsters bypassed multiple times to target other, further prey. The pair looked terrified, but also as though they couldn't believe their luck in evading attack or even the attention of the terrible things. Marri narrowed her eyes and took a sharp, deep breath. Even amid the smells of carnage, she caught the pair's scent.

Revenants. Interlopers. Invaders.

Only by destroying them, them and the glow monsters both, could she cleanse this place.

"I'm all ears for a plan on getting out of here," Karl said. The ground shook beneath them in another quake, as though to punctuate his words, and Marri shook herself as though snapping out of a trance. She'd been about to rush out there. What kind of idiot was she turning into?

Marri was trying to form an answer to his question when another shape rose up in between eye-blinks, seemingly from nowhere at all. In the middle of crossing streets he stood, directly blocking her approach. Marri inhaled sharply with surprise.

It was him. It was the Strange Man.

Feeling a sudden urge to call out, she opened her mouth to shout to him. Once again, she was sure he was staring right at her despite not being able to see his face beneath his wide-brimmed hat. Marri felt the force of his regard in a way she never had before. It seemed accusatory, that unseen gaze. It laid upon her a haze of blind rage that started white-hot and built from there, a brand within her mind. Her hands itched, as though they longed to be something else entirely. She marveled at how she hadn't remembered how to do this just a few moments ago.

Karl is here. Karl will see. Just like that, the spell was broken.

"We have to get out of here before this gets any worse," she said, but her voice sounded feeble in her ears. False. Like it wasn't even her that was talking.

Like it had never been her.

"Are you all right?" Karl asked, suddenly all fatherly concern despite their situation. But Marri barely heard him.

The Strange Man had recaptured her gaze. That invisible regard was somehow even more intense this time. Marri fought it, despite not wanting to fight it.

I can't do what you want. That isn't me. That can't be me. She didn't understand her own thoughts.

The sea of people parted around the Strange Man as though they didn't see him but still knew he was there. It was as though nobody in the world existed but him and Marri. As she stared, trying to interpret his wishes to mean something that wouldn't sweep her away, he moved without breaking his gaze with her, his body twisting into unnatural shapes as his head remained perfectly still. He reached out with both arms, seemingly at random. His hands little more than spindly shadows at the end of his wide sleeves, he gripped the shoulders of two passers-by.

Running, screaming people froze at his touch, stretching out rigid as if they'd been electrically shocked. Then, the two panicking bystanders became screaming, raging berserkers. They lunged back along the path they'd come, tearing at two of the police officers. Two gunshots went off, but fear of hypermutation didn't seem to stop the Strange Man's new warriors.

All of this she beheld out of the corners of her gaze, because she couldn't tear her eyes away from him, couldn't move. She thought Karl might be shaking her, pulling at her, but she resisted.

The Strange Man, by contrast, held her stare even as he continued his strange dance, grabbing two screaming people. Then Marri gasped, because the man didn't let go of either of the two he already had before snaring a third. Instead, a third arm had simply appeared from nowhere, and the man was now wearing a long coat that had three sleeves. Then a fourth arm appeared. A fifth.

More and more bystanders he touched, and more and more turned back to rush at their pursuers, fighting with that raging fury. Gradually, enough took up his call that they began to blunt the tide of the onslaught, cop-mob and glow-monster both. On this street anyway. Marri could hear the echoes of screams from neighboring streets.

She felt the full force of his attention resume just as a nearby wall burst outward, and two full revenants, their emerald and tourmaline-highlighted black carapaces gleaming in the streetlights, emerged, shaking off composicrete rubble.

Instead of simply attacking with abandon, slicing up the sea of humanity and glow-monster thus presented to them, they picked and chose their targets, ignoring the rebellious cops and their followers, and focusing on the screaming throngs trying to escape them. Several people died messily in this fashion in just the first few seconds. But instead of pausing to gorge, the revenants simply moved on, opening people as fast as they could flash their scythe-like forelimbs or lunging with mouths like jagged flowers.

Then one of the pair took aim at the Strange Man, lunging forward with preternatural speed. The Strange Man never took his shadowed gaze from Marri, even in the face of certain death.

He merely nodded solemnly at her.

Marri again inhaled sharply at the gesture, some reflex she didn't comprehend. The world seemed to slow. Instead of stale and mildewed, the night smelled suddenly vibrant, crackling with energy, like the tail-end of a thunderstorm.

A shiver passed through her then as something took hold. Any desire to get away from this place fell away. Any concern over being seen, being *known*, shriveled like worms trapped in the sun after a rain. A new push, to lay about her and kill and destroy all impurities, surged within her like a bonfire. Marri brought her hands up, and once again they were not hands, but bony blades like scythes.

"What?" Karl said, his shock breathless. "W-what are those? How?"

Marri didn't care what he was saying. She breathed in again, and that sense of burgeoning energy filled the air, suffusing Marri.

Red drenched her thoughts as she overflowed with a sudden rage. She stepped out from her flimsy shelter into the mad night. There were too many of them, but she didn't care. The rage, primal and deeper than anything she'd ever felt, crested like a storm-tossed wave, wrapping her in a warm embrace. It was both a new thing and so very old.

It felt good. Simple. Right. Like she had come alive for the first time. She gave into the feeling fully and transformed, at long last, into herself.

She would be too slow. She knew this. She watched with strange new eyes as the revenant took its brutal swipe, watched the Strange Man fly apart as though he'd exploded. Instead of blood, black and opalescent goo splattered outward in every direction from his ruined corpse.

Marri howled in unexpected anguish at the sight of the Strange Man's death, but at the same time she slipped into a kind of flow state. Perhaps the revenants had never expected to encounter anything like Marri. Perhaps something of the Strange Man's hypnotic powers affected them as well. But despite its size advantage, the first revenant died upon Marri's claws before it could so much as raise its own in defense. All its armor parted like butter before the knives that were her hands.

The second had warning, but still clearly suffered from surprise.

Marri was nothing but a lifetime of pent-up ferocity. When the revenant stabbed at her, her brutal parry took its arm off. *Interloper.* When it lashed its horrible maw outward on a scorpion-tail neck, she sliced off half its lozenge-shaped head. *Parasite.*

And when it scrambled away, its movements already acquiring the drunken clumsiness of hypermutation, she opened a wide, toothless maw, and disgorged green, clinging fluid all over it. It smoked and popped, screaming as its chitin armor was eaten through and the flesh underneath dissolved.

Marri exulted as it died.

"Marri?"

Something about the voice brought her up short, and she turned to see him. Like her, he was, but older and hurt.

And, most importantly, asleep. Totally unaware of what he really was. Hobbled in the leg, yes. But hobbled more by lies.

A part of her wanted to become like him, to become the girl. Maybe then, he would stop looking at her that way. But she knew if she did that, he would die, because she would not be able to protect him.

Destroying the invaders was important. It was why she existed. But protecting Karl was also important. And already, the space around them was filling back up with dangers. The peak of her rage had ebbed. It left her thoughts clearer, and clearer thoughts told her as good as that had felt, she could not cleanse them all from this place by herself.

Maybe, though, she could protect Karl.

So she rushed at him. Squeezing the acid pooling in her toothless mouth back into the gullet which produced it, she scooped him up, and scuttled on six bony legs for safety.

CHAPTER 48

LIFE AS A LANCER had shown Karl more than his share of strange sights, most of those having to do with the horrible things bodies, be they human or revenant, did as they died. Prior to becoming Iazmaena Delgassi's lance commander, he had just about convinced himself he'd seen everything.

The universe had, predictably, taken it upon itself to repeatedly prove him wrong.

Riding now inside the mouth of the bony-legged worm which had been Marri Palmieri, he resisted the urge to panic. It was not a choice so much as a constant struggle which grew more difficult the longer it lasted. A little like having to pee and not being near a bathroom, only with blind terror instead of a full bladder.

This is Marri. You saw her change. Somehow, somehow, this is her.

Despite his eyes telling him to believe what he'd seen, there were only two reasons he was able to keep that panic at bay as he was carried with surprising gentleness down rapidly emptying streets.

One was he'd seen Marri, or whatever Marri had become, kill two revenants with no more fuss than if she'd been making a sandwich. Anything that killed revenants couldn't be all bad.

But perhaps more important was his realization that he'd seen a creature like this before. The bony legs, the wormlike body, the glass bead eyes of alternating oily black and shiny white. Iazmaena Delgassi—the real one—had hypermutated into something very much like this when she died.

All of it left Karl wondering. If Iazmaena had been one of these, and Marri was one of these, how many other people in the city were?

It was not a pleasant thought. To avoid following its path, he twisted in his toothless perch to stare into the six eyes of Marri. They alternated between that black and white in two rows of three along the worm-like body's long axis. They looked more like obsidian or ceramic than eyes. He wasn't sure how they saw anyway but straight up until the front of the head bulged a little way back from the mouth, creating a slope that lifted the frontmost pair of eyes so they stared more or less forward.

"Hi," Karl said, suddenly feeling watched in a way that wasn't entirely comfortable. "Um ... thank you for saving me."

"What the hell is that?" came a shout from up ahead. Belatedly, Karl recognized the harsh lighting of a ward border crossing. They'd reached the border between Renewal and Illuminance, easily outpacing the chaos behind them.

And now they'd been spotted by the pair of lancers guarding the border.

"It's some kind of revenant!" came a second voice. "Gods below, look at that. And it's eating someone!"

"Call for backup!"

No, Karl wanted to shout. *You've got to get into Renewal. That's where it's happening.* As if to punctuate the words he could not force out, screams rode the night wind at their backs.

"Kill it!" said the first lancer, a lieutenant. "Center of mass. Try not to hit the civvy."

The last word hurt more than the prospect of dying by lancer fire, the ultimate irony. But worse than both was the thought that Marri might drop him and kill the lancers or be killed herself in the attempt.

But Marri simply bunched her bony legs and leaped.

Karl endured the sensation of weightlessness followed by the sensation of her tightening her grip on him. It wasn't exactly the most comfortable thought.

Up and over the barricade, wall, and fencing they vaulted. The landing on the other side was a bit jarring, as announced by Karl's hip. But judging by the shocked cries of the lancers they rapidly left behind, they'd been expecting it as little as Karl.

"Thank you," Karl said. "For not hurting them."

Marri didn't answer. Karl wasn't sure how she could. Maybe her mind was gone. Maybe she was carting him off somewhere private to devour him.

But he couldn't make himself believe it.

Several minutes went by before Karl understood where they were going. He recognized Stefani's building from down the street. Just as he wondered if Marri was going to transform back, and what they would do about clothes for the poor girl if she did, she started scaling the wall, digging her claws in such that at least four of them had contact at all times.

She moved like she'd been born to this shape. Karl just tried not to think how high he was. When Marri braced herself outside what must be one of her apartment windows, Karl had only a moment's warning before she dug into the window's frame, and ripped it entirely out of the building's wall, hurling it to the street below.

Marri's room lay beyond, and Karl found himself deposited on the floor. Marri gestured with a single claw, and Karl felt like he was being shooed.

The moment was so surreal that Karl felt faint, but he obeyed what he believed the message to be, opening Marri's door and closing it behind him.

He forgot everything when he saw Stefani stirring fitfully from where she'd been sprawled out on the floor of her living room.

CHAPTER 49

KARL HOBBLED into the apartment's main living area just as Giana entered through the front door. The woman, if that term applied, looked less than surprised at finding Stefani collapsed on the floor of the living room. Giana spoke, seemingly unaware that she and Stefani were not alone.

"Well. This explains a lot. I hate to be the bearer of bad news, but this is not the worst thing that's going to happen to you today."

Karl had heard enough. Determined to get to Stefani before Giana—whatever Giana was—could do whatever she intended to do, he surged forward. "Stay back!" he barked at Giana, setting Ella crying.

Giana, for a wonder, did back off, looking shocked at Karl's entrance and moving to the corner of the room, letting him approach Stefani.

"What happened?" he asked, more gently.

"Iaz was here," Stefani managed through a hoarse voice.

Karl cursed. "We've seen her too, just now. She's whipping the police up into a mob." He looked to Giana, his gaze half-question and half-glare. Unwise to assume she was any different than Arjun and Harken had been.

"I was at the Bridge site," Giana said calmly. "I didn't see any signs of a mob, but I certainly heard a disturbance of some kind." Her face was a picture of concern for Stefani, but there was something else underlying the emotion. It felt almost like impatience. "You said Delgassi was here, ma'am? What did she do to you?"

"Just showed me something I didn't want to see," Stefani croaked, then laughed as if it was the funniest joke she'd ever heard. That laugh made the hairs on Karl's neck stand up. It was not entirely sane. "Where's Marri? Is she all right? She was supposed to be here watching Ella. Did I hear crashing just now?"

Karl's stomach plummeted. In the frenzy to reach Stefani, he'd forgotten—

"I'm here," Marri said, and Karl nearly had a heart attack. He whirled to see Marri entering from her room. She wore fresh clothes and sweat matted some of her hair to her forehead, but the real give-away of something strange going on was the breeze that riffled the remainder of her hair, a breeze coming through the massive, newly made hole in her wall.

She carefully shut her bedroom door behind her.

"Where exactly did you two come from?" Giana asked. Her brow furrowed with suspicion.

"Step away from them, Karl," Marri said. She sniffed the air several times, scrubbing her nose. "They aren't who they claim."

Something within Karl despaired at these words. Some part of him didn't want to hear where they led. *And why is that, Karl?*

"Marri, I'm properly suspicious of Giana, believe me. But your mother is sick, and you ..." He trailed off, at a loss for words. "We need to get to a hospital," he said. He felt his mind scrambling for something, some authority he could invoke to make sense of things. When no one responded, he tried a different tack, hating the desperation in his voice. "At least we need to get somewhere safe and fortifiable. That mob will tear any government official they can find apart. We need to get Stefani somewhere no one can find her."

"We need," Giana said, her voice uncharacteristically full of authority, "to finish what we started with the Bridge. We need to leave this place. Now. That's the only chance any of us have of surviving this. Right, Stefani?" She clearly knew more than she was saying. More worrisome was her implication Stefani knew more than she was saying too.

"No," Marri said, and before Karl could even ask what *leave this place* meant, precisely, she addressed him. "Karl, I brought us here to be sure of something. And now I am. You and I are going. Come on." She turned a cold glare upon Stefani, who stared at her adoptive daughter, her expression a mix of hunted and hurt. "Don't try to follow us, whoever you are. Whatever you are." She turned her glare upon Giana. "You either."

"Will someone please explain to me what's going on?" Karl said. The despair was so close, now. *Are you sure you want to know?*

"You saw Iazmaena," Marri said.

No. No. Please, no.

"You know she's dead," Marri continued, oblivious to his pain. "That was a revenant, not a human." She opened her mouth to say the rest, and Karl was utterly powerless to stop her. "Stefani is the same. I can smell it on her. Stefani is dead, Karl. She has been for a long time. I understand that now. I understand why I didn't feel comfortable here. I *never* did. I think she died the same day Iazmaena died."

And the hell of it was, Karl believed her. Because Iazmaena—the false Iazmaena—had been perfect enough to fool anyone who hadn't *known* she was dead. Because Karl had asked Stefani why more wasn't being done about the revenants that could look human, and she had blown him off.

And because, deep down, he'd known something was wrong himself. That knowing had been as much the reason their relationship hadn't survived as anything else had.

So he didn't turn to Stefani and beg her to deny it, to say it wasn't true. Because he knew it was. And at the end, he didn't even feel despair. All he could manage was self-loathing. Because he should have seen it. He *had* seen it. He'd just been so desperate to ignore it that he'd found a way.

Marri seemed not to need Stefani's confession either. She had shifted her glare to Giana.

"I don't know what she is. A glow-monster, whatever they are. You saw them in the streets, Karl. She's one of them. Different, though. More sophisticated."

The two women behaved very differently. Giana went very still, drifting toward the door so gradually, Karl barely noticed her moving at all.

Stefani, though, she sagged.

"Marri isn't wrong," she said. She cast a wry glance toward Giana, one that almost looked admiring. "About either of us." She looked to be on the point of saying more when the entire apartment began to shake violently around them.

It took close to a minute for the tremors to subside. It was the worst earthquake Karl could ever remember experiencing.

"Magistrate, we need to go," Giana said, striding forward, seeming ready to pull Stefani to her feet as though only the quake mattered. "The Bridge is ready. All it needs is your authorization codes. Any discussions that need to be had can be had when we are safely on the other side."

"Neither of you are going anywhere," Marri declared. It sounded ridiculous unless you had been with Marri when she'd transformed, had watched her filet two revenants in under ten seconds. "You're both liars, and at least one of you is a murderer." She shifted her glare back to Giana. "Probably both. But you're for sure not human."

"On the contrary," Giana said. She seemed an entirely different person, a feat that ought to be impossible after speaking just three words. "If anyone in this apartment can be called a human, it's Stefani," she said. Then she shifted her dark-eyed gaze to Karl. "I think some of us here are well aware that the pot is calling the kettle black."

"All right," Karl said, a sudden anger suffusing him. "Someone, maybe everyone, is going to explain to me what's going on."

"What's going on," Giana said, "is that we have a very limited window to escape this world before it dies. These earthquakes? They are just the beginning, and the end is coming on very soon now."

"Okay, ignoring most of what needs to be unpacked there, how on earth would we 'escape this world?'" Karl asked.

"The Bridge," Stefani said. "The device you found in the warehouse, Karl. I told you it could do the impossible. It can open a gate to another world. Many other worlds! Instantaneous travel. It's ..." she trailed off, reluctant to speak the words. "It's one of the reasons why we invaded the city eight months ago. It's what we've been after this whole time."

"The revenants wanted this Bridge," Karl said.

"That's right," Stefani said. He still could not stop thinking of the thing as Stefani.

"And that's why you killed Stefani," Karl said flatly, willing his voice not to break.

"When we consume one of you," she said, casual as you please, "we can absorb the memories intact via the structure of the brain. We can recreate them. The appearance is a lot easier," she said. It. *It* said. "Any detailed knowledge of what you look like will do. But only one can hold the memories. We needed governmental access. We'd worked out a kind of deal with Iaz—the real Iaz—but it was obvious how unstable she was. How likely to fall from power. So we needed another way in."

"What did this 'deal' involve?" Karl asked. He found it was easier to just keep asking the questions. It was a way to kick the can full of his feelings down the road because it was always a problem for some future Karl.

"The real Iazmaena Delgassi wanted Gene Sequencing destroyed, its employees killed," Giana said evenly. "They were my coworkers," she said with all the inflection of a bored waiter announcing the special for the fifty-third time.

Stefani looked at Giana sharply.

"I'm afraid so," Giana said, responding to Stefani's unspoken accusation. "I worked for Gene Sequencing. I happened to call in sick the day her siege began, though I know now it wasn't nearly as simple as that. But regardless, I never got caught up in it."

Stefani shook her head in what looked to Karl like a combination of disbelief and admiration. "We helped Iaz with that, it's true. Though I, at least, wasn't there for that part."

"How did Stefani die?" Marri cut in, sounding as though she was just raw skin pressed against the edge of a razor.

Stefani regarded her with apparent sympathy, as though asking without words if the girl truly wanted to hear. Whatever she saw in Marri's face made her sigh, but she didn't refuse to answer.

"We needed access. I wasn't out to get Stefani, specifically. It was dumb luck that I ran into her and Ella. But it was an opportunity. I took it." Her eyes filled with tears, and despite the words she was saying, Karl felt his heart go out to her. "But the transition didn't work correctly for me. I had already taken a human form, memories and all. Trying to incorporate another person ... it produced some strange interactions. I forgot what I really was. Until Iaz forced me to remember just a little while ago."

Her shudder had all the appearance of an involuntary show of emotion. A single sob wracked her. "I'm sorry. I regret doing what I did to Stefani."

"You're lying," Marri said.

This time, there was nothing but hurt on Stefani's face. "I *am* her. I have her memories. How could I do anything but regret my actions? I saved your life, Marri. Back inside the cordon. That man in his fancy suit was going to kill you, and not quick and easy, either. Believe me. I have his memories too, so I know. I saved your life, and I gave you a piece of the truth, showed you my humanity. Let you go free. And then, when I wore this form, when I believed I was Stefani, I took you in off the street. That's what *she* wanted for you, so that's what I wanted for you. And you can't even listen to what I have to say?"

"This is what they do," Marri said, as though to batter the thing's words away with her own. "They play with our feelings. She isn't one of us." She stepped toward Stefani threateningly, and Karl didn't like the glint in the girl's eyes.

"Hold on," he said, stepping between them. "We need to hear everything before we make any kind of decisions." He turned back to Stefani. "Where does Iazmaena—this new Iazmaena—fit into all of this?"

"Once we'd successfully infiltrated the city, our first goal was to undo what had been done to us to make us into revenants. We believed it was possible, but we lacked the tools. We had some half-brained notion that radiation might be the key, but that just wound up getting a lot of us killed, thanks to Iaz and Karl and, well, me, I guess. "We decided what we could achieve on our own," she said, gesturing at herself, "was good enough.

"After that, our people split on our approach going forward. One side wanted to simply rebuild the Bridge and escape the planet. Bygones be bygones otherwise. They weren't going to help the people of the city, but they weren't going to go out of their way to hurt them, either."

"I'm guessing that was not Iazmaena's faction," Karl said. *Stop engaging. You are not talking with your Stefani. Your Stefani is dead. Because of this thing.*

But the truth was so very bleak, and the lies were so much more comforting.

"You're correct. The bygones be bygones group is not Iaz's group," Stefani said. "Iaz's group wants to use the Bridge too, but they are at least as interested in revenge as escape. They want to hurt and kill as many citizens of Coldgarden as possible," she clarified when Karl looked a question at her.

Giana, meanwhile, had moved into a very protective posture beside Stefani. Clearly, she was serious about keeping Stefani alive.

Karl couldn't help but feel that those two sticking together gave some credence to Marri's words about neither of them being trustworthy.

"You don't get a say in this," Marri said. "I've killed one of you already."

Stefani goggled, then turned and really looked at Giana. "It's really true, then? You're one of *them*?"

"We don't have time to get into that," Giana said, sounding annoyed it had come up. Stefani's laugh, by contrast, was scornful. Giana fixed Stefani with a penetrating gaze. All emotional affect dropped from her voice. It was chilling to Karl's ears. "If we don't leave now, we may miss our chance entirely. This opportunity at escape will not survive the night."

"I don't think Marri has any intention of letting us out of this apartment. And I don't know about you, but I have no intention of fighting her." Stefani looked and sounded grim.

Giana turned to Marri, her eyes considering. "You judge her for crimes committed before either of you were born, each of you acting in the best interests of your people, and you calling her a monster for it while she tries her best to give you a better life."

"She. Killed. Stefani."

"She is a different being now," Giana said, her voice surprisingly gentle. "And how can you expect her to feel bad about killing an enemy in a war? Only now, with her in possession of that enemy's memories, her identity, does she see the pain she caused to Stefani and her loved ones. But the point is that she *couldn't* have seen that before. She didn't have that information until the moment she committed the crime. So how can you hold her to blame?"

"You expect me to just forgive that thing?" Marri spat.

"I expect you to expand your mind for what the meaning of being a person really is."

"Easy for a non-person to say," Marri bit back.

"I've already told you," Giana said, unperturbed. "Stefani is the closest thing to a human in this apartment. So you'll need to expand your definition of what a person can be."

"Tell them," Stefani said to Giana. After a moment's reflection, Giana nodded. The gesture was mechanistic, like she'd stopped pretending to be a human and had revealed herself to be just a machine of meat.

"This world, which you believe to be the planet Earth, is not. The creatures you call revenants are in fact the descendants of humans from the actual Earth. They arrived here using the Bridge apparatus to establish a colony upon this world. But it was already inhabited by both my kind and yours." She gestured specifically at both Marri and Karl.

The gesture shook Karl. *How many others are like the real Iaz and Marri?* he asked himself again. *Is this another question I don't really want answered?*

"Not long into the colony's establishment conflict arose between the natives"—and here Giana pointed again at Marri and Karl—"and the humans." She pointed at Stefani. "Matters escalated. The human colonists attempted to eradicate the natives with genetic warfare. But the natives, gifted mimics, had already infiltrated that team. They altered the weapon, turned it back upon the humans.

"Those that survived were horribly mutated and forced out of their own colony and into the wilderness. Over time, their descendants became the so-called 'revenants.' The natives, meanwhile, eager to claim the galaxy-spanning technology of the fallen humans, made the decision to adopt the human ways in the hopes of reaching the stars themselves. Over time, they forgot they were ever not human, forgot their true origins entirely. And all of them, all the residents of this city, believe that to this day, all except for a few." She looked fixedly at Marri. "For it seems some are starting to remember."

"And which are you?" Karl asked her. "Human or native? He refused to dwell on her story at all. To think about it now would leave him a gibbering mess on the floor. No matter what else was happening or had happened, right here and right now Karl Yonnel needed his wits about him. He had to catch Giana in any lies.

But Giana turned smoothly to face him.

"I am something else. My kind is simpler. We arose later than the natives. Whereas they had intelligence thrust upon them, our search for it took some time." She gestured at herself as though she were the display model in a high-end appliance store. "But now we are all here. We are talking. And we all wish for the same thing, whether we realize it or not. I am here to tell you this world is dying. Stefani and her kind know it. You and Karl know it as well, Marri, though you have forgotten. The moment to do something about it is now. We can all depart it together, but we must do so now."

"I'll be the first to admit that my people don't fully understand what's going on here, the origin of this threat," Stefani said. "But it seems to me that bringing you along when we don't have to might not be the best idea."

"Not even if I could save your daughter?" Giana said.

The room fell deathly quiet.

"Yes, Stefani, she is dying. There is no father. You had her with the assistance of Gene Sequencing."

Stefani's words were full of tears. "I've never told you—"

"Then you should believe what I say. Because you didn't have to tell me. Even being this close, I can tell. She was one of our experiments. My kind's. We do not change ourselves the way you do. We lack your creativity, your intuition. We are creatures of brute force. Try a thing, and watch it fail. Try another thing, and watch it fail too. Over and over. Until at last, something works. I am the end result of the thing that worked. And some distance along that path, my kind gained access to Gene Sequencing. And when you went to them because you wanted a child, they took their opportunity. Another attempt. Another chance, however small, of achieving what I would ultimately become."

"And you think telling me this makes me inclined to help you?" Stefani growled.

"No. But this should. The experiment in Ella is failing. Slowly, but inexorably. Most aren't even that lucky. But Ella may be the luckiest of all. Because I can correct what went wrong in her."

"Make her like you, you mean," Stefani said. It was an accusation, but Karl could tell it was more bluster than not. She was wavering.

"Yes," Giana said. "It's not what you would choose, I'm sure. But it's better than death, surely."

"Death isn't always the worst thing," Karl said softly, choosing to weigh in at last. He meant it for Stefani, but he knew what she was going to say. He knew the desperation on her face too well.

"I'll go with you," Stefani said. "Save my child, give us all safe passage, both to and over the Bridge, and I'll make sure it's up and running."

"Done," Giana said before Karl could react. "But Ella only after we are all safely across."

"Now, hold on," But the rest of Karl's words were stolen from him as the building shook. If the previous quake had been the worst Karl had ever felt, this was at least an order of magnitude bigger. Another rumble, not as loud but much closer, sounded from Marri's room.

"What was that?" Stefani asked, sounding so much like herself that Karl's heart ached.

"Marri tore a hole in the wall of her room getting us back in here," he said.

"I didn't have any clothes," she muttered, flushing. "And I wasn't going to fit through the door like I was."

"I have a feeling that whole wall has given way," Karl said.

"We need to go," Giana said. "The trams will not be safe. The walk to the Bridge site may not be either, but—"

That was when Karl felt the dizziness wash over him. It staggered him, but even with his bad hip, he stayed upright. Marri was not so fortunate. She moaned and sagged, sliding to her knees.

CHAPTER 50

THE VERY AIR seemed to vibrate around them, as though the entire atmosphere was inside of a drum that someone had just pounded a single note upon. Marri spun automatically to face a random point on the wall. Somehow, in that moment, she knew exactly the origin point for the world-vibrating sound. It lay in that direction. Down the street, perhaps a couple of blocks away.

To her left, Karl gave himself a shake but returned to stare at Marri, concerned. Stefani-thing and Giana-thing didn't react at all.

A second thrumming boom, deeper than the first.

"You heard that, didn't you?" Marri said. It was barely a question. She knew he had, even if the other two hadn't. Something was speaking to them.

The Strange Man. It didn't make sense. He was dead. She'd just seen him die. But nothing made sense anymore. And she knew it was true.

"Just a little ringing in my ears," Karl said. "But when you've been shooting lances as long as I have, that happens."

Boom.

"There it was again," Marri said. Apparently the timing of this pronouncement impressed Karl, because he finally looked like he was really paying attention to her.

Stefani-thing and Giana-thing didn't speak. Both their gazes were fixed on Marri, each concerned.

Boom.

This time, Marri caught the subtleties of the tone. It wasn't the same beginning to end. There were modulations of some kind.

Words, her intuition whispered. *It's a message.*

Boom. She listened harder, picked out a few sounds. Marri felt as though she was falling into a trance.

Boom. A little bit more, and her intuition began to piece things together.

Boom. Come to me here.

"It's a message," Marri said dreamily. She felt as though she were talking from the edge of sleep. She was only dimly aware of Karl shaking his head as though to dispel cobwebs.

Boom. Come to me here.

"He's talking to me."

Boom. Come to me here.

"I'm supposed to go to him."

Come to me here.

CHAPTER 51

"THIS WASN'T a part of our deal," Giana said again, much to Stefani's annoyance. She'd dragged Giana off to the corner of the apartment. Marri had in turn pulled Karl back toward her room, to gaze out at whatever she had sensed.

"Well, I'm not going without them," Stefani said.

"It's interesting that you continue to show such loyalty to them. Marri, at least, seems quite willing to cut you loose and not look back."

Don't let her provoke you.

"Well, I'm not willing. Whatever else I am, the part of me that is Stefani Palmieri would never let me forgive myself if I left them behind to die. So if they are going down to whatever it is Marri thinks she heard, I'm going as well."

A moment passed between them, then. Stefani had the sense that the entity calling itself Giana was weighing its tactical options, whether it could overpower Stefani without killing her and be gone before Marri could react. Stefani would have been interested to see the calculus there, but regardless, it seemed to reach Stefani's desired conclusion.

"Very well. But I am not exaggerating when I say our time is almost up." Given that the building was shaking nearly constantly by this point, Stefani didn't doubt it. Whatever doom her people had predicted, it seemed close.

Giana obviously assumed they were done discussing the matter, but Stefani caught her before she could rejoin Karl and Marri.

"Tell me something," she said. "Did I ever meet the real Giana Novak?"

"A nonsensical question," Giana said. "If you are asking whether I was already undergoing the conversion process of my kind when we met, then the answer is yes. But it was still fairly early."

"What was it like for you? When you took her over, I mean. For me, it was this bright line where one awareness became two. That was with Volkes, Teodori's man. And then a much blurrier line later, with Stefani, when two became three and I became confused."

"Three different personas, three sets of memories sharing space in the same brain. Each person absorbed in total and at once." Giana shook her head. "It is not so for my kind. There was no line of division. There was no single moment. The process was gradual, then stepwise at certain key instants. But that is the reason your earlier question was nonsensical. I was Giana Novak when it began. All throughout the process, I was always Giana Novak. I am still Giana Novak. It is only that Giana Novak has not always been me."

Much to Stefani's surprise, it made a strange kind of sense. She lowered her voice, despite Giana's obvious impatience.

"What is it your kind did to doom this world? We came to understand it was doomed, but we lacked the tools to know how or why."

"Every living thing acts in accordance with its nature and based on its circumstances," Giana replied cryptically. "My kind is no different. But we're running out of time. You may insist that they come with us, but you must still convince them, I think." She paused, and for a moment sounded exactly like Giana Novak, Stefani Palmieri's assistant. "And I really think you should pack up Ella as well. We won't be coming back here."

CHAPTER 52

COME TO ME HERE.

"It's not far," Marri said. She was talking to Karl, *only* to Karl, though the other two were tagging along, a few paces behind them on the sidewalk outside the apartment building.

Marri hadn't precisely agreed to their coming, but she hadn't precisely forbidden it, either. For one thing, Stefani-thing had Ella, and for the first time ever, she couldn't bear to be parted from her mother, even by a few meters. For another, Marri could neither bring herself to willfully deprive Ella of the closest thing to her mother, nor be sure she'd wouldn't lose control and do so without precisely meaning to.

It would be so much easier if they just went away, but Marri couldn't bring herself to do that, either. Not with Ella in the mix.

So they followed, too close, but also not that close.

"If you say so," Karl said. Whereas the pulses, coming closer and closer together, spoke to Marri in a comprehensible language of urgency and command, they just seemed to make Karl feel ill. Or maybe it was the degree of change to his view of the world he was being forced to absorb all at once.

The street was empty, but that was not to say they weren't

watched as they walked down it. On the contrary, Marri saw faces in every lit window, and she guessed they were there in many of the dark ones as well.

It's not just me and Karl. The whole city can hear it. Those of us that are "natives" anyway. She was not certain how much to trust what Giana-thing said about anything, but it was impossible to ignore that Marri had felt more herself than at any point in her life when she'd held that other form, the one she'd first seen Magistrate Delgassi's corpse transform into eight months ago. It had fascinated her even then. Now that she'd understood what she'd seen, she thought it had awakened her as well.

It was a short walk, in truth, but it felt to Marri like walking toward the end of something, an end that had stretched forever into the future until precisely this moment.

She knew she would see the tall, rangy silhouette before she laid eyes upon it. Her happiness at seeing him alive was so great, it overwhelmed her confusion both at how he could be alive at all and why seeing him should make her so happy.

The Strange Man still sported the same outdated clothing, as though he didn't quite understand how to gauge an adequate disguise. But given that Marri knew he wasn't human, now—that she wasn't either—perhaps that wasn't such a surprise.

He stood in the middle of a split in the street's center, one that ran down its length for twenty meters at least. Something pushed up, bulbous and organic looking, from below that split, as though forcing its way up from underground. Even with the help of Illuminance's generous streetlights, it was hard to make out details in the dark. So Marri couldn't tell if it was part of the Strange Man or if the Strange Man was part of it.

But it was definitely one of those.

The message emanated both from him and from *beneath* him. But that it flowed through him was unquestionable, and though all were meant to hear, Marri knew with bone-deep certainty it was directed primarily at her. Marri obeyed her instincts instead of her experience and ran to him, ignoring the shouts of all three adults behind her.

She stopped just short of the split in the pavement, not quite trusting her footing on the unknown material jutting up from below. Still, she was within easy grabbing distance. But she did not back away. This was a sign of trust on her part, and the trust she felt in this man was real, however much hard-learned experience screeched that she was being a fool and would shortly die.

And she decided not to waste any more time, for as the world shook again, hard enough to stagger her, what time was there to waste?

"Are you him?" she asked, breathless.

The shadowed head tilted in silent regard. The coat and hat fell away, vanishing into nothingness like a magician's trick. In a horrific squelching sound, a being of pulsing, deflated sacs and asymmetric geometry stared down at her with clouded, white eyes that formed a clustered shape a bit like a flame frozen mid-flicker. Too many eyes, and too few. What had appeared to be broad shoulders unfurled into spindly, claw-tipped arms. Too many arms. Too many joints. Marri counted five of the former. Only the vaguest sense of human anatomy greeted her eyes, and Marri had a few heartbeats to think she'd made a terrible, fatal mistake before the thing's jagged, diagonal slash of a mouth dividing its cluster of eyes into two opened. The mouth was full of needle teeth that fit together like interlocking combs.

In a cultured, if strangely self-echoing, human voice, the Strange Man spoke. "At last. You have come at last, and your eyes are open, despite such ... mixed company as you keep."

Marri finally gave voice to the question that had haunted the back of her mind, never touching her consciousness, since she'd first seen him. "Are you my father?"

"Father ..." it said, as if musing over the word. "Father. Crude. Reductive. Essentially accurate. Yes, servant. I am your father. Or at least, my voice speaks through the vessel you see before you. A servant, twin to the one you saw perish earlier, and one of my very last."

The ground shook then, twice in rapid succession, and though Marri couldn't credit why, it sounded almost as though the world was coughing. She didn't know what to make of ... *any* of that.

"Well, you aren't my father in the way I was asking. That much is pretty obvious."

"So you say? If you speak true, it is only because your forebears abandoned me."

"I don't know what you're saying," Marri said.

"It grew within me," Father said.

"What grew?"

"Corruption. Perversion. Infection. I know not which, save that it feasted upon me. The gall of it still chafes. Mine own, immortal self, undone from within."

"You're sick," another voice interjected. The Stefani-thing had arrived, Ella in tow. Karl was hobbling up behind. Giana kept a wary distance. "Is that what you're talking about?"

Marri almost told the Stefani-thing to shut up and let her talk, that the man had come to *her,* not anyone else. Whatever this horrible thing was, it belonged to Marri in a way it did not to any of the others.

"Such a small term for something vast enough to slay such as myself," it said. "Perhaps yes. Perhaps no. The analogy is imperfect. But all would be. It is adequate."

And Marri found she was annoyed that the Stefani-thing had earned even tepid praise from the entity.

"What's the nature of the sickness?" the Stefani-thing asked, and Marri rounded on her, hissing.

"Stop. Talking," she said, putting as much force as she could into the words. Tears filled her eyes, however she willed them away. "You killed her? Do you understand that? However much you want to be her, you can't be her because you *killed her.* So *stop talking.*"

And the Stefani-thing did.

"Why did you visit me so many times?" Marri asked the sick monster.

"I felt you flailing at truth some significant time in your past," it said. "Your senses beheld it." And Marri understood what he meant. He was talking about the memory she'd thought lost, the moment when she'd seen Magistrate Delgassi's dead form. "Even if your mind rejected it for a time, you alone were on the cusp of remembering your betrayal. Remembering your forgotten duty to me."

"I never betrayed anyone!" Marri exclaimed.

"Shift the blame to your forbears if you must," it said. "But your duty is your duty, and your people shirk it collectively, generation upon generation. Only now, when it is too late, does one of you remember. A cruel joke."

Karl had joined them now. Looking back, Marri saw Giana had still approached no closer.

"Too late for what?" Marri asked before someone else could steal the question from her.

"Too late," the thing said, "for me. But not, perhaps, for you. But if you would survive me, I would have you know—"

"Who we are?"

"No, impudent mite! *What* you are."

CHAPTER 53

GIANA KEPT WELL AWAY of the Host's avatar, merely listening. But she knew it was aware of her, and it was only a matter of time before the confrontation.

She kept querying her strategy and kept coming up with no better alternative. She had first settled on merely kidnapping Stefani but had quickly deemed this plan unacceptably risky. Risk of death to either her or to Stefani was too great, particularly when the exact nature of Marri's intervention—or lack thereof—could not have been predicted with certainty.

A similar plan to kidnap Ella and use the girl as leverage, a combination of both carrot and stick, had been likewise deemed unworkable. All three would have surely turned on her, and while Karl was no threat, Stefani and Marri together would certainly outmatch Giana.

In the end, it was this path, the path of acquiescence to both Stefani's and Marri's demands, and of offering only the carrot in the form of saving Ella's life, that offered the best chance of success.

Even the presence of the Host did not change that fact.

"It was subtle at first, weak," the Host said to Marri, speaking of Giana's kind. "It could not strike openly, not with my defenders constantly on the hunt, eating its fellows. A million of its brothers died every day, swallowed and digested by your forebears. As was only right. As was your duty."

"You're talking about ... revenants?" Karl sounded so confused that Giana felt a vestigial stab of pity for him. "Or is that what you are?"

"Revenants ..." It rolled the word around, tasting it. "Parasites. Carrion-feeders. They are naught to me. My fate was written ere they tore the fabric with their arrival. Had I possessed the strength, had I not been betrayed, that which you call revenants or humans would have been snuffed out between two sunrises. No, my foe is far more insidious. Far more deadly. Is that not true?"

It had pitched its voice for Giana at the end, a beckoning taunt. Accordingly, she stepped forward, but not so close that she could be physically assaulted by any of them before reacting.

"Look at how far you've come, oh foe of mine," the Host said to Giana. Marri turned, looking furious that she'd lost the avatar's focus. "It was not this way at first. You were mindless. Lashing out blindly, ever changeable, ever looking for the approach that would let you survive my defenses. And you found it. Random stabs in the dark, yet you found the way, and those survivors replicated, ready to build upon their blind luck. But you must tell." It gestured one of those ropey arms at Giana. "Come. Do me the courtesy of allowing me one discourse with my assassin before I expire."

Giana once again ran through stratagems, modeled outcomes in her head. Playing along seemed best.

"We could not overcome your defenses," she said. "They were too strong. We had to subvert them instead. We didn't know any of this, of course. We didn't 'know' anything. It was random attempts, just as you said."

"Evolution," Stefani said.

"Just so, parasite," the Host said. "Just so." It gestured for Giana to continue, as though it were a host in a more metaphorical sense, and Giana an honored guest in its home.

Marri still stared daggers at her.

"We mutated at random," she said, "and chanced upon a solution. We lured a few of Marri's kind. Found the chemical signals that would draw them, but not trigger their rage until the right moment. When they drew close, we released a part of ourselves where Marri's kind were sure to snap it up, a tasty foreign object."

"You cursed them with minds," the Host said. "They were as mindless, as ruthless, as you. And then you transformed them, my defenders, into individuals. You gave them cause to worship you, even though they quickly forgot to whom they spoke when they referenced 'the gods below.'" It turned its gaze back upon Marri, and even in such an alien face, Giana could sense the anger, scarcely diminished after all these eons.

Judging by her face, Marri could clearly sense it too.

CHAPTER 54

SINCE THE MOMENT others had begun talking, all Marri had wanted was for Father's attention to return to her. Now that she had it again, she began to regret the desire.

"This was the moment of your betrayal," he said, his teeth clicking. "Your kind became curious. You began to strive for other things than serving me. You became selves, and so forgo your sire. And in my hour of direst need, you abandoned me. I possessed not the ability to recall you. Even this shell which speaks to you relies on the very corruption of my foe to do so."

One of those overlong, spindly arms hooked toward the thing's neck, or what passed for a neck, and Marri saw the soft, pulsing glow of a throbbing white mass protruding there.

"One of my last loyal servants must die such that you rebels may yet live. For make no mistake, I am dying. It took me an eon to accept this fact, and it was my intention to make certain that every one of you perished with me. For the crime of my slaying, and all your roles in it, you would find only the grave as your just reward.

"Yet now, with oblivion looming, I find that my mind spins off its axis into new directions. In the throes of my end, I desire some part of me to live on. And that leaves only the part of me that is separate, if not by my choice."

"Hold on," Karl said, and Marri knew that tone of voice. It was the I've-stayed-quiet-long-enough-and-now-I'm-going-to-get-some-damned-answers voice. "What is speaking to us? I feel compelled to listen for some reason. But why? You say you're not a revenant. You say we betrayed you, that we were your defenders. Are you some other kind of alien, then? Some kind of king that sees us as his servants?"

"Alien ..." Father considered. "Irony. Insult. That which is alien is everything that is *not* myself. It is axiomatic that I, and that which sprang from me, are the only non-aliens here."

"What, on this whole world?" Karl pressed, sounding ever more frustrated. "I get that this isn't Earth, even if I can scarcely wrap my brain around it, but what world is this, and how do you lay claim to it?"

"This world ... Petulant child, this world is *me*. I *am* this world. The two cannot be separated."

"Awfully full of yourself, whatever kind of not-alien you are," Karl said. Marri glared at him, willing him to shut up.

"No," she said, when he looked a challenge back at her. "I think he means it literally."

"Wisest of my fools," Father said to Marri, and she felt a warmth blossom within her. The shaking had resumed, and to Marri's alarm, it was building. "Closest to redemption. The one who almost remembers duty speaks true, Blind One." He seemed to direct that at Karl.

The shaking became a roar, and the split in the street widened with crackling pops. Whatever bulged up from beneath was no longer content to stay put. A bulbous shadow rose, lifting Father into the air.

"When you stand upon this ground, you stand upon *me*," he cried from his newly lofty perch. "The air you breathe clings to this world by virtue of the fabric of space warping around *my* mass."

The giant shape lifting free of the ground tore up the full width of the street and beyond, causing several buildings to partially collapse against it. Marri thought she could hear screaming from those buildings, but she was forced to back up rapidly to avoid getting swallowed up as a sinkhole opened underneath the mass lifting itself free. She dragged Karl with her, and after a glance at Ella upon Stefani's back, she pulled Stefani as well, backing up until she nearly collided with Giana.

The mass which had lifted itself free of the ground was a great, curving stalk of flesh. She couldn't describe its color, because in the glow of the lights it both glistened and shone iridescent, except for the places where glowing, white blobs pulsed as they fed. Black corruption laced with angry red surrounded each of those throbbing masses of glow-monster. From the shifting of shadows in the sinkhole below, Marri could tell it was attached to a far greater mass.

But the main thing that held her rapt was the circular dome at the end of the stalk. It was somehow both white and black, depending on the angle Marri viewed it from. It was also wider than the street it had destroyed to emerge.

It reminded her of an eye while obviously being something entirely more. Somehow, though, it regarded them in ways beyond Marri's imagining.

"Behold," Father called from his perch atop the lobe of corrupted flesh, "I summoned you here, at the end of all, to look upon me as I now look upon you, though I can muster but a fraction of myself to act now." All five of its spindly arms in a spiral, sweeping motion, as though to encompass all things.

"So you exist as, what?" Stefani-thing said after many moments of shocked silence. "As a whole world?"

"Perhaps it was the parasites that should have been gifted with minds," it called down with undisguised contempt. "Hardly. When I took ill, I took refuge. Curled in upon myself to save my strength, I accreted this shell of stone and dust. Nature took its course."

Marri had never felt such awe. Into the dumbfounded silence

around her, she spoke the question surely both Karl and Stefani-thing were thinking.

"You got sick, went on bedrest and ... *became a planet?* How long ago was this?"

"A pointless query. The answer would be meaningless in its magnitude. It would beggar your very concept of time. Long and long and long again in the past, as you would reckon."

"Billions of years," Stefani-thing wondered aloud. "So if you are everything," she ventured, "what are we?"

"You are a parasite. Interloper. Pest. Unworthy of my attention, even in my dire state."

"What are the natives, then?" Karl asked. "Me and Marri."

But Father didn't need to answer. Not to Marri, at least. She saw. She understood. All those things it had said about their betrayal, their duty to protect. About how the infection, the cancer, whatever it was, had undermined them. "We're its immune system," she said. "Or we were."

"Wisest of my fools," Father said. And it seemed perversely grateful, almost proud, she had spoken this truth. "Not the whole of my defenses were lost. But enough to doom me. Tempted away from my service by my foe. It was free to eat me with abandon, then. And now its feasting draws to a close."

"Does that mean," Stefani-thing began. Marri started, momentarily falling out of her daze. She had never heard Stefani-thing, either version of her, sound this excited. "Does that mean that ... that your foe is *Mutagen Prime?*"

"Mutagen Prime ..." It tasted the words. "In a sense, correct. But also too simple. My foe was the source of my servants' transformation, their rebellion." It ignored Stefani-thing again, turning back to Marri. "When my foe gifted my defenses with minds, they also imprinted upon you some of their changeability. Which you then cursed the human parasites with when you banished their kind from their place of imagined safety, the city. And then you used that same changeability in turn to blaspheme me in your mimicry of those same human parasites.

"Incomplete to say my foe is ... Mutagen Prime," it said with obvious disdain for the term. "Less wrong to say that whether servant or parasite, my foe cursed you with a deadly weapon. But my servants chose to change yourselves, to defy your natures, to be other than you ought. In doing so, you primed that weapon, you turned it upon yourselves. In that way, you chose to damn yourselves. In that way, Mutagen Prime is you."

"I don't understand," Marri said.

"I believe I can help," said Giana-thing.

CHAPTER 55

GIANA WATCHED KARL, Stefani, and Marri struggle with the enormity of the truths being forced upon them. How much easier it had been to wake fully to her improved self in that bathtub and have the information already there, totally integrated and accessible. How superior her kinds' methods were.

"I don't understand," Marri said.

"I believe I can help," Giana interjected. "The Host means that my kind's mutational ability has been imprinted on both your kinds. Upon the immune system natives," she said, gesturing to Marri and Karl, "when we gifted them with minds. Whereas for the human colonists"—and here she gestured at Stefani—"when the natives mutated them and drove them from the city."

"That's the part I understand," Marri said, voice dripping with venom.

"Quite," Giana said, unperturbed. "The part you are stumbling on is the why of how this mutational ability turns on you and kills you. It is because neither of your kinds hold your true forms. The natives have changed themselves by choice. The humans have not. But choice doesn't matter here. Neither of you are yourselves. That aspect of my kind, the ability to hypermutate, recognizes this. And so, when you are injured, or sick, when your physical forms require healing or restoration in some way, that mutational ability steps in and tries to restore you to what you ought to be."

"He said it was our fault," Karl said flatly. "How is any of that our fault?"

"Because you resist," Giana said. "Unconsciously, unknowingly, but resistance is resistance. That one part of you tries to correct you, while all the rest fights against it. And so you die."

"Humans, *real* humans, don't want to be revenants," Stefani-thing protested.

"This matters not. You have your answers, all you shall have," the Host called down. "The only choice that mattered was my servants' choice to abandon me. Had you remained, I might have triumphed. By all rights, you should die with me. Yet, I am merciful. You shall live on, my legacy, yet in full awareness of your sins against me."

"And what's going to happen to this world when you die?" asked Karl, ever the lancer worried about the safety of the populace.

"Every living thing still upon it will perish, Blind One. Once the life has left me, that which has been clenched closed all this time will come unclenched."

The other three looked confused, but Giana, conscious of how rapidly their time was running out, did not give them a chance to process this information on their own schedule.

"There's only a planet here because the Host has been curled into a ball orbiting this system's star for a few billion years. Once it dies—"

"It comes uncurled," Karl said, eyes wide as he stared into Giana's impassive expression. "Gods below."

"The entire planet will come apart," Giana said with a nod.

"Just so," the creature said. "As you reckon time, it will be very soon. As I reckon it, it has already begun."

"Which is why have to use the Bridge," Giana said. "Now."

"'We?'" The Host's reverberating voice grew dangerous. "You

believe you shall be permitted to flee with these others, after what you have done?"

Giana didn't flinch, but she did tense. She had known this moment would come. Now it came down to the argument she could muster, as well as over the degree of control she could summon up.

"You said it yourself, Host. Look how far I've come. From mindless, brute force luck to a thinking being you can converse with. You wish to save those creatures which sprang from you. Am I not one such? My kind could never have achieved so much within a lesser creature. Do parents not often give their all to their children? Even their very lives? We are your offspring as much as anyone else can claim."

Rather feeble as arguments went, but it just had to have a thread of rationalization. For the rest, Giana reached out, sensing the vast, decaying mind of the host deep beneath them.

Or rather, sensing the threads of her kind which had burrowed into that mind, twining themselves into its thoughts, wrapping themselves around its decisions. Those filaments were far more influential than their victim could ever have guessed. Giana suspected they were the only reason the Host was choosing mercy over revenge in helping any of them escape at all. The filaments sensed their input was needed, and they flexed.

"It is true, what you say," the Host's avatar said after the silence had stretched. "Though I could wish matters had gone otherwise, the more of me that can be saved, the better. Very well, you shall go. Wisest of my Fools, you are charged with her safety. Make sure she escapes this world with you."

Marri looked about to protest, or maybe swallow her tongue. Gainsaying the being before them was an act Giana could not imagine the outcome of, even if a part of her longed to see what that would look like. Perhaps Marri made the same calculation, though, because for what must have been the first time in her life, she merely gritted her teeth and nodded stiffly at a command she disagreed with.

"But," the Host said, and Giana's moment of self-congratulatory elation rebounded back to tension. "I would ask you one final question first, one dying question, oh foe of mine."

"Name it," Giana said, feeling a wash of relief. She even gave a little bow as though to a monarch. "If it is in my power to answer, I will."

"Why me?" it said, and the vestigial Giana, she of native biology and human personality, felt another stab of pity. "I should have carried us into eternity. I should have seen the very universe die with me. Why did this fate befall me?"

Because you were on a list.

"Sometimes things just happen," Giana lied.

CHAPTER 56

"MORE AND MORE ARE JOINING US," Karl said nervously.

"No," Marri said of the many Coldgarden citizens, the *natives* who were emerging from their homes to walk in the direction of the Bridge site, silent as though in a trance. "They're obeying Father's command."

Marri had to give it to Father. When he said he wanted them to live, he meant all of them. *All* of them, he'd warned as they left. That included feral natives who he claimed still lived as themselves outside Coldgarden, never choosing to join the ones mimicking the human invaders.

None of Marri's group seemed interested in hanging around long enough to see those arrive in the city, herself included. Maybe they'd be unable to get past the wall.

The trip was long on foot with Karl's limp, but the tremors meant taking the tram was out of the question. Marri considered transforming again, picking Karl up, and making a break for it. But that left Ella, and Father had, for some inexplicable reason, charged her with safeguarding Giana as well.

His words had clearly impacted her because she felt she couldn't disobey him in this.

Then she considered at least transforming to carry Karl, but she still didn't know if she could do so and not turn on Stefani, Giana, or both.

"We're going to make it," Karl said, trying to force the tightness of his pained leg from his voice. Probably he could sense her tension. "We are."

Marri wasn't so sure, especially based on the number of detours they had to take. The street a few blocks down from Stefani's apartment had not been the only one rendered impassable by Father's breaching of the surface. But Marri said nothing, trying to keep her negativity to herself. Perhaps Father had done this on purpose to breach the wall and allow his wayward children from the wilderness beyond a chance to get inside.

Stefani spent much of the walk on her handheld, trying to reach Dolce.

"He's not answering," she said after what must have been the fourth attempt. "This isn't a good sign. If the quakes have damaged the apparatus, or the power grid running to it ..."

"I think Iazmaena is the worry," Karl said, almost in perfect lockstep with Giana-thing. Giana-thing looked amused. Karl looked annoyed.

Stefani-thing put her handheld away with a stressed sigh. "I guess we'll find out soon enough," she said. She really seemed to take in her surroundings, and all the people walking in trances, for the first time.

"This is better than my plan to try and get the archon to claim the Bridge site was a shelter from the earthquakes and get everyone there that way. But it's still pretty creepy." She looked to Marri with a tentative smile, hoping to get one in return for the weak humor.

Marri looked away, keeping her face hard as stone.

"Speaking of the archon," Giana-thing said. "I find it ominous that we haven't heard from her at all in this."

"So do I," Stefani-thing said. Marri almost found it comforting, hearing the two women discuss political analysis. She'd certainly heard it enough over the past months to create a sense of familiarity.

"But Iaz more so. If she doesn't know I'm needed to activate the Bridge, she will soon, and she'll come for me. If she does know, why hasn't she come for me already?"

Marri stared hard into every darkened alley and side street after that, scanned the faces of every dazed citizen that drew too close to them.

"You can't take other shapes, right?" Marri asked Stefani-thing, hating herself for having to do so. "Now that you're ... her?"

"I can," Stefani-thing said warily. "But without the, um, person to work with, it wouldn't be very convincing except from a distance. Even the movement would seem off."

"Sorry to be the one to point this out," Karl said, "but that could apply to literally any of these people."

They all stared more warily at their unwitting companions after that.

When the walls of the Bridge site at last hove into view and they had not been assaulted, Marri began to feel a little bit better. The world did not appear to be flying apart at the seams. Maybe they would get the Bridge operational in time to save at least some of the city.

CHAPTER 57

SOMETHING about the control tower and the Bridge beyond, the former standing stark against the deep of night, the latter bathed in harsh work lights, made Stefani's hackles rise. Judging by the many darting and rushing shadows cast by the work lights, the Bridge site was bustling, which was how she would have expected it to be ... provided she had given the affirmative order to get the Bridge online.

Which, since she hadn't been able to reach Dolce, she had not.

"Don't even bother asking me to stay with Ella," Marri said, staring her own set of daggers up at the tower.

The ground shook before Stefani could reply. The quakes were ramping up steadily with time. Stefani saw no obvious damage to the tower, which meant the Bridge was likely intact as well, since it was a more robust structure. But that might not be true for either much longer.

"We don't have time to leave anyone behind," she said. "We're just going to have to see what's waiting for us." *And hope for the best,* she didn't add.

But she thought Karl's and Giana's suspicions about who waited there for them were correct.

As soon as they opened the ground floor door, the smell of blood assaulted them. Squirming smears of it lay everywhere, far too much loss of blood to suggest survivors, but despite this, there were no bodies in sight.

"Iazmaena is here," Stefani said, recognizing what they were going to find.

They climbed the stairs, four piles of nervous energy plus a jittery almost-toddler kicking Stefani's lower back. More blood. More death without bodies. Stefani wondered if Dolce was even alive to speak to.

"Madam Magistrate!" Dolce cried as Stefani and her companions stalked slowly into the command center. She recognized his voice only. Dolce was shrouded in shadow, as all the lights remained off. There was some other kind of shadow behind him, though. Stefani had her eyes wide, trying to see in the darkness when the lights came on all at once, dazzling her.

Iaz stood behind Dolce, the palm of one hand pressed against the side of his neck. It would have looked strange to anyone not familiar with Iaz's true nature. But Stefani knew that the hand could become a claw in an instant. This was the equivalent of holding a knife to her lead researcher's throat.

"It will be all right, Dolce," Stefani said, hoping she sounded only half as tense as she felt. "It's me she wants. I have the codes she needs."

"Hi, Steffi," Iaz said, and with a little jerk of her head, she indicated the rest of the room. Up until that moment, Stefani had only had eyes for Dolce, but now she saw that the rest of the research team was present as well.

Only they weren't really the research team, of course. She recalled all the blood below. They were revenants with the team's memories. Enough to operate the Bridge, at least.

That, plus several of them had police-issue guns which they trained on Stefani's group.

"I'm surprised you left any of them alive," Stefani said, indicating Dolce.

"Always so cruel," Iaz said with a very un-Iaz-like pout. "I had to leave someone to be my hostage."

"So now what?" Stefani demanded. "You trade Dolce in exchange for my access codes?"

"Oh, no, not at all," Iaz said with a bark of laughter. "I already found something better." She jerked her head toward someone Stefani couldn't see. "Bring her in!"

One of the research-team revenants, a woman named Petra Bischoff when she'd still been alive, entered the control room from the adjacent conference room. Behind her, she dragged Archon Graysteel.

"Ritala," Stefani said reflexively, horrified. Both their questions answered, then. And in the worst possible way. The magistrate of Illuminance had the access codes for any Grand Project, but the archon could override any magistrate.

Ritala looked terrible. Her skin was blotchy, flushed red with anger in some places and alarmingly pale in ragged swatches between. She turned a bleak gaze upon Stefani.

"I see we didn't move fast enough, did we, Stefani?"

"No, ma'am," Stefani said. "We didn't."

"Stefani," Ritala said. She looked profoundly disappointed. "Back when I debriefed Lance Commander Yonnel there, he claimed that the revenants could look like humans. When I asked you to corroborate that, you told me that was delirium induced by his injuries. That he'd made it up. You lied to me, didn't you?"

"I did, ma'am," Stefani said. Karl was out of her eyeline, but she could sense him stiffen at this revelation. It was infuriating how much it hurt to say. *I don't want to be Stefani Palmieri anymore.* But she would never be free of Stefani, no matter what other form she might take.

"Because you're one of them," Ritala said.

"I am."

Dolce gasped, but Stefani ignored him. Everyone might as well know.

"Devils beyond, I was such a fool," Ritala said. She sounded inexpressibly weary.

We were idiots, Iaz, Stefani thought. *We never should have taken the forms of actual people. All we wanted was our humanity back, but now we're saddled with theirs. We can never be free, no matter what.*

Iaz rolled her eyes, almost as if she'd heard Stefani speak. "I'm going to spare us all any further shocking revelations and get on with this." Dragging Dolce with her, she stepped to the console which communicated with the personnel in shelters below.

"This is your archon speaking, Bridge site," Iaz said, seeming to relish the way *archon* rolled off her tongue. "Full initiation in one minute, please." She glanced at Ritala. "Input your codes. Now."

Stefani had never imagined she'd see the day where stiff and proper Ritala Graysteel would bow before the demands of terrorists and hostage takers. But the woman looked utterly broken when she leaned over to the console and input her code, allowing full powerup of the device.

The sound of the device powering up was familiar to Stefani after the last time. And because she didn't really see a way around this trap, at least, not until it was fully up and running, she tried to make use of that experience to stall.

"How can you be sure there's no Kyne Libretta surprise, like last time?"

She'd expected defiance or anger, but Iaz just shrugged again.

"Can't," Iaz said. "The woman is a colony of cockroaches. You'll never stamp all of them out." The tower shook with the latest quake. "But we're out of time to keep checking."

"What happened to Ali?"

"You know, I don't know. She made herself scarce after your apartment. They all did. Maybe they're hoping to slip through once the Bridge is open. Who knows? I might even let them."

Poor Dolce's face was a mix of confusion and terror. His gaze pleaded for help. But help had to wait. She couldn't operate the Bridge herself. Neither could he, alone.

This time, instead of shaking, the tower vibrated. Flashes of violet light lit the night sky outside, coming faster and faster. The roar was building. The tension in the room felt like a steel cable ready to snap.

"So, did you actually speak to the ones behind all this?" Iaz asked.

"I got called a parasite a lot," Stefani replied. She had no idea how much Iaz knew about the thing Marri called her father and wondered if sharing more might work as some sort of a distraction, when Ritala spoke.

"I saw it on my kitchen floor," the woman said, her gaze suddenly gone vacant, her skin ashen. Her tone had shifted entirely. Instead of despairing, she sounded thoughtful, as though she was simply working through some knotty puzzle in her mind. "Months ago, this was."

"All right, then," Iaz said. "Safe to say that whatever is going on, your suffering will be over soon, Graysteel."

But the archon wasn't listening to Iaz. "A little white glob of something," she said as though she hadn't been interrupted. "It looked like it had popped out of my sink drain. It looked absolutely revolting. It was just some bit of old food growing mold, I was sure, and yet I couldn't stop thinking about it. For hours I left it there because I couldn't bear the thought of throwing it away. I couldn't get the notion out of my head that throwing it out or flushing it down the drain wasn't enough. That I had to ... destroy it. Utterly destroy it. Purge it from the world to make it a cleaner, healthier place. It was small enough to crush between two fingers. Just bend over, pick it up, and squeeze it to nothingness."

The entire room was captivated now. Every single pair of eyes was fixed on Ritala Graysteel. Even Stefani could not see past the strangeness of what was happening to how she might utilize the distraction.

"So I did," Ritala said. "I picked it up, and I crushed it. And it vanished. For a second, I thought I'd truly squeezed it into nothingness." For some reason, she fixed her haunted gaze on Stefani specifically.

"Then I felt it moving *inside me*."

Something was happening to her skin. It had gone beyond gray. She was white as a corpse.

"And then I forgot about it," she said. "It just vanished from my mind. For months, I forgot. Until now. Until this very moment."

Stefani felt a squeeze on her shoulder. It was Giana. Stefani turned slightly, glanced at the woman out of the corner of one eye. Giana had a very particular stare fixed on the archon. It was a stare of recognition.

Then Ritala Graysteel shuddered as if in great pain, and all that corpse-white skin began to glow blindingly bright.

"Help m—" But Graysteel could not finish, and what next came out of her mouth was not words, but blood. Black, oily blood.

As though the blood were acid, the skin to either side of the archon's mouth began to tear. Her face peeled itself, then collapsed like a rotten melon that had been stepped on. Whatever had been inside the woman's head, now clusters of glowing white globules sprang forth, slumping to one side and glistening obscenely.

"Well, that was horrible," Iaz said. "You know, I was just bullshitting that story about the city's leadership being corrupted." She turned a sickly smile on the rest of her captives. "Turns out I was right."

One of the researchers spoke up into the horrid silence.

"The startup sequence is locked in. Bridge activation should proceed without us now."

"Time to go then," Iaz said. She jerked her chin, and the researchers holding them at gunpoint took more careful aim. One for each. Iaz turned back to Stefani. "Any last words?"

As if the infection that had claimed her life were made of pure spite, the monstrous Ritala-thing lurched into motion suddenly. It lunged at Iaz, blurred with speed. Gunfire erupted.

Stefani felt Karl's calming hands on her shoulders, felt him sliding Ella's sling from her back.

"Now," Giana hissed in her ear.

Stefani's heart hammered. "Marri, now."

CHAPTER 58

MARRI INHALED DEEPLY, taking in the scent of so many revenants. The rest was as easy as falling.

One surprise could be recovered from. Two surprises in rapid succession was a lot harder. And Iazmaena's revenants were definitely double-surprised.

Marri surged forward, riding that shock. The rage was all. *Parasites! Invaders! In the name of my Father, I cleanse him of you!*

The first gunman was in pieces before he could even adjust his aim back to the real threat. Marri felt bullets dance along her hide, deflecting elsewhere, leaving only pinpricks of annoyance. She impaled the second gunman, the one shooting her, with all six legs, then splayed them wide, shredding him.

The third gunman got halfway into his transformation before Giana-thing took him, a glowing, vaguely human-shaped mass with the right number of limbs but ten times too many joints. She moved like sped-up video footage and tore through the half of the man that wasn't yet revenant, before moving on to help the golden-hued, boneless flow of blackness that was Stefani-thing fight the fourth gunman, similarly transformed into his revenant form.

Freed of any further obstacles, Marri turned toward the

Iazmaena-thing, intent on ending her. But she was cagier than her fellows and shoved Dolce at Marri to foul her approach.

The scientist screeched at the sight of Marri skidding sideways, claws struggling to find purchase in all the blood.

"Quite a show," Iazmaena-thing crowed, "but I'll see you on the other side!" Karl made a valiant attempt to trip her, but she sidestepped him with contemptuous ease, not even bothering to strike back as she darted out the door to the stairwell. Marri heard her shoes clapping the stairs as she ran. Marri almost lunged after, but something crashed into her hard and latched on tight.

Marri thrashed as a burning feeling settled across her hide wherever the thing touched. She flailed, but her bony claws could find no purchase, and her attacker was not in range of her mouth and its acid vomit.

"We didn't move fast enough, did we?" Ritala Graysteel howled in a horrible monster's voice as she draped herself across Marri's back, touching as much of her hide as she could.

"Marri!" Stefani-thing's voice echoed in strange ways, but she was there abruptly in her revenant form, and with a heaving effort, she peeled the Graysteel-thing off Marri and heaved her away. Marri howled silently at the pain striping her back wherever the Graysteel-thing had touched her.

"Marri!" Stefani-thing shouted in her strange echo-voice. "Are you all right?" Marri recoiled from her touch at first, shuddering, but at last consented to be examined. Giana, meanwhile, leaped atop Graysteel and grabbed both wrists, still white and glowing all over.

After a few moments the shining mass that was Graysteel turned back into an older woman, but just for an instant before she opened her mouth in a silent scream and came apart in gelatinous chunks dripping with black blood.

"Too far gone," Giana-thing said. It was strange to hear a perfectly human voice coming out of the glowing white silhouette. "Unsalvageable." She turned to look at Marri and Stefani.

"Let me see." she said.

"Don't you do anything to her!" Stefani-thing said fiercely.

"I may have to in order to save her," Giana-thing retorted. "Let me see so I can know."

The glow against Marri's many eyes became painful as Giana-thing bent close, examining. Her touch was sharply cold against the fire, but too brief to bring much in the way of relief. Maybe she was afraid of what Stefani-thing would do if she touched Marri for too long, considering what Giana-thing was capable of.

"Looks like surface damage, only," she said at last. Marri felt a wash of relief radiate through her despite the source of the comforting words. "It wasn't developed enough to know how to efficiently turn you, and it didn't have contact for long enough. You'll be all right. Transform back and forth a few times, and it should heal quickly."

Karl at last approached the three. He seemed hesitant. Considering what each of them looked like, Marri supposed she couldn't blame him. He had some kind of bundle in his hands and Ella on his back.

"Considering I contributed absolutely nothing, I thought the least I could manage was to help you three maintain your dignity. They had them in a locker in an adjoining room."

He held out three jumpsuits of various sizes. Then he went to check on Dolce, who was cowering in the corner.

"Come on, there, friend," Karl said, bracing himself to hoist the man up with a grimace of pain. "We still need you to tell us what the Bridge thing is doing."

Once Marri, Stefani, and Giana-thing were back to their human forms and dressed—Marri's suit at least a size too big—they walked over to the compglass window.

The groan which emanated from the waking Bridge battled with the planet's death throes for pride of place. But at least they could still watch it opening. The concentric rings which filled nearly the whole of the square outside the command center began to rotate, each in the opposite direction of the rings immediately inside and outside of itself.

This continued for several revolutions, as near as Marri could make out, like a dog turning in repeating circles before it finally bedded down, but in this case the machinery was waking up. Then, as if by magic, the outermost ring lifted itself from the ground, supported by nothing Marri could see beyond purple light. Once the largest of the rings was perhaps five meters off the ground, the others followed suit in quick succession, moving inward one by one. Each successive ring elevated itself higher than the previous. The cumulative effect was something like a dome described in the air by the hovering rings.

"S-systems functioning within normal parameters," came Dolce's shaking voice. Marri turned. He looked like he was about to faint and flinched away from every gaze but Karl's, though focusing on his work seemed to stiffen his spine. Then he frowned. "There is a small drain on the power, however." He tapped some controls. "A few percent at most. Well within the safety margins." At this point, his voice sounded almost normal. "I wouldn't mention it at all except that it seems to be coming from ..." He shook his head, tapping furiously.

"From?" Stefani asked. She looked half as though she expected him to run away screaming when she talked, but he only shook his head some more, his frown deepening.

"From elsewhere on the planet," he said wonderingly. "I don't see how that's possible."

Stefani winced. "I have a guess," she said. "But it doesn't matter. We're leaving."

And so, Marri saw, was Dolce. Whatever message Father had beamed out across the surface, it seemed to be too weak to overcome imminent fear of death. But now that Dolce wasn't in danger of dying, Marri could see the pulsing signal taking root behind his eyes. They gradually lost focus, and without a word, he began shuffling toward the door.

"We should go too," Marri said.

"Hold on," Stefani said, coming up behind her. She reached out a hand to touch Marri's back then thought better of it, probably for multiple reasons. "Are you all right?"

Marri could only laugh at that. What did a question like that even mean anymore?

"I know it's hard to understand," Stefani said. "But I'm not the same person I was ... before."

"Before you killed her."

"Before I killed her," she said grimly. "I saw what we needed, and I took it. And then I was her, and even if I knew something was wrong, I forgot I'd ever been anything else but her. I'm sorry I did what I did. But I can't take it back. And you need to know that all Stefani was is alive in me, still. She loved you with a fierceness that frightens me. All the more so because that means I love you with that same fierceness."

"You aren't her," Marri said defiantly.

But no one ever will be, whispered an equally defiant voice in her mind. Her own voice, not Father's. *And she's as close as you can ever get again.*

"I know I'm not," Stefani said. "But at the same time, I know I am."

It would never be the same between them. How could it? And that hurt more than Marri was willing to admit. Yet she found the edges of her hate had been filed down somehow. Maybe it had only been that Stefani had saved her. Maybe.

"Well, I won't eat you, anyway," she said.

Stefani's smile was tremulous, but it looked real. It looked like her.

"It's happening," Giana-thing said from the window.

The light that kindled in the center of the dome was a violet beyond violet, something at the edge of what Marri's eyes could perceive. She felt a powerful urge to look away but forced herself to ignore it.

The spark of light flared larger into a sphere, widening even as

Marri continued to gaze into it. It became easier to gaze into the more the light attenuated with the sphere's size. Gradually, that light grew less uniform, becoming denser in some spots and less so in others. Almost as though it was describing shapes of its own in some unseen place beyond.

Then there came the moment. Amid the hum of the machine rising until it passed beyond Stefani's ability to hear it, the violet color faded entirely.

In its place was a window into another world. It flickered fitfully, the image within seeming to shift a little each time, but it was unmistakable.

Orange rock, as though blasted by a furnace, shone through everywhere she looked. The sun was a massive, orange orb of nearly the same shade as the rock. It dominated most of the sky to a degree that terrified Marri.

"The Bridge is open," Giana-thing said. "Time to go."

CHAPTER 59

THEY CAME IN THEIR HUNDREDS, in their thousands. They came in the culmination of an infiltration plan long in the making, or at the silent, mysterious urging of a dying being that might as well have been a god. Revenants that looked like people. Scythe-legged worms that looked like people. Or just revenants, and just worms. And hidden among them were the turned, the infected. The ones that only looked like people, and the ones that had made that final leap and, in a sense, really were.

For so long, they'd been killing one another. Now they crowded the square's limited space, and every space beyond that they could pack full. All seeking the same thing: survival.

CHAPTER 60

MARRI AND STEFANI stood closest to the dome that would lead them from this world, wordlessly staring into it as though waiting for some signal or invitation. Marri itched to go but dreaded it as well. She felt like she was walking through a waking dream that threatened to become a nightmare the moment she crossed that threshold.

Iaz and her underlings had surely already crossed over.

But behind Marri, the silent multitudes waited for someone else to be the first through of the rest. Their body language conveyed the same jittery energy no matter their biology. Father's spell was enough to bring them here, tell them what they must do, but there was still that final hurdle to get over, the fear of the utterly unknown.

Even Giana-thing hesitated.

Perhaps they would have hung there forever, poised on the cusp of death until it claimed them. But then the ground took away the last of their time. Marri sensed it an instant before it happened. The ground split from one edge of the Bridge rings outward, tearing a building that fronted the square in half as it spread. This was no mere sinkhole. Huge chunks of the building disappeared into the fissure, and heat and foulness blasted up from it. Worse than either of those, though, was a ruddy light.

The shaking was irresistible in its ferocity. Marri went down hard, the breath driven from her, her head dangling over the newfound lip in the pavement as the crack spread, widening. Hot air and the stench of rot blasted her face.

"Go!" she yelled as loud as she could for anyone who might still be able to hear her. "Go!"

She needn't have worried. The masses hadn't waited.

Beside her, Stefani went sprawling as well, but by this time the ground had tilted dangerously, and she couldn't stop her slide. Moving by instinct, Marri gripped the woman's arm with both fists just as she went pitching over the side. But her adoptive mother was too heavy, especially with Ella slung across her back, and Marri began to slide to the edge. Instead of saving Stefani, she was about to be dragged into the abyss with her.

She slid as far as having to bend her waist over the lip when she felt two pairs of hands grip her, one set for each leg. Her forward motion slowed, then stopped with painful pressure along the top of her thighs.

"Hold on," Karl's voice called.

"We've got you!" Giana-thing chorused.

Marri met Stefani's eyes as the pair of them were dragged back from the brink. They were filled with gratitude and brimming with tears. Marri looked away uncomfortably, which led her gaze beyond Stefani, down into that red, hellish abyss.

Everywhere there was dust and debris choking the hot wind which rushed up from that place. But there was a moment where everything cleared, and in the fiery light, Marri could improbably see all the way down.

And what she beheld was Father. Father as he really was. And what he really was turned out to be vast on a scale that beggared imagination. He had not exaggerated. Lit in the light of its own feverish body heat, Marri beheld a single creature as large as a planet.

The world is him. He is the world.

Asymmetric legs the size of continents splayed slowly out in the relaxation of impending death. In place of a planetary core and of similar scale was a head that was all eyes. Eyes on stalks, some long enough to reach the surface, as they'd already seen. Hemispheres of eyes. Eyes that seemed more like pools of liquid.

But centering them all were a central pair of eyes so massive Marri could easily see them thousands of kilometers down. They seemed the closest to what she thought of as normal eyes, lidded and spaced such that Marri kept trying to meet them with her own.

Then his voice was in her head again, as weak and faint as the last gasps of dying breath.

Leave now, child. But one last thing I would have you know. I did not hide here in my illness solely to rest and recuperate. I hid because I feared what might find me in my time of weakness. Devils beyond the stars.

Karl and Giana finally succeeded in dragging Marri past the lip just as she watched that immense pair of eyes drift closed.

Then they were dragging her to her feet, Stefani and Ella with her.

The four of them turned to stare at the masses surging forward on the Bridge's span, beings of every shape and size. And that was the literal truth, for Marri had to hold back a wail as she watched several people morph into blinding glow-monsters before hurling themselves through, both at people and simply over the Bridge. But there was nothing to be done about it. They were through now. They would have to be dealt with on the other side.

"Come on," she said, feeling another quake building and suddenly unsure their footing would hold. "We have to go."

Wasting no more time, the quartet moved as fast as Karl's injury would allow, stepping as one into that all-consuming orange light.

CHAPTER 61

FAR AWAY FROM the dying city, elsewhere on the dying planet, matters worked out well for Kyne Libretta, as they always seemed to. She stared into the glowing ring of the miniature Bridge she'd found after months on the hunt, and the circular window depicting the world beyond. Someone long ago had taken it upon themselves to recreate the larger Bridge at smaller scale, and after months of searching, Kyne had found the fruits of their labor.

Those months had been spent poring through data she'd stolen before fleeing Coldgarden, extrapolating the location of the buildings Delgassi had destroyed. Comparing those results to the location and signatures of test objects sent through, she'd concluded a smaller version of the Bridge currently rebuilt in Coldgarden had to exist out in the abandoned wilds of the planet.

She had rejoiced when she'd found it at last, buried in an unnatural cave of strange-looking stone. Rejoiced, and then despaired. For she'd quickly learned this miniature replica Bridge could only be powered on when the other, larger Bridge was also online. Somehow, it parasitically fed off the source, a stroke of genius of the builder, if an inconvenient one for Kyne. Because she'd spent a good amount of her last days in the city sabotaging the reconstruction of that larger Bridge to the greatest degree she was able.

"Better for me that it didn't delay their rebuilding efforts too much," she said, laughing to herself. She talked and laughed to herself quite a lot these days. It had worried her at first, until eventually, it no longer did.

The knowledge that Palmieri and those in the city had different sets of coordinates than she, that she could not follow them, that they would see places she wouldn't, grated. It was the one rotten sore spoiling the fruit.

"Easy, Kyne. One good turn. You have coordinates they don't have, too." She had made sure of that. And the one set that mattered most, only she possessed.

That was the set she had input during her interminable wait.

Wasting no time—there was no telling when they might shut their Bridge off, robbing her of her long-awaited chance—Kyne stepped through. She didn't dare waste a breath when the portal might snap shut at any moment if a quake severed the wrong power line.

Crossing over felt like dying. It felt like being born. It felt like existing everywhere in the universe at once. Kyne concluded hallucinogenic drugs had nothing on Bridge travel.

She emerged into a world shrouded in the deepest darkness of night and walked confidently away, secure in her belief that she would see them all again, all those who had wronged her, all those with the gall not to die when she wished it.

As it happened, her Bridge did not retract immediately. It remained open for some time, long after Kyne had left it well behind her. What was more, the immense amounts of energy it shed drew the attention of other things, things which had lain close, but dormant, for a long time. They reawakened, squirming and writhed in apparent pleasure, their brilliant white glow pulsed in strange patterns almost like communication.

For these particular instances of that which had killed the planet had learned to feed upon the miniature Bridge's particular stew of energy emissions, and then to go dormant like stone otherwise. Like stone of the sort that had formed a strange, artificial cave around the miniature Bridge's structure. Now awake and moving once more, they approached cautiously, as though not believing their luck after so much time. And then they slithered and oozed their way toward that source of delicious energy.

Toward, and ultimately through.

And if all Kyne Libretta's stolen knowledge was correct, the world she and they emerged separately onto, asleep and as yet unaware of this invasion in miniature, was Earth.

BELL ADJUSTED her office chair endlessly, trying to find a spot of perfect comfort she knew deep down didn't exist. The little squeak the chair made each time she tweaked its position would have annoyed her to no end if she hadn't known it annoyed Pietro even more.

No, her annoyance, aside from it not being Vierday all-goddamn-ready, was at least as familiar to her as her incessant chair-squeaking must have seemed to Pietro.

Boredom.

"If you're finished working," Pietro said, right on cue, "I recall a message saying the supply closet needs to be inventoried."

"I didn't take this job," Bell said, punctuating the sentence fragment with a squeak, "to do that kind of work." *Squeeeak.*

"It seems to me," Pietro responded, his unnatural unflappability decidedly unflapped, "that you didn't take this job to do *any* work."

"Now, see," Bell said, pausing after one, no, two more squeaks, "I'm the linguist here, but you put it much better than I could have." She put her hand to her heart. "That hurts me, Pete." She thumped her chest to drive home how sarcastic she was being. "Right here."

Pietro was either too smart or too experienced to take the bait.

Bell knew where she'd place her bets. "Why are you here if you don't want to work?"

"Well," Bell said, as if they hadn't already had this conversation a thousand times, the galaxy's most dysfunctional work marriage. "I'm here because I like getting paid. I don't want to work because I don't want to work. The two things might seem related, but they really aren't."

"What we do is important," Pietro said peevishly. "It's—"

"Not important at all. And before you get up on your high horse about me being 'just a linguist,' I'll explain why to you." This, at least, was new material. She'd been researching since last time, when he'd run brainiac circles around her. "First, it's been a really long time. If Earth was still capable of reaching out to us, they would have by now. Which means Earth was fucked a long time ago. Is fucked? Is in a continual state of being fucked. Nobody is home who is capable of saying hello, or they would have by now."

"I'll grant you that seems like the obvious conclu—"

"Second," Bell said, voice rising in impending triumph, "we are well over ten-thousand light years from Earth. So even if they reached out to us through good old-fashioned boring EM, it would take so long to get here, it's unlikely we'll still be a functioning world by the time it does. *And even if we were,* absolutely nobody is interested in having a conversation that takes twenty thousand years between responses."

"One of the colonies could reach out if they're able to recreate the Bridge technology!" Pietro spoke the words very fast, as though desperate to get a complete thought ventilated from his body.

"Technically true," Bell said, mock pondering. "But we haven't managed to recreate it, despite trying since the moment we arrived. And what are the odds we're the *only* colony that hasn't? Seems much more likely to me that we got sold a bill of goods on those plans they gave us when our intrepid ancestors crossed over their Bridge and arrived here."

"This is *important work.*"

"If it's so important," Bell said with faux sweetness, "then why do I keep seeing you typing and deleting requests for transfer to another department—*any* other department—when you think I'm not looking?"

It was a low blow. People like Pietro—which meant anyone who wasn't Bell, so far as she knew—couldn't help but be meek and unassuming and willing to put aside their own wants for the common good. It was disgusting, but it wasn't his fault.

She'd been born luckier than most.

"Maybe I'm just trying to get away from *you*," he said venomously, ruining the moment she was having entirely in her own head.

"I'd say get in line," Bell said, her smile laconic as she gestured at the room full of empty desks, the two of theirs the only ones with monitors on their surface, "but it's clear you were already last in that particular line. And you know the regs. There's always got to be two."

Squeak. Squeak. Squeak.

"I'm going to get myself a snack!"

Bell actually felt a little bad. Pietro rarely snapped, and almost never ate snacks off his rigid schedule. She must really have gotten to him, she thought as she squeaked even faster, hoping he'd just decide to go home for the day.

A beeping from her own console interrupted Bell's symphony of squeaks. It was a very *particular* beeping, one she'd only ever heard in drills.

"What in the ever-loving fuck-a-duck?" With some difficulty—she'd really been abusing her chair—Bell managed to scrape it back along the floor toward her terminal, cursing the Xenocomms Department, Exocomms Subdepartment's founding-aged furniture all the while.

She waited for the announcement that it was a drill, though they usually announced those ahead of time, somewhat spoiling the purpose. There was no counter-indication, no separate alert on her screen, no text informing her of the whole episode's fakeness.

There was just the text. The text that she'd theoretically been waiting for her entire professional life.

Signal Detected — Initial Strength Analysis Indicates Bridge Carrier Wave — Probable Colonial Origin — Confidence: 99.8%

Bell could have double-checked the analysis. It was technically her job, the thing she'd been drilled to do, especially when the confidence level was so high. Computers still made mistakes that needed humans to correct, even though the line between those two types of thinking machines grew blurrier every day. Bell herself was somewhere north of 70 percent cybernetic. Probably more. She'd stopped counting a while back.

Instead of double-checking anything, which wasn't really her jam, she just keyed the message to audio. The buzz of the haptic feedback felt almost like a shock, but that was surely just nerves.

A voice, one Bell's own internal software identified preliminarily as both human and masculine-presenting, spoke in a near monotone. For some reason, instead of elation, icy fingers of dread clutched Bell's heart tighter with each syllable.

"If anyone is still alive to hear this message, please respond. This is the city of Calgary, now known as Coldgarden. We are surrounded by hostile alien life forms, and we fear we are the last humans alive on Earth. Please, prove us wrong. Please. We don't want to lose hope."

The message repeated. Repeated. Repeated again. All Bell could focus on was the dread. At last her conscious mind caught up to her limbic system, meaning the various computational modules that made up her brain's language center provided their refined analysis. What her fear had responded to by instinct now had a name.

Her language module whispered to her as a kind of wordless intuition, a warning. *That thing speaking sounds* almost *human.*

But it's not.

ACKNOWLEDGMENTS

Those who say that writing is a solitary pursuit are only thinking about the up-front part. In truth, once we writers exhaustedly collapse over a completed first draft in a puddle of tears and possibly bourbon, a legion of talented people rush in to help shepherd our ramshackle drafts to their complete, polished, published form.

I'd like to give special thanks to Sara George for once again gritting her teeth and plowing through a proofread of my grammatical atrocities with skill and grace, René Kim for lending her supreme narrating talents on this series, the artist extraordinaire Stefanie Saw for the gorgeous cover art of this series, and Kevin Colby for keeping the gears turning behind the scenes at Cursed Dragon Ship Publishing.

Extra-super-special thanks to Kelly Lynn Colby, who not only took a chance on this weird little nightmare of a story but who once again found all the weak joints in the first draft and said "nope, try again," in that way she has where it doesn't crush my spirit.

But most of all, I'd like to thank my wife Debbie for her infinite well of patience and willingness to let me squirrel myself away in these made-up worlds for hours on end. She's the best wife a writer, or a person in general, could ask for.

ABOUT THE AUTHOR

Gregory D. Little is the author of the Unwilling Souls, Mutagen Deception, and the forthcoming Bell Begrudgingly Solves It series. As a writer, you would think he could find a better way to sugarcoat the following statement, but you'd be wrong. So, just to say it straight, he really enjoys tricking people. As such, one of his greatest joys in life is laughing maniacally whenever he senses a reader has reached That Part in one of his books. Fantasy, sci-fi, horror, it doesn't matter. They all have That Part. You'll know it when you get to it, promise. *Or will you?* He lives in Virginia with his wife, and he is uncommonly fond of spiders.

Join Greg's newsletter and get a free story:

facebook.com/gregorydlittleauthor
x.com/litgreg
instagram.com/authorgregorydlittle

9 781951 445430